In the Shadows of Savannah

In the Shadows of Savannah

Dianne Daniels

ISBN: 978-1-944662-57-8

This is a work of fiction. Names, characters, places and incidents are the product of the author's imagination or are used fictitiously. Any resemblance to actual events, locals, or persons, living or dead, is entirely coincidental.

Cover Design by Devon M. Tuttle, Tuttle_Recall

Dedication

For Mom with love.

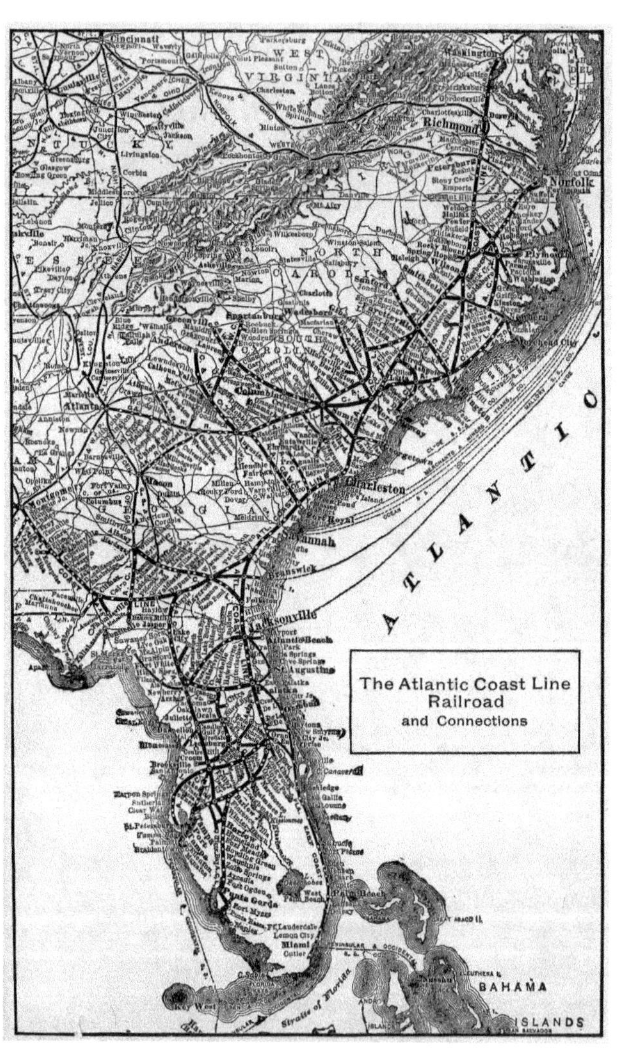
The Atlantic Coast Line
Railroad
and Connections

Table of Contents

Prologue

Josephine Thayer Davies &
Allison Edyth Davies –

Shards of blood orange, tinctured with magenta, gold, and iodine violet, pierced the diminishing night clouds still casting shadows over the Atlantic. Emerging brilliantly on the horizon, this dawn seemed in stark juxtaposition to the recent cruelly dark days.

Allison Edyth Davies, "Ali" as her Mama called her, kneaded her eyes to awaken, and a tremor shot through her numbness. Was it grief? Trepidation? Anticipation? She surmised perhaps a smidgen of each, and she accepted it as a sign of life in her battered soul. She was enswathed in a dark shroud of unbearable grief, and the momentary spark offered hope. Surviving the worst circumstance she could conjure, her beloved mother's death, she somehow still possessed the crust to board this train alone in Wilmington and venture South to the unknown of Savannah. *I can do this, Mama promised me.*

In the passing distance, Allison could just make out hazy shadows of live oaks in the morning mist, limbs heavily laden with Spanish Moss intertwined here and there with lavender wisteria—even more than in the backyard at home along the Cape Fear. *Home. Mama's home. Our home.* Now Mama was gone and with her all vestiges of what made the stately salmon-colored Queen Anne house on Ann Street a warm and welcoming home. Her memory was fading to grayscale and caused her a moment of panic. Ali swallowed back the sorrow that threatened to overcome her, concentrating instead on the passing small towns, sharecroppers in tattered clothing working the cotton fields, and the occasional glimpse of sandy beaches.

The Atlantic Coastline train rhythmically clickity-clacked over the uneven rails. She had slept fitfully. A dream, train whistle, bump or squealing brakes deprived her of rest. The deep burgundy seat, upholstered with scratchy velvet mohair and stuffed no doubt with horsehair, was unyielding. Ali had not splurged for a sleeping berth or private cabin, rather parsimoniously guarding her coin, as each penny saved now assuaged her fear of being without funds later. As of last night, upon climbing the steps of this southbound train, she was an independent woman. Mama saved enough money for her to start over in Savannah but not without the admonition to use it wisely.

Mama, God rest her soul, left a miracle for me. Ali unconsciously crossed herself. Josephine Thayer Davies, "Jo," left her daughter the means she had denied herself to start a new life on her own in Savannah far away from her abusive father James Davies. In Savannah, she told Ali, she could become a wholly different version of herself—anything she chose—without the encumbrances of the past.

Jo died just two short yet interminably long days ago, precipitating this forced migration south. In the instant of death, Ali's life drained of any semblance of happiness. It became a dirge composed of extreme emotions flatly orchestrating her steps. Her mother's sweet voice, now silenced, was replaced by a macabre cacophony screaming in her brain that only she could hear. Dazed, Ali somehow made the appropriate arrangements for her mother's mass, wake, interment in the family mausoleum, and, of course, the obligatory mourners' luncheon. In truth, Ali hated this tradition, thinking it odd that people wanted to be sociable and have a meal prepared by those who mourned after a death. Her heart had only been invested to ensure proper honor was paid to her mother in Wilmington society. *Mama deserved the best.*

Months before, Mama prepared her for this eventual outcome in consideration of her failing health and general frailness. She etched the unthinkable details upon Ali's heart and mind so, when the time arrived, Ali was able to rotely accomplish the task as a dumb animal returns by the same worn path at twilight. As much as she resisted her mother's discussion of her impending death, she was now grateful for her instruction because Mama was correct—she wasn't able to think. Ali survived the worst—the final farewell—and completed her preparation to affect the second act of this precise plan.

This was an entirely different type of plan, one secretly devised by the two of them for the express purpose of Ali's escape from her abusive father when her mother's protection was no longer available to her. Both Jo and Ali knew once Ali was alone she would become nothing more than a degraded servant in her own home to James Davies and his two older daughters from a previous marriage as well as their husbands and ghastly spoilt progeny. Jo knew the keen mind of her daughter and her skills and talents and refused even in death to allow Ali to be used by people of such ilk.

Ali clung to those plans as a life-saver in a black sea of grief, guiding her one leaden foot after the other.

Edyth Thayer Leonard – Cousin "Edy"

The train was passing near Beaufort, South Carolina, after a stop in Charleston to pick up passengers and allow others to disembark. As the train continued south, Ali rehearsed possible scenarios about finally meeting Cousin Edy today. She wrote to Edy at Mama's request two weeks prior and told her of her mother's illness and plan for her, if Cousin Edy agreed.

In this letter Ali asked Cousin Edy if she had an available room where she could stay upon her arrival until she got on her feet if and when her mother passed, though Ali herself could barely acknowledge this possibility. Mama hadn't wanted her to be alone, Ali explained, and asked her to write at that time saying it would give her comfort to know Ali would be welcome. While Ali did not anticipate anything but recovery for her mother, she said she wrote to please her mother and to pass along her regards.

One of her earliest memories was of sitting on her mother's lap as she told Ali stories about how she and Cousin Edy were as close as sisters when they were young. Of course, time passed, Ali's mother married James Davies, and each had her own family and life to live many miles apart. They stayed in touch by writing long and frequent letters to one another filled with all their news and gossip.

Able Leonard, a businessman from Savannah, and a man who was the complete antithesis of James Davies, was invited to visit a friend in Wilmington. The gentlemen attended a theater performance at the ornate Thalian Hall. It was on that fated evening shortly after Jo married James that Edy and Jo were also attending the performance. It was a rare moment when James was out of town and Jo was free to be with her cousin.

Edy and Able were introduced by their mutual friend that night. Edy was attracted to Able, who appeared to be a quiet and gentle man. He owned a farmers' exchange and lumber business in Savannah and was moderately successful financially, but certainly not of the social status Edy's family had enjoyed in Wilmington.

Edy, though, was unconcerned with the trappings of society and the wealth which supported it. Edy did not enjoy nor did she thrive on the debutante's cycle of social life. Edy was a genuine and refined young lady and much preferred reading and needlework to parties and balls.

Edy was acutely aware of her cousin's recent unhappy marriage to James Davies. It was a bad match from the very beginning, which made her even more resolute to marry for nothing less than love as her kind heart ached for her dear Jo.

Since they had been little girls playing tea party together, Edy and Jo had sworn to be each other's attendant at their respective marriages. Though unhappy with Jo's choice of husband, as if "choice" had anything to do with the debacle, Edy stood faithfully by her side as she married James, determined to support her as much as possible, for she knew Jo would need it.

As it happened, when the time came for her own wedding to Able several months later after a brief, yet lovely courtship, her cousin Jo was heavy with child, Allison Edyth Davies, after her dear cousin, and was unable to leave her confinement to be by her beloved cousin's side. Edy and Able married in Wilmington then moved to Savannah where Able had his business and began their life together.

Once in Savannah, Edy easily and joyfully assumed the role of wife and, nine and one-half months after her wedding, mother. She too gave birth to a daughter, Hannah Josephine Leonard, whom she named after her cousin Jo. She and Able were over the moon with delight. They lived a joyful life together, though tragically, for only a brief whisper of time.

The influenza epidemic of 1898 claimed both her beloved Able and Hannah. Edy contracted the dreaded illness as well, and upon the beginnings of her recovery learned, in the midst of her fever, that her loving husband and precious daughter had died and were already buried. Edy had no opportunity to say goodbye to her cherished family, which had cruelty heaped upon sorrow. Sadly, Ali was never to meet her only cousin Hannah.

Devastated, Edy slowly recovered but rather than sell the farmers' exchange and lumberyard her husband had so cleverly built, she brokered a deal with Able's manager to keep the business running as joint owners with her acting as a silent partner. In return, she would receive an adequate stipend each month for the rest of her life or until the business was sold or closed. At such time she would receive one large and final sum.

Edy did not live lavishly, but she found great comfort and eventually happiness in the cozy red brick rowhouse home

Able purchased for them and where Hannah was born. It was also where both Able and Hannah departed, and she frequently heard the faint whisper of their gentle spirits around her like angels keeping watch. She kept her home immaculate with a constant fragrance of food cooking on the stove as if her family would walk through the door at any moment.

Edy always knew that her cousin Jo's daughter might one day come to her for refuge to escape her brute of a father. Sadly, Edy also knew it would be after the unthinkable passing of her cousin. Now, at the Savannah Atlantic Coastline Railway Station, Edy awaited Ali's arrival with mixed emotions—the grief of losing her cousin and the exhilaration of welcoming Jo's daughter into her life. Though no one could ever take the place of her Hannah in her heart, at least with Allison she would have a "daughter" to spoil and care for. She missed having a family and this filled her heart.

Only recently Ali had written her on behalf of her mother, requesting a home with Edy if it became necessary. Edy knew Jo was gravely ill, though she did not suspect she was on her deathbed. Ali had minimized her mother's sickness, and Edy knew it was at her mother's request as Jo kept her difficulties well-hidden throughout her life. Immediately after her mother's death, Ali sent a telegram to Edy informing her that her dearest cousin had passed. The next day after the funeral mass, Ali surreptitiously boarded the train to Savannah to her new home with Edy. There were few preparations necessary for Ali's arrival as Edy had kept on the ready for her if indeed that day came. Today was that day.

"Next stop — Savannah"

Ali was startled out of her deep thoughts when the conductor called out, "Next stop Savannah!" She was excited about the prospect of her new life in Savannah and a tad fearful at the same time. She wrote a letter to her father before she left and received a promise from her neighbor's son Walter to post the letter the day *after* she boarded the train. Walter could be trusted, and Ali was thankful for his kindness. She knew his help was a Godsend to her.

What will Father do when he reads the letter? Well, what can he do? I will be long gone, and he will have no idea where. Ali turned twenty-nine years old that year, and her father had no further say in any matter concerning her or her life. Mama had seen to that. *Thank you, Mama,* Ali softly lifted her eyes towards Heaven and crossed herself.

Ali was counting on being able to find a position using her accounting skills, but she had Mama's money tucked away safely and Mama's jewels as well if funds ran short. *Dear Mama.* She felt the tears well up in her eyes once again as she absently looked out the window of the Pullman coach. She thought surely she had cried all the tears in her body. How could there be any tears left? Mama would not want her to cry, she knew, but deep down she realized she would never run out of tears for Mama, and she would never stop missing her. *Please God, let me be half the woman my Mama was.*

As the train rocked along the rails, she thought back through the convoluted path that led her to her present circumstances.

Chapter 1
Uncertain Origins

From her first memory, Ali's father let her know she was a deep disappointment to him—sometimes overtly, sometimes through sarcasm or innuendo. Ali didn't understand why he felt that way, and, as it would any child, it haunted her. *What is wrong with me?* She constantly searched herself for any flaws that might have caused her father's wrath. She knew it just wasn't natural for a parent to hate a child so. Perhaps Father had wanted a boychild? Maybe she wasn't as pretty as her two half-sisters, Anna and Marie? In fact, her perpetually discontented half-sisters seemed to feel the same about Ali as her father. She was aware of their sideways glances and general impatience and lack of acceptance of their younger half-sister. They needn't have said a word to her. Their attitudes spoke volumes—and loudly. Their carping was constant and Ali inwardly cringed with each slight.

With huffs of disapproval, they expressed their condemnation when she came home after spending a day walking along the Cape Fear waterfront—her bonnet hanging down her back allowing her auburn hair to fall to her shoulders disheveled, freckles appearing on her nose and sun-kissed cheeks. Ali was unfashionably sun-tanned for a lady of standing and, even worse, physically fit and strong. She knew she was a complete disappointment to her half-sisters and father—to everyone except her dear Mama.

Ali had no desire to live the debutante life, much the same as Edy had felt at her age. She was more practical and enjoyed walking on the beach in her bare feet, skirt tied in a knot just above her ankles, worshipping the sun, craving one of the new bicycles to scoot around, and reading every book she could check out of the new library in town. She had already exhausted her parents' library at home. She also enjoyed the challenge of doing sums. So unladylike, everyone said! Now, however, she was counting on this unladylike skill to support her in Savannah if given the opportunity. Ali poured over any news of the Suffragists' movement, now feeling more akin to them.

Both half-sisters were older than Ali and married well to socially prominent young men they met at their "coming out" balls—those debutante soirees of great importance when young girls from prominent families are presented to society as a woman, ready to be captured in marriage and begin making babies. Mama's prominent family was the only reason Anna and Marie were eligible to be debutantes. Their father, her father, had nothing to offer other than acquired prominence through Mama. Anna was married to William Pettigrew, certainly a blue blood family of Southern ideals, and they had two children, a boy Willie, and a girl, Annalise. Marie accepted Beau Cooper's proposal, though Ali was convinced she must have given him some voodoo potion to be so blind as to marry Marie, and she was expecting her third child with two daughters already, Prissy and Sissy. Ali had to suppress her urge to laugh when hearing their names called together. Prissy and Sissy—it sounded like names for a team of mules pulling a plow in the field! She remembered laughing with her mother until the tears flowed down their cheeks, wondering if they would call the new baby "Pissy," or "Hissy." Her mother clucked her tongue, shaking her head.

"Now, Ali, be a lady. You know it is impolite to harbor unkind thoughts about your half-sisters," her mother said reprovingly but half-heartedly, and they both had a good laugh.

"Oh Mama, it may be too late for you to make me into a lady. I am quite a lost cause, I fear."

"My dear girl, you are the loveliest of ladies, with a heart of gold and a mind as sharp as a darning needle. You are quite more than even my dreams for you, and I am very proud to be your mother. One day, I am certain a kind and wonderful man will meet you and see what I see and make you his wife. But in the meantime, you must learn to hold yourself."

All but her mother considered her a failure in the realm of marriage, but it wasn't as if she hadn't been courted. She had. She was just discriminating about whom she would agree to marry. She never wanted to end up as Mama had with a demeaning, cold, and abusive husband. Ali never could understand why Mama stayed with her father rather than return to her family's home. In fact, it made no sense to her why her mother married him in the first place. Mama was cultured and from an excellent family of high social regard. She could not fathom their pairing.

For her part, Ali's very first beau was Benjamin Blacknell, who was but one year older and a student at the University of North Carolina in Chapel Hill, studying to be a scientist. He was serious about his studies, enthusiastic about all he was learning, and planned a long stay at the university to study for his doctorate. Benjamin rarely came home to Wilmington; thus, their budding relationship died on the vine despite the obvious efforts of his mother admonishing Ali to wait for her son, "the genius." His mother was quite mistaken to think that her son or any son was worth pining her youth away. She politely declined.

A year after ending that relationship, Terrance Beauloir, a graduate of the College of South Carolina in Columbia who fancied himself a poet, became her next beau. Ali thought he was a particularly romantic and beautiful man—if one could say such about a man—with dark, curly hair and dark soulful eyes that seemed to look into her very heart. Sadly, Terrance needed a constant muse for his poetry, which necessitated frequently changing his romantic partners as the inspiration waned. His poetry was not well-received nor was his reputation in society, and his constant lack of financial means of support was troubling to Ali. Father spoke with him early on before there was any true attachment, and she no longer was courted by Terrance.

When she was twenty-four years old, Ali met Daniel Roberts at a Thalian Hall Harvest Moon Cotillion. Handsome and unusually kind, he and Ali quickly established a "steady relationship" that lasted for several years but with no proposal. Ali did not understand Daniel's reluctance to marry. Everyone expected them to wed, but, when marriage inevitably came up in conversation, Daniel changed the subject or he offered dozens of superficial reasons why this or that time "wasn't right." After so long in courtship, his reticence to make her his wife was unseemly.

She felt dear Daniel was insecure and unmotivated for success (neither of which Ali felt were shared traits), and she suspected there was a volatile temper simmering just beneath the surface of his kind outward demeanor. Daniel tended to be controlling, often speaking for her and making decisions that were hers to make. Ali prickled at this as she had seen this same behavior in her father's treatment her mother. Though overall Daniel was a good man, she was repelled by this particular trait. She was not a possession to be used and controlled. She had a mind and a will that could not be owned. Ali uncharacteristically found herself fearful of appearing too intelligent with Daniel because of his insecurity about his education and lack of success. Finally, choosing not to give him one more day of her life waiting for a marriage proposal that apparently was not forthcoming, she ended the relationship and broke her own heart at the same time.

Her father was not pleased nor understanding. Instead he told her she would always be a spinster and a drain on the family with her peculiar thoughts about the equality of women. Ali desperately wanted to have a career and money of her own. She wanted to make her own decisions. This, however, was unthinkable and scandalous for a young lady of her social standing, her father had declared, and she would learn to be an adept homemaker so she could find a suitable husband to support her.

Ali devoured any news about the Suffragettes, most of which, of course, was negative, and poured over every booklet or pamphlet she could get her hands on. Mama told her about the Seneca Falls Convention of 1848, which effectively started the women's suffrage discussion, and she knew she possessed the same philosophy and desires as they. No one could intelligently explain to her why women should not be allowed to vote. She and her mother discussed it in guarded conversations in her mother's room where less enlightened ears would not overhear—namely, Anna, Marie, and her father.

It was soon after the failed courtship with Daniel that Ali noticed Collier Thompson who worked with her father. Father coarsely called him a "coon-ass" from Baton Rouge, which meant he was Creole—partly of French or Spanish descent, partly "who-knows-what," he would snarl. Father felt he was totally unsuitable for a young lady of society and especially *his* daughter, and he "spoke funny English," the "pidgin English" of a Louisiana Cajun. All of this made Collier even more enticing to Ali.

He was a handsome man to be sure with raven, shoulder-length wavy hair and emerald eyes. He wore the latest trend set by Prince Edward of England, a trimmed full beard and mustache, which Ali found quite distinguished. He sent a thrill through Ali, and yet she sensed a dangerous streak, knowing he had a reputation as a "ladies' man." Raw sexuality seemed to ooze from his pores. He made her feel beautiful just because he had chosen to court her when he could have his choice of any of the young ladies. Collier was well aware of the effect he had on young ladies and even older women, knowing exactly how to charm—with his slightly tilted head, crooked smile, just a fleeting touch on the hand or forearm, with deadly charisma.

His charm clearly was not lost on Ali. Collier quickly swept her off her feet with his sexual inklings, their stolen kisses when no one was about, his quick wit, and, most irresistible, his intelligence. This was a man with whom Ali was certain she could have a life of adventure, enlightened conversation, and shared nights of passion. He was surely her first truly adult love. Collier made her heart race, and she experienced a foreign tingling between her legs and a mysterious wetness. Ali didn't quite understand these reactions, but it wasn't unpleasant and foretold of possible future rapture in his arms.

Collier addled and thrilled her all at the same time and made her heart race like a rabbit. For his part, Collier was much more experienced than she at six years her senior, and she wanted him to teach her everything he knew, and she didn't give a fig about consequences. She was in love.

Predictably, her father couldn't wait to steal her joy and soon nixed the relationship. Without so much as a word to her, Collier was terminated from his position with her father without warning, packed off without ceremony to Baton Rouge, and never contacted her again. She was inconsolable for nearly a year. It was as if Collier had died and she was robbed of even a farewell.

After Collier, Ali did not consider any other young men's attentions nor requests from suitors. Ali closed down her heart and felt as if she had fulfilled her father's prophecy: she was a spinster. Only her mother could console her and somehow sympathize with her sorrow. Ali intuited that her mother must have experienced some similar heartbreak at some point to be able to experience this pain with Ali.

As the trip to Savannah wore on, she felt tears again threatening to spill down her cheeks. She missed her mother. *Oh, Mama, you were so beautiful and kind. What did you see in me that I cannot? You made me feel special and even beautiful.* Ali hadn't felt beautiful since Collier left. Only Mama could bring her out of her despondency.

Ali continued puzzling out the events that placed her on this train to Georgia, and these were not pleasant thoughts. Her father, James Davies, was cold and cruel—unloving to her and even to her dear Mama who treated him with such respect. He tried in all his evilness to convince Ali she was an embarrassment to the family. In reality, because of the benevolence of Grandfather Thayer, her maternal grandfather, he and his daughters from his first marriage were living off of Grandfather's good graces. Her father let her know the only reason she was still under his roof was to placate her mother, but she suspected Grandfather Thayer may have had something to say about that. He, Anna, and Marie constantly reminded Ali, because she had not accepted any of the few proposals she had received, she was now "past her prime." *He and his daughters? Aren't I also one of his daughters?*

Why would I ever want to be married, Ali wondered. *So I could be treated the way Mama was?* Her father's controlling behavior towards her mother was the cause of the alienation of nearly all of Mama's family and friends. They rarely called to visit anymore, because it was obvious Mama was on pins and needles and Father was simply rude. They would occasionally send a note or card on special occasions, but after a time Mama rarely had tea or luncheon with her lady friends. This, her father thought, put Mama squarely under his complete control. She was as much his property as the team of horses that pulled his carriage. *He even treated the horses better than Mama!* How Jo had suffered under James' tyrannical rule, but her mind and her will were never surrendered to him. He was not nearly as intelligent as she, and Mama was never obviously rebellious towards him but was able to communicate in such a way that outwardly he puffed up with what he thought was his dominance, but he must have had a fleeting thought in the back of his pea brain that he had just been bested. Nothing he could accuse her of but enough to be a grain of sand in his socks.

Once when she and her mother were having their tea in Mother's room, Ali asked about her father.

"Mama, why is Father so angry? Why does he hate me so? And why is he so despicable to you?"

Her mother put her teacup down and gazed out the window into her beloved garden. She had one of those faces that even in rest always wore a smile, and a light shone around her. When Ali asked her this question, a rare shadow hung in her eyes.

"Ali, you never met your father's parents, your grandparents, Evan and Clara Davies. I met them only once, at our marriage. They were two of the unhappiest people I ever laid eyes on. Their despondence and gloom seemed to engulf them—and anyone connected to them—like a black cloud. One night I asked your father to tell me about his childhood as I simply could not fathom how they came to be so wretched. It was not a pretty tale, but I will tell you so perhaps you may be able to understand your father.

"Your father's parents, it seems, had what is crudely referred to as a 'shotgun wedding.'"

Jo noted Ali's raised eyebrows and look of surprise, but she continued.

"Clara Rickhardt came from a strict German Catholic family in Columbus. They lived in a section known as German Village, a small and separate enclave of immigrants. She had three sisters—Anna, Catherine, and Hilda, though Hilda died in childbirth. The girls had enjoyed an active social life and were considered affluent in their little community. Her father was a well-respected carpenter who created many of the lovely "gingerbread" houses that distinguish the area. All the girls made suitable and advantageous marriages—all but Clara, your father's mother, and the apple of her father Francis' eye.

"She became infatuated with a handsome young Welsh lad, Evan Davies, who was the fire chief of the German Village area. His parents were Welsh immigrants who settled in southern Ohio and attempted to farm a small and rocky patch of land. Evan was very poor and he lacked any formal education, but he was a hard worker and quite the jokester, I'm told. He left home for Columbus at the age of fourteen because his parents simply could not afford to feed him and his younger siblings.

"Clara's parents were very much against this pairing, as I'm sure you can understand. Her father forbade Clara to see Evan, but she was strong-willed, a bit spoilt, and rebellious. Her father's edict made Evan all the more attractive to her."

Ali's thoughts immediately went to Collier and her enhanced feelings for him as a result of her father's disapproval.

Her mother continued, "Then the inevitable happened when forbidden love is continued in secret—your father's mother was with child at the time she married Evan. What other choice did she have? Her parents would put her out and Evan was her only option.

"Your father's older brother, John Thomas Davies, was born only six months after their quiet, family marriage ceremony, and they tried to convince society he was premature, yet he was clearly a full-term baby. Their small community took notice as small minds in small communities will do and would surely never let them forget this faux pas."

Ali's mother directed her to the table in her room where she picked up James Davies' large family Bible. As it was very old, she opened it carefully to the family records' page, where Ali discovered the truth herself through the dates of marriage and the birth of John Thomas Davies. She looked at her mother and gasped.

"Yes, Ali, Evan Davies had gotten Clara with child and effectively ruined any worthy prospects for her life. She had no choice but to marry him because no other decent man would have her. Needless to say, their passion was quickly doused with the news that she was carrying Evan's child. Clara was disowned by her own family, married to a dirt-poor, uneducated man with few prospects, and certainly well beneath her social station. Marriage was no longer a fanciful game.

"Her childish rebellion had thrust her into a world of poverty for which she was ill-prepared. Neither truly loved the other, and the passion of a moment had brought ruin on them both. Clara took in laundry to help the family make ends meet, but then things went from bad to worse. Evan was struck down by an apoplexy at the young age of twenty-seven, and his left leg was left lame so that his foot dragged and he had to walk with a cane. He was, needless to say, forced to give up his position with the fire department, and other work that he could do was hard to come by, walking with a gimpy leg. He drove a vegetable wagon for a time, selling directly from it.

"Because of Clara's father's rage and contempt for Evan, and because they were ostracized by their community, Evan was forced to take his new wife to the country, where he purchased a few acres to farm but not nearly enough to sustain a growing family. Times were very hard for them with no family support, and the resentment between them grew.

"Your father's birth just ten months after his brother's was an unwelcome additional burden, and he represented a deeper devolution into abject poverty. Your father was evidently viewed as just another mouth to feed, just as his father had been. His desperately unhappy and unloving parents raised their two boys under harsh circumstances no child should experience, and as a result John and your father clung to each other for survival, always looking out for one another.

"As much as John was cherished by his mother in spite of the circumstances, partly because, I've been told, he favored his mother in complexion and build though thankfully not in temperament, but also because of his frailty. Your father, on the other hand, was despised, neglected, and treated inhumanly. Beginning at the tender age of four, his father worked him in the fields with grown field hands during harvest, lifting sheaths of hay and baskets of corn that weighed more than his own tiny body.

"Your father never held any resentment towards John and, in fact, told me that John was brilliant, a wonderful student at the small school they attended. Sickly and frail, he was spared from much of the hard, manual labor your father was forced to do. John was very kind and unselfish to your father, and they were very close—the best of friends with less than a year between them in age."

She continued, "John became very ill near his sixteenth birthday. It seems he had contracted an unknown disease.

No one quite knew what it was or how to treat him even if they had possessed the money to obtain medical treatment. He began losing his coordination at first; then his mental faculties began to fail as well.

"Each day your father would help him bathe and dress for school, where your father would sit beside him to help so that he still felt a part of this life. He shared his lunch with him and then brought him home again after the school bell rang at the end of the day. Your father did this until John was completely bedridden and had lost all mental faculties.

"Soon thereafter, at the age of eighteen, John died and left your father, then seventeen, to carry on without him in the cold and harsh family."

Mama then withdrew John's death certificate from the Bible that listed the reason for his death as "moron."

"Oh, Mama, how tragic," Ali said, tears forming in her eyes.

"Unfortunately, my sweet girl, that was not the worst of it."

Ali couldn't imagine how anything could get worse than the sorrowful tale she had just heard.

"On the day of John's funeral at the Old Creek Church just across the road from their farm, the little school girls all dressed in white and carried flower wreaths they had made from wildflowers. You father and some school chums carried the coffin to the gravesite just across the road from their farm. After the service at the gravesite, his mother turned to her youngest son James, your father, and said, 'I wish it had been you in that grave instead of my John!'"

Ali gasped at this unthinkable, brutal comment to her father. This indeed explained much about his disposition.

"Why in the world would anyone, let alone his mother, say such a horrible thing to her own boy? And especially after Father had done so much to care for John and obviously loved him so? It is cruel beyond words, Mama."

"That I cannot tell you, my darling, but, when your father is overly harsh, perhaps knowing this may help you bear his anger, knowing the sadness and cruelty of his life. He knows nothing else."

Jo concluded, "The family was unhappy in their rural community but too poor to move elsewhere. They tended their hardscrabble farm until they died. You see, Ali, the consequences of her youthful rebellion followed her throughout her life."

As Ali continued to ponder the horror of his story, she resolved to be kinder to her father if indeed he would allow it. With each kindness she showed her father, his cruel treatment of her mother and of Ali intensified. No amount of bad luck or unhappiness could justify his wrath.

Chapter 2
Blest Be the
Tie That Binds

The unthinkable crashed into Ali's life mercilessly, crushing the breath from her lungs and shattering her heart. *Could it have been just two short yet agonizingly long days ago?* It all was so devastating to her.

Ali had spent what was to be her mother's final morning of life at Wrightsville Beach, looking for interesting treasures for the vase of seashells Jo kept on her bedside table. It was a beautiful, cool morning with a good breeze when she stepped onto the street car and later the ferry to get there. She had hoped Jo would be well enough to accompany her on this little adventure, but she had not been feeling well of late, so Ali was determined to bring a bit of the beach and sunshine to her with the shells. As always, Ali let her bonnet fall to her back without a care about the inevitable freckles forming on her light skin. Her hair pins had been removed and her tangled head of hair blew about her face in the strong ocean breeze. It was no use trying to command the bonnet on a day such as this nor her unruly mane. The wind won, not that it was much of a battle. She loved it.

The ocean was her refuge where she escaped the oppressive atmosphere created by her father when he was home. At the beach, Ali felt she was face to face with God. She communed with Him here where the warm sand sifted between her toes and the briny air filled her lungs. No judgment, no clock ticking, no criticism—just Ali and God. It was here she prayed fervently, even more than in mass, for her mother's health and happiness and for her own.

As the sun peaked in the noonday sky, Ali thought to head back to her family's home on Ann Street in downtown Wilmington so she could help prepare dinner. If she were lucky, she would miss Anna, Marie, and their cloying children's almost daily visit to see James. Certainly, they cared nothing for Mama. Their own mother had died long before Ali was born. Her father was left a widower with two little girls to raise alone, which was untenable, so he married Jo. Ali would not and could not ever understand this coupling. *He and Mama are polar opposites in every way. I understand his attraction to Mama; she was kind and lovely, but what was Mama thinking?*

Arriving at their large home, Ali immediately noticed things were amiss. Her half-sisters were at the kitchen table, talking softly, pretending to dab tears from their cheeks. *What now?* Ali thought.

"Anna…Marie…what…is…wrong. Is Mama all ri…" and before she could get the word out, she saw their faces and knew instantly it was Mama.

She ran up the stairs, two at a time, skirt hoisted above her knees, as she rushed to Mama's room and slowly, cautiously, with her heart in her throat, praying over and over, "God, please let her be all right," opened the door.

The room was unusually dark for this time of day. Normally the afternoon sun shone in through the chintz curtains. She saw her mother lying peacefully on her bed. She looked as if she were sleeping, as beautiful as ever even in repose. She was breathing so faintly Ali could barely detect breath.

Drawing close and taking her hand, Ali whispered, "Mama? How are you feeling? I've brought you some beautiful shells from Wrightsville." Ali spoke as if everything was normal and her mother was listening to her. "I think you will like the hole-y ones I found. They have such character," she said, afraid to glance her mother's direction.

"Allison, for God's sake, can you not see that your mother is gravely ill—dying? Honestly, you are the most thoughtless young woman!" James snarled at her, unaware that the words he flung at her had cut her to the bone—not his judgment of her but what he said about her mother. She felt the blood drain from her, causing her to feel faint.

Ali's father rose to leave the room once Ali entered but had taken some perverse pleasure in telling her abruptly, with such detachment and coldness, the shocking, heartbreaking news of her mother's imminent death.

"No, Father. Mama is just resting. She was feeling much better before I left. She asked me to bring her shells. See how pretty they are, Mama?"

"What is wrong with you? Your mother is nearly dead!"

Her mama turned her head towards Ali. In a soft but hoarse whisper she said, "Oh, Ali, I'm so sorry, but I fear I must leave you soon."

Mama lay there in her lovely room, normally bright and joyful, with clusters of violets on her wallpaper and soft moss green stripes in the background. A lavender rug covered the heart pine floors, and the small walnut dressing table displayed Mama's lovely perfume bottles. The perfume bottles, Ali knew, were guilt gifts whenever Father came home after one of his out-of-town trysts, full of insincere apologies and smelling of whiskey and women. His "business trips" became more and more frequent as Mama fought off this lingering illness and grew weaker. Ali remembered her father telling her mother that she was never to allow Allison to touch her expensive perfumes as there was no reason for a spinster to smell pretty. Her mama ignored his insults and each night gave her a choice of fragrance to dab on her wrists.

When bedtime was near, her mother would sit on the small bench, covered in the same chintz as the draperies. Ali picked up the silver brush on the table and brushed her mother's long hair a full hundred strokes. She knew her mama would rest easier after this little ritual. She wanted to brush Mama's hair now—a full one hundred times.

This was the room where she and Mama exchanged all of their deepest secrets and latest gossip in conspiratorial whispers and giggles.

Ali gently sat down on her mama's bed and whispered close to her ear, "I'm here, Mama, but please don't leave me; please don't go. I'll have no one if you go. I love you so much. I can't live without you. No one in this world has a more precious Mama than I."

Ali gently stroked her mother's forehead as tears fell unabated down her sun-kissed cheeks. Her mother's eyes opened slowly, and, looking at her daughter with tears in her eyes, she lifted her hand to Ali's face and managed to whisper into her ear, "Ali, my beauty, my love, you will be fine. Remember what we have discussed and please follow my directions. Remember always that you and your Papa have been the joy of my life."

Ali thought this was curious as Mama had never referred to her father as *Papa*. Perhaps she was thinking of her own dear Papa, Grandfather Thayer.

Her face buried in her mother's hair, crying softly, Ali could smell the same citrusy orange blossom scent of the perfume they had shared just last night. She inhaled deeply, hoping the scent would stay with her forever as she tried to memorize each of Mama's features. The velvety skin of her cheeks, elegant fingers, now grown thin with lingering ill health, and shiny manicured nails. *Mama's one luxury*, Ali thought. Each week, Gracie came to their home to buff Mama's nails to a shine. She always offered to have Gracie also manicure Ali's nails, but hers were always raggedy from working in the garden and digging in sand at the beach.

"Ali," her mother whispered breathlessly, barely audible, "pro…promise me you will leave here and never come back. Don't let him hurt you anymore."

"I promise, Mama, just as we planned. My trunk is packed."

"Do not forget, Ali, my jewels, and the small box— bottom drawer; take it please and go to Cousin Edy. I love you, my precious girl. You and your dear Papa have been the joy of my life. Find happiness, Ali." Ali saw the effort it took to say every one of these, her last words on earth.

"I will, Mama…I will."

Her mother's face was peaceful and lovely. She was an angel now. Ali saw her spirit leave her spent body. Her hand slid from her bereft daughter's, and Josephine Thayer Davies expelled her final breath. A smile, still visible on her soft, beautiful face, made it look as if she were seeing Jesus face to face in Heaven that very moment. It comforted Ali when she saw her smile.

"Farewell, my dear Mama. I will see you again one day, I promise," Ali whispered into her ear, and she knew her Mama heard her. She sat touching her mother's hand as the sun began its afternoon trek downward toward the western horizon. The birds stopped singing, Ali noticed, as if mourning their loss too. It was silent and Ali prayed the rosary for her mother.

"Hail Mary full of grace, the Lord is with thee. Blessed art thou among women and blessed is the fruit of thy womb Jesus. Holy Mary, Mother of God, pray for us sinners now and at the hour of our death. Amen."

Ali barely had said her "Amen" and crossed herself before the door abruptly opened, and her private time with her mother came to an end. Her father barged into the room in his usual uncouth manner followed by two men in black morning coats and white gloves.

"She is gone, Father." Checking his gold pocket watch, James acted as if this was all too inconvenient for him, as if time was of paramount importance at this moment. *Mama's body is still warm!* Ali was repulsed at her father's crass behavior.

What were these strange men doing in her Mama's room? Who were they and why was her father looking so intently at his watch? Ali was aghast. After thirty years together, James seemed to have no feelings whatsoever about his wife's death. He had not shed one tear. There was no pain etched into his hard, frowning face. He never moved closer to touch or kiss her goodbye.

The two men efficiently and gently lifted her mother off of her bed and placed her body on a hard stretcher covered her with a black velvet shroud with the McCabe Mortuary name emblazoned in gold thread. They then carried her from the once cheerful, bright space where Ali and her mother had spent so many happy hours.

Anna and Marie entered the room while the men were preparing the body. Their annoying wailing came in great torrents, but Ali knew it was false emotion. They were only interested in what they could grab in Mama's room and take home as their own. Their eyes greedily darted from one thing to the next around the room, searching vainly for Jo's jewels.

They have no clue that all of Mama's things…clothes, jewelry and money…would soon be in my trunk and on its way to Savannah, and I with it. They will never touch a thing that belongs to my mother!

"Girls, silence this noise and kindly remove yourselves to the parlor and allow these men to do their jobs."

Ali noticed that at their father's dictate, their disconsolate sobbing stopped abruptly, and their eyes were dry as a parched bone. Appalled by her father's abrupt removal of Mama's body from the home, Ali was on his heels going out of the room.

"But Father!" Ali protested. "Mama has only just passed! Surely you will allow me to spend a bit more time with her! May I please be allowed a brief moment?" Ali begged to no avail.

"Ali, step aside this moment! I will speak with you later in my office. Your mother is dead. There is no reason to postpone the inevitable. Now do as you're told."

Stunned as if struck by lightning at her father's blunt pronouncement of her mother's passing, even given his usual coldness, she felt this was beyond the pale. Ali knew her father had been "entertaining" another woman during her mother's illness. He appeared to be in a hurry to erase Mama's presence and move his harlot into her home! *God will deal with him*, Ali thought and crossed herself.

Poor dear Mama, Father hadn't even allowed for Father Maloney to be called to give her the Sacrament of Last Rites. He didn't know that Ali had slipped her rosary into her hands and prayed before he came into the room. She also had brought some holy water home in a small vial from mass last Sunday at the Shrine Basilica of Saint Mary just down Ann Street from her home. She had sprinkled it on her mother after tracing a cross on her forehead with it. It wasn't Father Maloney's blessed anointing oil, but it would have to suffice. She believed God would allow her into Heaven without the Last Rites.

Her father held the heavy carved wooden front door open as the men gently carried her mother down the stairs. Ali quickly grabbed her bonnet and small black reticule before moving to depart with the men.

"Where do you think you are going, Ali?" Her father nearly bellowed at her.

"I will stay with Mama until the men have prepared her," Ali said defiantly. Her father dared not cross her now, not when it involved her Mama. Or so she thought.

"No! You will *not*!" he yelled. "Stay out of their way!" At this, he turned on his heel, then shouted back, "See me in my office. Now!" he ordered, exiting the room.

Behind the two men stood Mr. McCabe, the owner of the mortuary and the undertaker. Ali spoke with him quietly, "Please, Mr. McCabe, be extra kind and gentle with my precious Mama. She deserves to be treated with dignity. She is a lovely woman," Ali pleaded.

"Of course, Miss Ali, we always treat each of our clients with the utmost respect. We will take special care of your beloved mother. I knew her well and agree she was a lovely woman, so kind. My sincerest condolences."

"Mr. McCabe," Ali said softly, "I will send clothing for her shortly, and, if you will, I beg you to conceal the rosary in her hand. I know Mama would be ever so grateful as will I. I will come later to prepare her hair and makeup."

He patted her hand with sympathy as if he knew the dynamics of her family. She felt her face flush with embarrassment and touched her cheek where her mother had stroked it as she took her last breath. It was then she felt the full weight of her passing, and the first of what seemed like endless tears began rolling down her face. It would be a long night, but first she must face her father's wrath. She passed through the parlor walking slowly to her father's study. He was standing behind his large desk, his back to the door. Suddenly, Ali turned and bolted up the stairs before her father could see her. *I will speak with Father later when I choose to do so.*

Quietly and quickly, Ali climbed the stairs and entered her room. She locked the door behind her and lay on her bed with the fishnet canopy made in the Blue Ridge mountains. Ali cried herself into a deep sleep in the same clothing she had worn to the beach earlier that day. She was exhausted and there would be much to occupy her time in the coming days.

She awoke to an impatient pounding on her heavy door, and her father's voice bellowed, "Alison! All-i-sonnn!" She had awakened with a start, looked around the room, and realized it was dark. Confused, slowly the day came back to her, and she moaned in her grief.

Ali walked unsteadily across the room, reaching to unlatch the door. She heard her father's angry shouts.

"Open this door this instant! How dare you lock a door in my home! I will not be locked out of any room in my home!" he thundered.

As she tried to open the door just a mere crack so she could see her father, he forcefully shoved it wide. It struck Ali in the middle of her forehead, knocking her to the floor. She lay stunned, her head exploding, seeing stars. She reached up to the trickle of blood catching in her eyebrow, a large bump forming at its origin.

"Forgive me, Father. I fell asleep and lost track of time," she said, hoping to assuage her father's temper somewhat as she dabbed a handkerchief to her forehead to stop the bleeding. She hoped her response would be enough so he would go away, but she knew that was more than he could ever deliver. Even her dear Mama could not calm his temper tantrums. He had an uncontrollable rage inside of him. Ali tried to remember her father's wretched upbringing and life before meeting Mama, but this was unforgivable.

Ali momentarily wished she could have passed with her Mama, certainly a better alternative to her father's wrath. But escape she would once Mama's funeral was over. She would put her mother's plan in motion tonight. For now, she must face him, and her stomach roiled with fear.

"How *dare* you! How dare you talk back to me in front of Mr. McCabe and his assistant! How dare you disobey my orders in *my own home!*" She caught his emphasis on *my own home*. This was her Mama's home, because Grandfather Thayer had gifted it to her on her wedding day.

He raged on, "Mr. McCabe is my peer and you brought shame to me in front of him! Not to mention I am paying them to prepare your mother for burial, and we must get on with it so as not to drain my accounts!"

There it is, Ali thought, *he is too cheap to provide Mama with the dignity and burial she deserves.* She tried to speak, "But, Father, she had only just passed a moment before. Surely you would allow me to have a few moments with my precious Mama?"

"Your sisters (she cringed when he said *sisters*, not half-sisters) said their goodbyes and went home to tend to their families. They had no need for your theatrics."

Of course, Ali thought, *because they didn't love her.* They hadn't just lost their mother. They were too young when their mother died to even understand her grief. They had what they wanted now—their "Papa" all to themselves with *"that woman*" out of the way. They had their prominent husbands and perfect children and their stations in Wilmington society. They never lifted a finger to care for Mama, but that was fine with Ali. She knew Mama preferred her to care for her. No, they could *never* be expected to help with anything, not when their "Papa" had an unemployed and unmarried spinster living in *his* house. Let her earn her keep caring for Mama, cleaning the home, preparing their meals, and entertaining her half-sister's families.

What they didn't know, could never experience, was the precious privilege Ali felt caring for her dear Mama, and being there to hold her as she transitioned to Heaven. *And now that Mama is gone,* Ali thought, her mind making a checklist, *I must carry out the plan Mama and I made, and I must rush to have all in order.* She must remove the rest of Mama's things from her room tonight after her father was fast asleep. She would leave immediately after Mama's funeral, asking the neighbor boy Walter to take her trunk to the train station while they were at the funeral.

She was thinking deeply when her father once again raged at her, "Get up off the floor and get supper on the table! The girls and their families will be here soon expecting a meal!"

Jolted to awareness by her father's anger, Ali looked up defiantly into his angry eyes, her head aching intensely but her chin held high, and immediately she felt the cold hard slap of his hand hitting her full force across her already injured face. She cried out in pain, not only from the slap, but because it landed on the very spot where the door had nearly just knocked her out.

Even more than the physical abuse, her own father felt justified in beating his daughter the very day her beloved mother died. *I loathe him. He hates me. I have no other option but to go before he throws me out. Or kills me,* which Ali now believed was a real possibility. *Soon, Mama, soon I will be in Savannah.* Ali knew she would have to work quickly and secretly to put Mama's plan in motion. If he caught her leaving, there was no telling what he might do to her.

"We will be going to the mortuary at seven this evening for a brief viewing of your mother. Mr. McCabe will inter her in the family vault tomorrow morning. Now get up and prepare supper. I will be back directly to eat and then we will leave by six-thirty. Do not disobey me again, Ali, or you will find yourself on the street with no means of support."

And there it is, the threat she had been waiting for, and the one Mama had told her to expect. *Yes, he would like that,* Ali thought, so he could more openly carry on with that harlot of his, Rebecca Bard. *Yes, I know her name, Father.* Ali once followed her home from the millinery shop where she worked. Ali had been bold enough to inquire of Rebecca's neighbors who she was. Decent people, they were more than happy to accommodate her with not only her name but other details of what they had noticed.

Father will have her in this house before Mama's body is cold. Mama's house. The house Grandfather Thayer had given her. He would have nothing if not for Mama. He came from dirt and he will one day return to dirt, where he belongs. Ali felt that the house was rightly hers, but, of course, as an unmarried woman, she could not legally own property. She hated these constraints society put on her life.

She dared to protest. "But, Father, Mr. McCabe cannot possibly have Mama prepared for the viewing by seven this evening!"

"There is to be no public viewing. This is simply a short family service and burial will proceed in the morning. I have work to attend to. We have not the time nor money for such a waste. She is dead. Nothing can be done about it, and we must carry on with our lives."

At this, Ali stood and steeled herself. She knew she was risking his physical abuse once more, but she would not allow him to simply bury her mother without friends or family to mourn her. It wasn't right.

"Father," she said as sternly as she could, having taken a step backwards beyond his striking distance, "Mama was a wonderful wife and mother. She has many friends and her family, especially Grandfather Thayer, who care about her! She deserves more than a pauper's funeral, and certainly Grandfather Thayer will never allow this!

We must have time to notify everyone and prepare refreshments for afterwards for the mourners. I must select an appropriate dress for her burial, and I would like to coif Mama's hair myself. I know exactly how she liked to have it done. We simply cannot bury her in the morning; it would not be decent!" And delivering the final blow she added, "All of society will be revolted by such a crass handling of Mama. It simply isn't done." She knew she was out of range of his strong arm already drawn back and prepared to strike her again.

"No! You will *not* strike me again! I will see to it that my sweet Mama has a dignified burial befitting her station in society, and you will work with me to that end. She was your wife. She deserves honor. And she will have it! Do you understand?" Ali shocked herself but not nearly as much as she had taken her father by surprise.

His face betrayed that he was startled and put off balance. She could tell he was rolling the effect of his plans on his social standing. His arm dropped and he turned to walk out the door. He turned back towards her.

"Seven this evening, Ali. Oh, and your Grandfather Thayer has nothing to say about this matter. Josephine was my wife, and I make the decisions in my home regarding my family. I will allow one extra day for mourners and not one minute more. If you want a luncheon, you will plan, prepare, and serve it yourself. You will not ask Anna or Marie to leave their families for such frivolous nonsense."

He moved towards the door, stopped, and turned to her and hissed, "If you dare ever again to speak to me in such a disrespectful manner, I will not merely strike you, I will throw you from this house to navigate life on your own. As a matter of fact," he added with hatred written on his reddened face, "when this ghastly business is complete, we will discuss your new responsibilities if you wish to continue to call my home your residence. I suggest you give it some serious thought." He walked out the door, slamming it in his retreat.

No, Father, we will not discuss anything of the kind! Mama saw to that. I will leave this house forever, and you will have nothing to say about it. Ali knew she would be on the first train to Savannah and to Cousin Edy at least a full day before her father knew she was gone. This knowledge empowered her over the next twenty-four hours. Her heart skipped a beat in anticipation. Her heart was torn in so many different directions by such intense emotions. Sorrow. Excitement. Fear. Anticipation. Trepidation.

Ali had no black dresses in her chifforobe, so she instinctively went to her mother's room to find a dress. She stepped in the door of her mother's room where just a few hours ago Mama still lived and breathed. And then she didn't. It was all so sudden. She wasn't prepared to lose her mother. Ali tried not to look at the bed, now stripped of its coverings—the soft, cotton sheets and coverlet on which Mama had embroidered small violets. Her velvety hands expertly worked the needle making delicate stitches. The laundress hadn't wasted any time stripping all vestiges of her mama from the room, no doubt on Father's orders.

Ali moved quietly to Mama's chifforobe and opened the large birds-eye maple doors. Mama ordered the wardrobe directly from Harrods in London. There were full-length mirrors on each of the three doors, and, when she saw herself, Ali noticed the still oozing gash above her eyebrow, and the red welt on her pale skin where her father's blow had landed on her cheekbone just below her eye. It was swollen and soon would turn all shades of blue and purple, but she had no intention of trying to cover either wound with face powder.

No, Ali thought, *I will allow Father to feel the shame of his brutality towards me and let the rest of those at Mama's funeral know what she and Mama had endured from this horrible man. There is a day of reckoning coming, James Davies, and I only wish I could see it.* But Ali would be long gone.

She was ashamed that he was her father. How could his blood be in my veins? She would never understand. Nor could she understand how her Mama could have fallen in love with much less married such a brute. No, she would go defiantly and let them stare.

Her senses were flooded with her mother's scent, and hot tears rolled down her raw, injured cheek, stinging. Her mind filled with precious memories the fragrance evoked, memories of being a child in Mama's arms, wrapping her in love and protection. As if embracing her mother, Ali wrapped her arms around the few dresses left, holding them close, breathing in Mama's scent as if being hugged by Mama, safely held to her bosom. *Oh, to be held just one more time in her embrace—everything would be made right.*

But this time, without Mama to protect her, she pushed her father too far, and there would be no turning back. She must give careful thought to her plans. As much as she feared leaving this house, there was a growing anticipation of the freedom her mother had engineered for her, out from under the cruel and critical oversight of her father. She silently thanked her mother again and crossed herself in a prayer for Mama's repose in Heaven. If she stayed, the consequences of her open defiance of her father would be unbearable. And she made a promise to her mother to carry out the plan they had devised.

Ali chose one of the few dresses left in Mama's chifforobe, a black taffeta gown with a matching velvet bodice and small covered buttons. It had a detachable black lace collar, but Ali felt lace would be inappropriate for this sad occasion. She remembered Mama had worn this dress to her own mother's funeral when she passed three years ago. She and Mama had always shared clothes. This would be the final time here in this home, and she felt closer to Mama somehow, wearing her dress.

Ali stripped to her undergarments and pulled the dress over her head. She buttoned it in the front and would not need anyone's help dressing. She caught a glimpse of herself in the mirror and realized she looked like an adult. And for the first time in her life, with her mother gone, she knew she was an adult. All day she felt like an orphaned child, but the mirror did not lie. It reminded her that she had grown-up work to do to escape the hell her father had made in this home. She must honor her mother's final request of her, and this she did with pleasure.

She had taken the rest of her mama's clothes to her room, one by one as directed, and packed them into the steamer trunk, preparing for her flight to Savannah. Only this black dress was left along with a few "day dresses" Mama wore at home or to do the gardening she loved so much.

Ali carefully removed the lovely lavender evening dress Mama requested she wear "if something happened." This was Mama's favorite gown, a soft organza pastel with small embroidered clusters of violets dotting the full skirt here and there, much as her bed sheets and wallpaper. Mama loved the delicate spring flowers and their color. They reminded her of the renewal of nature. The bodice had attached mutton sleeves and delicate pearl buttons down the back. It was cinched at Mama's tiny waist with a very light mint-colored belt that tied in a bow at the back. Mama always finished the look with a small lace collar and a single strand of pearls that her own mother left for her.

Ali wanted to have these things delivered to the funeral home before her half-sisters arrived and began bickering about her choice. She knew what Mama wanted because she *knew* Mama. For her half-sisters, it would be all about perception and society, not about Mama's wishes. Ali also did not want Anne and Marie rummaging through Mama's room and discovering the jewels and clothing were missing. She knew they would greedily dig for anything they could appropriate when no one was watching.

Ali would ask the neighbor boy, Walter, who was sweet on her, to take the dress and other articles of clothing to Mr. McCabe as quickly as possible for Mama. Her precious Mama would be a lovely vision just as she always was. Salty tears flowed stinging her fresh slap mark.

Before leaving, Ali stooped to pull open the bottom drawer. Near the back she found the box Mama left there for her. Ali remembered this painted wooden box from her childhood. It was black and had a dreamlike Russian winter scene painted on top and lacquered all over. Ali gently lifted the lid, gasping at its contents. There were several rolls of one-hundred-dollar bills—enough for her to live on for several years. Ali knew her mother secreted this money away for her from the stipend Grandfather Thayer had a man deliver every month—only to her mother for her discretionary use. Mama had told her that only she, Grandfather, and now Ali knew of this arrangement, and she must tell no one. Ali understood instinctively this money was for use in the event her mother ever needed the means to leave if necessary.

There were still a few jewels left as well. She wrapped everything inside the folds of Mama's dress so no one would notice. Taking one last glance around Mama's room, trying to etch it into her memory, Ali quietly unlocked the door and silently moved toward her own room.

As soon as she heard the front door slam, Ali knew her father was probably going to see his whore. Even today of all days, the day his wife and her dear Mama died, Father would be thinking only about his own physical desires and his whore. But this was the time she needed to set their plan in motion. His sins were no longer her burden.

Chapter 3
An Earnest Ally

After carefully pressing it, Ali wrapped Mama's dress and other items for the mortuary in delicate white tissue, then brown paper and string. She had seen Walter in his backyard working earlier. She opened the side door just off the kitchen and called to him through the screened door.

"Walter, might I trouble you for your assistance, please?"

"Aw, Miss Ali, you could never trouble me; I am happy to help you in any way I may," Walter bashfully said, looking at his feet. Walter had just turned sixteen and still had the red plump cheeks of a boy.

"Thank you, Walter. As you may have heard, Mama passed earlier today, and I must have this package delivered to McCabe's Mortuary as quickly as possible. Would you be kind enough to carry it there for me? I would greatly appreciate it," she said pressing a shiny half-dollar into his palm.

"Miss Ali, there's no need for you to pay me anything at all. I am happy to help. I surely am sorry about Missus Davies' passing. She was always cheerful, like a breath of morning air. I will miss her," Walter said, tearing up. Ali was touched by his sympathy and obvious love of her Mama.

"Thank you, Walter. You are very kind to say so. She was wonderful, wasn't she?"

"Yes, ma'am, and if you don't mind my saying so, you favor her," Walter said, again looking at his feet. Ali knew Walter would be her ally in carrying out her plan.

"Thank you again, Walter. There is nothing you could have said to make me happier than that. If I can be half the woman my mother was, I would be satisfied. Now, please run along and deliver this package to Mr. McCabe. And, Walter, I will need your help with some other things later tomorrow. Do you think you will be available?"

"Oh course, Miss Ali; I will make myself available to help you in any way I may tomorrow."

"Oh, and Walter, please keep this between us," she asked and could tell Walter knew the reason for the secrecy. Her bruised cheek and awful forehead cut as well as those in the past told him a tale he desperately wanted to be untrue, but, from hearing the shouting coming from their home, he knew the truth of the matter. Walter felt sorry for Miss Ali. She was always kind to him. *I will help her*, he thought, *always*.

To avoid drawing attention, Ali knew she must prepare a meal for the family tonight before the viewing hour as well assemble food for the funeral reception tomorrow, and she knew she could expect no help from her lazy, entitled half-sisters. Ali was determined it would be the best funeral reception ever, to honor Mama.

She was relieved Father had relented in burying Mama without a proper service; yet she knew it was also another cruel test of his, thinking he had assigned her an impossible task, assuming she would fail and prove to everyone her father was right—she was indeed worthless. If the reception went badly, it would offer him another opportunity to demean her publicly in front of his other two *perfect* daughters with their perfect husbands and perfect children and their perfect places in society as well as the other family and friends gathering.

But Father underestimates me again. Mama taught me well. Ali had become an accomplished chef and decorator thanks to her mother's tutelage. Though she had little time to prepare, she would do this for her mother. *For Mama*, she whispered to herself. She set about making her plans.

Walter returned about half an hour later to let her know all was well with the package she sent to Mr. McCabe, and he asked Walter to assure Ali that he would take special care of her lovely mother.

"Walter," Ali began, "you said you would help me if I needed it. Did you mean that?"

"Why, yes, of course, Miss Ali—anything! How may I help you?"

"I have to prepare supper for my family tonight, and I must prepare food for the funeral reception tomorrow. I've made a list of things I need from the market. There will be many people here, and the task is mine to prepare all the refreshments for them. I want this to be perfect and honor my mother. If I give you the list, will you take it to Mr. Meier and ask him to gather the items I need? Please have him put it on Father's account. This is a very large favor I am asking you, Walter, and I insist you allow me to pay you."

"Miss Ali, I would be happy to do this for you. I'll go right away, and we can settle up after the service if that is all right with you," Walter offered graciously.

"Oh, I do thank you, Walter," she said and kissed him on the cheek. Embarrassed, Walter took the list from her and nearly stumbled out the door.

Ali went about her work all the while making plans in her mind. As Father also had demanded she prepare food for her half-sisters and their families before the private family viewing at McClure's this evening, Ali opted for a cold plate dinner.

She removed her apron, needing to walk, to escape the overwhelming sadness she felt and the oppressive cloud that had descended on her home. She simply needed to breathe. Ali walked to the mortuary to attend to her mother's hair and make-up.

Chapter 4
Preparations

After lovingly styling her mother's gray-streaked hair and applying the slightest trace of powder, rouge, and a bit of color on her lips, Mama looked as beautiful as if she were just resting. Oh, how Ali wished she was but resting! She began to cry, sobbing uncontrollably, and Mr. McCabe and his staff allowed her the privacy to mourn.

As Ali left the mortuary, she walked briskly, not giving thought to where she was going. Unconsciously her walk brought her to the waterfront. As she wandered alongside the Cape Fear River, she saw the tall ships at anchor and longshoremen still scrambling to unload the cargo that would make for busy trading at the warehouses tomorrow morning. She loved to watch this scene, and most days she tried to venture the few blocks from home to observe. If her father had known of her whereabouts, he would have been furious. Ali would be accused once again of bringing shame down upon the family.

"Seems as if all I need to do is breathe to bring shame to the family," she said aloud to no one but herself. Nevertheless,

Ali was committed to the plan she and Mama made and to live her life fully—for herself and for Mama. *No, I will never be stuck in a kitchen, preparing food for ungrateful people. I will never sit in a parlor entertaining the gossips with mindless conversation.* She had a brain and ambition, and she would find a way to support herself. Ali turned and walked the short distance home. She was ready to face the viewing for Mama tonight.

She slipped into the back door quietly, hoping not to be noticed, and lightly stepped up the back stairway to her room. There she bathed and donned the black dress of Mama's. She caught a glimpse of herself in the mirror, tucked an errant auburn lock behind her ear. Not the most becoming color on her, but, on the saddest day of her life, it seemed fitting to wear black. It matched her heartbreak and her attitude towards her family.

Ali knew the next day would bring the final resting of her mother in the family crypt. Her father had the gaudy edifice of granite and gargoyles built at the Oakdale Cemetery on the edge of Wilmington. He hired stone masons from Italy, and she had to admit their work was exquisite.

The crypt was finished with a custom hand-wrought iron gate covering frosted glass. Inside were spaces for four bodies. Ali assumed hers would not be one of them. But she would be able to visit her Mama here quite easily. It was just a short distance from home. There was a small stone bench within the crypt where, if she hadn't been leaving, she could have sat and talked with her Mama. *Mama always said she would never leave me—she said she will always be just a heartbeat away.* Ali held that thought tightly. It would sustain her in the days ahead. But now Ali must concentrate on getting through the next few hours of the viewing.

The reality was Ali wouldn't be there to spend this private time with her mama. Her father made himself very clear—Ali was not welcome in her own home. She wondered how long he had been planning this? Since Mama became ill? *Oh, Mama, this would break your heart. I am relieved you are not here to witness this final scurrilous action.*

At six p.m. just like clockwork, Father came home expecting his supper on the table and smelling of cheap perfume and sweat. *He has no decency*, Ail seethed.

Anna and William and their two children Willy and Annalise as well as Marie and Beau, Sissy, and Prissy arrived hungry at 5:45.

The dining table was set with silverware and napkins as well as crystal water glasses. When her half-sisters seated themselves, they eyed each other, perplexed by the lack of plates. They then looked at the table where Ali had spread a lovely cold buffet. The plates were stacked at one side so they could serve themselves from the proffered dishes—sliced ham and roast beef, fresh vegetables from the garden, fruit from the stand down the street, potato salad, and fresh breads and rolls Mr. Meier had selected for her.

Father was the first to remark, "Do you intend that we serve ourselves, Ali?"

"Why, yes, Father. I had no help in preparing the supper, so I imagine you will have no impediment to serving your own plates."

Her half-sisters huffed, obviously unhappy that they weren't being served as was to be expected at their station in society, and Anna was also expected to help her children? Well, it just wasn't proper. They complained as they filled their plates and went back for seconds.

"My dear Mama died today. There is much I must do to prepare for our guests tomorrow after the funeral. Because I am the only one available to make preparations, a cold supper before the viewing is a matter of convenience. For *me.* You may eat what I have prepared, and I notice you seem to be enjoying the food I have laid out for you," Ali said while eyeing her half-sisters nearly choking on their heaped plates of food, "or if you prefer my feelings will not be hurt if you choose to find a restaurant downtown. It is entirely your preference. I really do not care what you do."

Having spewed this on her family, her second bout of bravery today, though her stomach was in knots, Ali abruptly turned on her heel and left the room. She retrieved her cloak from the hall tree and left the house with mouths agape behind her.

On her way out, she prepared a heaping plate for Walter. At least someone deserved to be served, and Walter would appreciate her efforts.

Her day had been one unending nightmare, and the family viewing was as devastating as she expected. In the morning she must face the unspeakable—the final interment of her precious mama.

Dear God, if you are listening, my precious mama is with you now. Please, God, give her all the joy she was cheated out of in this life. Help me, oh God, I pray, to somehow get through her funeral, and later aid me in the escape my mama never had. Please give your angels watch over me, and if possible, God, make one of those angels my mama. Amen.

She crossed herself and climbed into her soft bed, knowing this would be the last night she would ever sleep in this bed, in this room, in her mama's house again.

Chapter 5
Farewells

She slept fitfully that long night and awoke to a grey drizzle. *Even Heaven is crying great torrents today. But only for her. Mama is going home today, and the angels will rejoice.* Ali put on her black cotton stockings under the black dress she had chosen from Mama's wardrobe. She wore a black cameo mourning pin that belonged to Mama, the one she wore at her own Mama's funeral.

Descending the staircase slowly, knowing the hell that awaited her downstairs, Ali wondered if her father and Anna and Marie's families would be expecting her to prepare breakfast for them. Ali had taken her time dressing so as to leave no time to cook for all of them. She was not hungry. In fact, her stomach was a bit queasy, not only because she was about to inter the dearest person in her world but because later she would leave this house forever.

Waiting in the foyer for the others, Ali could hear their loud protestations coming from the dining room.

"But Papa! Ali has nothing to do but lie about all day long. We have children and husbands to care for. Surely preparing a light breakfast for us is not asking too much, is it?"

Ali decided she would rather walk alone to the basilica. She retrieved her cloak, hat, and an umbrella and slipped out the front door unnoticed. It was a short walk down Ann Street to the cathedral. Arriving at the front door of the basilica, she saw one of McCabe's gentlemen who had assisted taking her mother's body from the home. Recognizing her, he opened the door.

"Hello, Miss Davies. My deepest condolences. You will find your mother reposed in the chapel. So many beautiful flowers have been delivered. Mrs. Davies must have had many friends and loved ones. Such an outpouring."

"Th-thank you," Ali said, quickly shifting her eyes downward to hide the tears that were threatening. She knew she would only have a few moments to herself before the family entourage arrived, probably peeved at her for leaving them to prepare their own cold breakfast and wondering where she had disappeared to. But Ali no longer cared. She only wanted to capture these few precious, last moments with her dear mama.

The chapel was empty but for Ali and her mother, who lay in the inexpensive coffin her father had chosen. *Of course, he would choose the cheapest wooden box available for Mama. But it doesn't matter because you look lovely, Mama. And look at all these lovely flowers! You would love them!* She was even more beautiful in death than in life if that were possible. *Perhaps because now you are an angel, Mama. Please, Mama, please—watch over me.*

Ali was more than aware how difficult her next moves would prove. Moments after her mother passed, Ali found the newspaper and scanned it for positions in Savannah. It was a long shot, but she had to try. She found an advertisement for an accounting assistant at the Southern Atlantic Merchants' & Farmers' Bank in Savannah. She immediately sent a telegram regarding this position and another to Cousin Edy to notify her of Mama's death and to let her know which train she would be on to Savannah.

Ali received immediate replies to her telegrams from Cousin Edy and a Mr. John Meadows, vice president of accounts at the bank and both in the affirmative. She had a home to go to as well as an interview with Mr. Meadows for a new position as an accounting assistant. She silently thanked her mother for the trunk full of sophisticated work clothing.

Wouldn't Mama be proud if she knew about my interview at the bank? Ali would feel even more confident wearing the beautiful clothes Mama had commissioned for her. Mr. Meadows requested that she report to the bank for an interview as soon as she was settled in at Cousin Edy's. This would make boarding the train tonight even easier than she anticipated. She always had been proficient at figures, and now she would put that talent to use. *I can support myself, Mama!*

Now, she had to quickly and carefully put their plans—hers and Mama's—into action to leave Wilmington for Savannah. Thank God she had Walter to help her pull this off.

For the last few months, Ali had been packing the large steamer trunk from the attic that she had hidden with a tablecloth and her pitcher and bowl for washing up. Rarely did anyone other than the cleaning lady enter her room, so she wasn't too afraid of its discovery. Still, she needed to be cautious. Because she and Mama wore the same size clothing, her mother told her to begin taking her dresses, new ones she had recently commissioned her dressmaker to make for her, one at a time and pack them in the trunk.

Jo had exquisite taste, and the clothing included nightdresses and undergarments, day dresses for home, evening attire for dinner and special occasions, and clothing that would be suitable to her new position at the bank if she were hired. There were beautiful new starched white lace collars and one with pearls sewn into the design. There were new high, lace-up walking shoes, satin evening shoes to match the gowns, and sensible everyday shoes for work and . Her mother said if she were to begin a new life and be employed, she must have appropriate clothing suitable for the position she desired.

As her mother inevitably learned of her father's indiscretions, which became more flagrant, her father would shower Jo with parfum from Paris and expensive jewelry— broaches, earbobs, bracelets and necklaces, even jeweled hair combs and a tiara for evening wear. Jo donned her beautiful dresses, accessorized with the exquisite jewels, held her head erect as she walked down the aisle of the Basilica of St. Mary for mass as if she hadn't a care in the world.

Though she could almost hear the wagging tongues of the gossips, she would not allow her husband to sully her name even if he had his own. Because he was cruel and abusive in life as well as in the marital bed, she felt his affairs relieved her of the wifely duties. The "act" was, after all, calculated purely for his pleasure, certainly not hers, so she contented herself with her gardening and her quiet conversations with Ali.

For Jo, Ali was her perfect and, yes, beautiful daughter—intelligent, gifted, ambitious, and loving. Jo taught her to rise above her abusive father and thrive.

She was a strong and graceful woman, Ali thought.

Her mother was painfully aware that her husband would never be faithful to her, so she was committed to making his filthy infidelity work for her. After making him squirm a bit so he thought she cared, she accepted his guilt gifts, collecting them for her daughter Ali, for the day would surely come when she would need them. Ali knew this was the time Mama had envisioned, remembering their conversation of just days ago. *She must have known she was dying. Why didn't I see it?*

"Ali, my darling daughter, in the event anything happens to me, I want you to take this box and do not let anyone know about it," her mother said. Jo didn't open the box but said, "On my wedding day, my father gave me this box with instructions to keep it a secret. It was to be used if ever I changed my mind about my marriage and I needed it to start a new life with you elsewhere. There were many times I was tempted to use it, but I learned how to make your father's ill treatment work to my advantage, and I did not want any shame to besmirch your reputation on account of us. If something should happen to me," she began.

"Mama, *no!* Do not speak of it!"

"But, Ali, my dear, I am not well, and I fear we do not have much time left, so please listen carefully to what I am saying. When I pass, come into this room and immediately retrieve this box and let no one see you. Take it and all the other things we have packed and go. Start a new life with Cousin Edy in Savannah.

Take my jewels a bit at a time starting today. I will give you pieces to secret away. No one will notice and I do not want Anna and Marie to have anything of mine. These are for you only. For years now your father has spoilt them and lavished them with everything their selfish hearts desired and much to their ruin. But you, my darling girl, never asked for anything and never received anything. For that reason and because I love you more than anyone in this world, everything I have is yours alone. I want you to take this box and use the money to travel to Cousin Edy's home in Savannah. She and I have had a pact to always care for each other if anything should happen. She will take you in and help you just as I would have done the same for her daughter Hannah, God rest her poor sweet soul. She will take you in and help you get on your feet in your new life. There is enough here that you can live comfortably as long as you take care not to spend carelessly and you secure a position.

You may have noticed that I have attempted to add clothing suitable for a working woman in an office. You see, my love, intelligent women can make their own plans. I want you to be free of this life here in Wilmington. So depart with haste, my precious girl, if God should give you this option.

You must make your arrangements quickly after I pass and tell no one. Board the train and post a letter to your father, but do not tell him where you are going. By the time he receives it, you will be in Savannah before he has the opportunity to devise a plan to keep you here and use you—and he will, Ali. He will use you until there is nothing left of your life. Don't let him do that, my sweet. You are so gifted, so intelligent and lovely. The world is yours.

I dare say your father will replace me very quickly with one of his mistresses. In this situation, the abuse will be unbearable for you. You must promise me you will take my jewels, this money, and my clothes and leave. And, Ali, never look back."

With open and teary eyes, Ali listened to everything her mother told her. She could barely speak; it was all so overwhelming and sudden.

"Oh, Mama, I cannot bear to imagine my life without you. I am happy here at home because we are together. I hope, pray, that this illness will pass and you will never leave me," Ali choked out through the deep sorrow that engulfed her at even the thought of her mother's passing.

"Ali, darling, it will happen one day—though I too hope not for a long time—but it is important that I prepare you for a life on your own without me. That is part of a mother's responsibilities as well as protecting her child. And I also must provide you with the means to escape this oppressive environment. Now you have it, and you know where to go, and you will not be alone with Cousin Edy. Bring down the steamer trunk in the attic. Pack everything and hide it." She handed Ali a small key for the trunk.

"Mama, thank you from the bottom of my heart. Bless you for doing all of this for me."

"Ali, to be truthful, I am so excited for you! You will have a fresh start. Oh my, how wonderful! And you will love Edy just as I always have. Never let the harsh words you have heard here enter your mind again. You are beautiful, so lovely. You are a good person. You are much more intelligent than even your father knows, and that is how you'll be able to escape!"

"Mama, it sounds as if you have been planning this for years!" Ali said.

"I have, Ali, with your grandfather, from the day of my marriage to your father. The plan originally was for both of us to leave together. I have made my peace with your father, and I am too old and ill to uproot now. I would only slow you down because I would want to hold you too close. You must do this for yourself."

"Mama, may we please change this dreadful subject? I cannot bear any more sadness. But, Mama, I adore you and I have no way to repay you for your sacrifice for me, but I will never forget it. I promise you that if that day comes, God forbid," Ali crossed herself, "I will do exactly as you have planned and make this new start for both of us." Ali stroked her mother's soft hands as she spoke.

"This was no sacrifice, dear child. This has been my dream, and I delighted in every jewel your father gave me, in every dollar I have secreted away, and every dress that was sewn for you. Though I likely will not be here to watch as you bring our plans to fruition, I will always be with you, but you must watch for the signs and know it is your mama. Edy will be good to you, and I have a feeling you will recognize her when you meet as we are a great deal alike, she and I." At that, Ali kissed her mother goodnight and went to her room to sleep, though fitfully after all she had learned that night.

Just two days later, Ali stood in the basilica next to her mother, her hand lying on her mother's, talking quietly to her as tears flowed down her cheeks. She touched her mother's cheek, remembering how exquisitely soft her skin was. Each night Mama applied Pond's Cold Cream to her face and décolletage, a habit Ali herself adopted. And today Mama's skin was glowing.

"Mama, I'm leaving tonight. I'm going to Cousin Edy's just as we planned. Walter is helping me. He reserved a ticket for me on the last train to Savannah and will collect my trunk and take it to the train station during the service. I know your heart goes with me, Mama. I love you and thank you for being the most wonderful mother in the world. Rest in perfect peace among the angels, Mama," Ali whispered, then lightly kissed her mother's cheek.

Ali noticed that the gentleman at the door had asked mourners to wait in the vestibule to give Ali a little time, and she was deeply grateful to him. As he allowed mourners to enter, the chapel filled with her mother's friends, those who had learned of her death by word of mouth and a small obituary in the *Morning News*. Soon, to Ali's astonishment, there was standing room only. *Mama, you were so beloved by so many!*

Hearing her father's and half-sisters' voices, she braced herself for what was coming.

"Ali, it would have been appropriate for you to have prepared a breakfast for the family and travelled to the service with us as a family. We had no idea what had happened to you, and I do not appreciate your rude behavior," her father said in a voice loud enough for all to hear in the small chapel. Most shifted uncomfortably and pretended not to hear out of embarrassment for Ali. Several came up to her to give their condolences in the hope her father would be distracted.

Not backing down, Ali faced her father, and in a much quieter voice, said, "Since when, Father, have you ever treated me as a member of your family?"

James Davies stood there, mouth agape, stunned, and perhaps even a bit embarrassed, into silence. Any other time, Ali would have prepared for a stern reprimand or even a caning. It was then he noticed the large bruise and angry-looking cut on her forehead, and his face reddened in contempt, but he was unable to do or say anything further in public. Ali was certain everyone there knew exactly why her face was beaten.

Not today, Father. You will not abuse me today. Ali knew that with the reception afterwards at their home, Father would not have the opportunity to scold or beat her surrounded by so many people whose respect he craved but would probably never have. *These people are here for Mama, and Mama only, not you.*

She sat down in the pew to the left of her father with her half-sisters on his right. Ali was on the aisle, edging as close to the end of the pew as possible, where she could be closest to Mama and as far from her father as possible.

Mama wore the lovely lavender dress she had requested, and Ali had coifed her hair and applied her powder and rouge just as she had watched Mama do every morning as long as she could remember. Mama always looked flawless with just enough makeup to enhance her natural beauty. *Still, Ali could see the smile on her lovely face.* Ali thought, *and she is happy now. You've escaped that vile man, Mama, and soon I will as well.*

Father Maloney conducted the service and the following interment at the Oakdale Cemetery, which seemed over in minutes, not hours. Ali clung to the last visage of her Mama until the coffin lid was secured. She rode with the family to the cemetery, where the carriages pulled to a stop in front of the ostentatious Davies mausoleum.

Her father took an ornate key from his vest pocket, unlocked the iron gate, then stepped aside as Mr. McCabe's gentlemen carried the coffin into the mausoleum and placed it on the top granite shelf. Mama was the first interred here and was alone, Ali noted sadly. It would have broken her heart but for the strong Catholic faith that assured her Mama was at this very moment in Heaven, rejoicing with the angels. *Mama is an angel.* Ali knew Father Maloney and the other parish members would be praying for Mama's release from Purgatory, but Ali found it impossible to believe that God would send her there and not directly to Heaven. Surely he knew her goodness and faith.

Because Father Maloney was certain James Davies had not had his elaborate mausoleum consecrated, he began the blessing of the place of committal of Josephine Thayer Davies' body.

Father Maloney crossed himself and intoned, "In the name of the Father, the Son, and the Holy Spirit, amen. Blessed is the Lord our God," and the congregants around the mausoleum who were Catholic crossed themselves and replied, "Blessed is the Lord our God" in unison.

"Almighty and everlasting God, remember the mercy with which you graced your servant Josephine in life. Receive her, we pray, into the mansions of the saints. As we make ready our sister's resting place, look also with fervor on those who mourn and comfort them in their loss. Grant this through Christ our Lord. Amen," Father Maloney continued. At the mention of "those who mourn," Ali began to weep softly.

"In You we place our trust and hope. In You the dead whose bodies were temples of the Spirit find everlasting peace. As we take leave of our sister Josephine, give our hearts peace in the firm hope that one day Josephine will live with You in Heaven which You have prepared for her. Amen."

Ali heard a loud, obnoxious, and rude "harrumph" rise out of her father's throat as he motioned with his hand to signal Father Maloney to move along. Father Maloney ignored his disrespect, sprinkled holy water onto the mausoleum, and moved to the interment sacrament.

"Father!" Ali hissed, "How *dare* you show such disrespect towards Father Maloney and Mama, and how dare you interrupt Mama's service!"

"Get on with it then!" James Davies growled under his breath, casting a threatening look at Ali. She knew there would be hell to pay when she got home, but she would not allow him to deprive her mama of a proper committal service.

"Ahem," Father Maloney uttered, picking up where he had left off. "Trusting in God, we have prayed together for Josephine, and now we come to the last farewell. May our farewell express our affection for her; may it ease our sadness and strengthen our hope that one day we shall joyfully greet her again when the love of Christ, which conquers all things, destroys even death itself. Amen."

At this, Father Maloney sprinkled the coffin with holy water, and the altar boy handed him the incense, which he in turn wafted over the coffin, the last earthly sacrament Mama would receive.

"To You, O Lord, we commend the soul of Josephine Thayer Davies. Receive her soul and present her to God the Most High. I breathe forth my spirit to you, my Creator, and in my flesh I shall see God. On the last day I shall rise again." Placing his hand on Josephine's coffin, as did Ali standing next to him, he said, "Grant your servant rest, a haven of pardon and peace."

Again, Ali wept openly and unabated.

"Yes, dearest Lord," Ali said softly, "give my mama some peace at last and joy beyond anything she could have hoped for in her wretched life here."

Father Maloney blessed her in the name of the Father, the Son, and Holy Spirit as Ali and those gathered crossed themselves. She noted her father and half-sisters did not, which Ali took as the final insult to her mama.

James seemed almost pleased to close the ironclad door and lock it, placing the only key into his watch pocket. He was quite proud of his ornate mausoleum. He was smiling. *Smiling!* Ali wanted to scream at his insulting and disrespectful treatment of her dear mother even to the end.

He herded her half-sisters and their families into the two waiting black funeral carriages. Ali instead turned to Father Maloney, almost hoping her father would leave without her. But her father knew the reception at the house depended upon Ali, so he impatiently cooled his heels as she spoke one final time to Father Maloney.

"Thank you, Father, for your blessing and prayers for my dear mama. Your service was lovely. Mama would've been so pleased," Ali said softly.

Father Maloney placed his hand on Ali's head and whispered a prayer. "Father in Heaven, we have commended the soul of our dear Jo to your love and care, and I now ask that you go with her precious daughter Ali as she begins this new chapter in life." He made the sign of the cross over her. Ali looked up into his eyes, and he nodded in affirmation that her mother had confided their secret in him.

"Thank you, Father Maloney, for everything. You have been here for me my whole life. I will miss you terribly," Ali whispered, holding his hand a bit longer than usual, both knowing they were not likely to see each other again in this life.

"Goodbye, dear girl. God go with you and keep you in His care," Father Maloney said.

She then felt her father take her arm brusquely, his fingers digging into her tender flesh, knowing it would leave a bruise for her to remind her he was in charge. *Not for long though, Father. Not much longer now.*

"Ali, time to turn off your tears and provide refreshments for the mourners as you said you could do. We shall see."

As if her tears were controlled by a faucet! *Oh, I loathe him, how I loathe him,* Ali thought. *But tonight—tonight I will never be demeaned, insulted, or abused by you and your nasty daughters again. Never again!* As she rode home with the family in their carriage, she looked around Wilmington, taking in the sites of her childhood mingled with memories of Mama, wistfully thinking, *I will never see you again, my beautiful Cape Fear.* Of course, Ali had no idea that this would indeed be her last glimpse of her beloved river town.

"Ali, will you be kind enough to listen to the conversation when it directly involves you!" Her father bellowed loudly enough that any passersby could hear, jolting Ali out of one of her many farewells today. *Still trying to shame me, Father? No more!*

"How may I serve you, my *dear* family?" Ali replied sarcastically, which was not lost on her father or half-sisters. They clucked their tongues in disapproval, shaking their heads, and exchanging looks between them.

"You may assure us that we will not be embarrassed by your lack of preparations for the upcoming reception for my guests," he answered, meeting her eyes directly as if challenging Ali to say anything in retort.

"Father, I have made everything perfectly ready for *Mama's* guests as *Mama* taught me to do. No one will be disappointed—*or shamed*," Ali added pointedly, "unless of course he or she," Ali looked directly at her father and half-sisters in turn as she said this, "might do so on his or her own account. It will certainly not be because I have not provided adequate, proper, and delicious refreshments."

Ali looked back out the window of the carriage, leaving her family to ponder all she had just said. *Oh, if looks could kill,* Ali thought, knowing their eyes were boring into her turned head. *Tonight. I only have to get through the rest of this wretched day.* Ali felt her stomach flip flop in anticipation.

Thanks in large part to Walter's help, the funeral reception was as perfect as she had hoped it would be, and she knew she might not have been able to pull it off without Walter picking up the food and finishing preparations while she was at the interment. Her father and half-sisters looked for flaws and missteps but found none. The silver was polished and Ali used her mother's best china. The food was plentiful and delicious. There were no complaints; in fact, the opposite. Ali could hear many guests whispering their astonishment that she was able to prepare such an event by herself while suffering the loss of her mother, and they commented that her mother would have been so proud of her. At that, Ali's heart warmed.

The mourners lingered for a little over two hours, coming in and out. Ali made a point of speaking to each one of them, thanking them for their friendship and kindness to her mother, until the front door closed after the last mourner departed. Ali quickly removed the dishes from the dining room and placed them in the kitchen on the counters and butcher block. She would let everyone think she would attend to the cleanup later. But she knew she would be gone and smiled at the thought of her half-sisters washing dishes.

Ali went up the back stairs to her room without comment to anyone. These stairs were rarely used by anyone else, but she took them many times to escape prying eyes and avoid intrusive questions about where she had been, what she had been doing, and with whom. She slipped easily into her bedroom without detection.

She had spoken with Walter earlier, apprising him of her plan to leave and asking him to assist her. While she and her family were at the funeral, he slipped into the house, removed her now heavy trunk from her room, and delivered it to the

Atlantic Coastline Station. Mr. Bradley, the stationmaster, was kind enough to hold the trunk for her. Walter purchased a ticket for her on the last train out of Wilmington that day to Savannah. Mr. Bradley would also hold the ticket for Ali. She gave Walter a letter for her father that he was to post the next morning, giving her ample time to arrive in Savannah before he discovered her departure and after any effort on his part to stop her would be dashed.

Ali stayed in her room until she heard her half-sisters leaving with their families for their own homes. At last the front door closed, and she knew her father was leaving, just as she had suspected, to go to Rebecca Bard's home, for he could not go long without his whore. She knew he would come home very late and very drunk, if at all, and this would be her opportunity to escape. Ali wondered how long it would be before he moved that slut into her Mama's home.

She picked up her reticule and looked around her light pink room, memorizing this chamber she had occupied since she was a child—her books, pictures, the large canopied bed, the fireplace—she suspected she would miss this a bit, but without her Mama this house meant nothing to her anymore. She had packed a few small mementos in the trunk, a photo of Mama and Grandfather and Grandmother Thayer, and a small Bible her mother gave her when she was confirmed into the Catholic Church. Those were the only things she wanted to remember about Wilmington and her old life here. Her life was about to open up in ways she could only imagine. *Oh, Mama! I'm going now! Watch over me. Be my angel in Heaven as you were here.*

After she heard the front door slam shut, she knew James had left. Ali moved quickly down the back staircase to the kitchen where she retrieved her cloak and hat and the small basket of food on the butcher block that she had prepared for the train trip. Ali slipped out the side door, where Walter was waiting to escort her to the train station.

Chapter 6
Peace Be with You

She wasn't about to give her father the satisfaction of telling her to go. She telegraphed Cousin Edy and Mr. Meadows and was on the last train out. She wanted to leave Wilmington long behind.

Walter had kindly walked with Ali to the Atlantic Coastal Railway Station where Mr. Bradley gave her the ticket he had been holding for her in the drawer under his ticket window. He assured her that her trunk was already stowed in the baggage car.

"Have a pleasant trip, Miss Davies. I was awfully sorry to hear of your mother's passing. Jo was a lovely lady, always kind to everyone she encountered. Forgive me for being so nosey, but I noticed this is a one-way ticket. I do hope you will be coming back."

"Thank you, Mr. Bradley. I will, of course, return for visits but not for a time. Thank you for your service to me, and, Mr. Bradley, please, could we keep this trip just between us? I would very much appreciate it."

"Of course, Miss Davies. I would never gossip about other folks' business. Your trip will be kept in confidence. Again, pleasant journeys."

Ali nodded and turned to Walter one last time. "Walter, there is no possible way for me to ever repay your kindness during this very difficult time. None of this would have been possible without your assistance and discretion. I will never forget you," she said and stood on tiptoes to kiss the deeply blushing Walter on his cheek.

Scuffing his feet and looking down, Walter drawled, "Aw, you're welcome, Miss Ali. You have been kind to me as well. In fact, I halfway wish you weren't leaving, but I am hopeful that your new life will bring you the happiness you could not find here, especially now with your mama gone."

With that, Walter reciprocated Ali's kiss on her cheek, catching her off guard. Blushing again, Walter said goodbye, then reluctantly turned to leave Ali alone on the platform to await her train to Savannah. There was a chill coming off the Cape Fear River. Ali pulled her cloak closer and soon heard the train whistle announcing its arrival.

Once she was safely settled on the stiff burgundy-colored mohair seat, she heard the shrill train whistle blow again, alerting travelers it was about to depart. Still with butterflies in her stomach, Ali tried to start making sense of all that had happened in the course of less than a week. The escape itself passed by in a blur—the station, Mr. Bradley handing her the ticket, getting on the train. Walter had the letter to post to her father. As her mother had warned her, Ali had not told her father where she was going, only away from Wilmington, from him, her half-sisters, her home—to safety and peace and freedom. She would be in Savannah by dawn well before he noticed she was gone and before the letter arrived. She was free. *Free, Mama, I'm free. Peace be with you now, dear Mama.*

After many hours, the train rolled past Calabash, Charleston, and Beaufort, South Carolina, past the Hilton Head station, the conductor calling out each stop in succession until Ali heard the station she had been awaiting.

"Next stop Savannah, Georgia!" the conductor shouted.

Ali gathered up her belongings, and, when the train screeched to a stop, she entered the aisle walking towards the door of the carriage. She glanced out the windows as she passed by, hoping she would recognize Cousin Edy. The conductor offered his hand to Ali, helping her disembark. As she walked through the steam from the idling train engine, she saw a smiling woman who resembled her mama. *Oh my,* Ali thought, somewhat startled, she could not fail to see the resemblance as she smiled and waved back to the woman she was sure was her Mama's cousin Edy.

"You must be Ali! I'm so happy you have made it safe and sound. I was so worried about you, knowing you had to leave surreptitiously. Thank our dear Lord, you have made it. You are safe now, my dear," Cousin Edy said with a sigh of relief.

"Cousin Edy! You look so much like Mama! I recognized you immediately! I too am relieved to be here, and I have Mama to thank for that and you too, dear cousin! Thank you for the plan you and Mama made to help me escape that horrible situation. I am forever in your debt," Ali said, giving Edy a warm hug and kiss on the cheek. She felt as if she had known Edy forever through Mama's stories of their childhood.

"Come, my dear girl, and we shall go to your new home directly. And I *do* want you to consider *my* home *your* home. It will be *our* home," Cousin Edy said with great delight, as if she had been expecting Ali for years. Edy took Ali's arm, gently directing her to Mr. Russell's carriage. Mr. Russell was Edy's neighbor, and he had graciously offered to accompany Edy to the train station in his carriage to retrieve Ali and her baggage. Unlike her father and others of prominence in Wilmington as well as Savannah, she suspected, Mr. Russell couldn't afford one of the new motor cars. She found his carriage with matched chestnut horses charming. Ali indicated to Mr. Russell her large trunk and carpetbag that held her immediate needs.

"Thank you kindly, Mr. Russell. It is very thoughtful of you to greet me and provide your carriage for Cousin Edy and me. What a wonderful welcome I have received today! I already feel at home in Savannah!" Ali said.

"Everyone I know will do everything possible to make you feel welcomed and at home. For now, I have a nice luncheon prepared for you at home. Shall we?" Edy asked, nudging Ali forward and into the carriage.

Mr. Russell offered his hand to help Ali and Edy climb into their seats. Ali was unused to such politeness. Her own father had never offered her a hand—in any way.

By now Father should be walking downstairs, expecting me to have his breakfast hot and plated. Won't he get a surprise? Ali smiled to herself, knowing she was safe here with Edy. There was no reason for her father to come for her even if he knew where she had gone. In fact, truth be told, he would probably be happy to be rid of her. *But he won't be happy about breakfast.* Ali nearly laughed aloud at the thought. *Don't be smug, Ali,* she cautioned herself. She didn't want to jinx her escape. *No, he won't come. Father has everything he wants now—Mama's wealth, Mama's home, Mama's entrée into the social position he so fervently coveted, a successful business that Mama financed, or rather Grandfather Thayer— all he could possibly want without ever lifting a finger to earn it himself.* How Ali loathed his abject laziness and sense of entitlement. *Now he can entertain his whore and his precious daughters 'til his heart's content.* Ali nearly spat the words out aloud. Her disgust washing over her as a toxic liquid must have certainly shown on her face.

"Ali, are you quite all right?" Edy asked with concern etched into her aging face.

Ali patted her gloved hand, "Oh, yes, Edy, forgive me. I was just thinking about Father and wondering what he will do when he finds me gone," Ali said.

"Ali, that has all been taken care of. Your father knows nothing of me. And we have presumed to change your last name. From this day, you will be Allison Thayer Malone. And, Ali, your grandfather knows where you are. As soon as he can make arrangements, he will be traveling to Savannah to reunite with you. Please have peace. All will be well," Edy covered her hand with her own in reassurance.

Ali smiled and nodded her understanding. *Peace. What a wonderful, and rare thought.* It had been many years since she felt peace in her heart.

"A new chapter," Ali said, smiling at Edy. "Indeed," Edy answered.

Ali rolled the name "Ali Thayer Malone" over in her mind trying it on for size. She wasn't sure how Edy had come up with it, but it was a good name if a bit Irish. Father would never find her now. "Malone. It is a good name," Ali told Edy.

"Yes, a very good name, Ali. You will come to cherish it I am certain."

She wasn't sure what Edy meant by "cherish," but perhaps she was reading too much into it. She turned to Cousin Edy, extended her right hand to her, and Edy took her hand in her own. Ali shook her hand and said, "It is my pleasure to meet you Edy Thayer Leonard. I am Ali Thayer Malone."

They both laughed as Mr. Russell urged the horses to drive them to her new home and new life in Savannah.

Chapter 7
A New Life

The drive to Edy's house was not long, only a mile or so. Mr. Russell pulled the carriage to a stop in front of a lovely red birck rowhouse with an iron fence in front, heavy with running roses. The smell was glorious. It was a small home but so charming with its gingerbread trim around the eaves and black shutters on the windows in the event of hurricanes. Ali was familiar with the high winds of hurricanes as they sometimes hit the coast near Wilmington and caused great hardship on so many. One Hundred Forty-one Lincoln Avenue was to be her address, the new home of the new woman, Ali Thayer Malone. Ali was smiling and, for the first time in a very long time, she was optimistic about her life.

"Cousin Edy, it is lovely!" Ali said, surveying the home where she was to live with Edy.

"Well, I am very pleased that you have come to me, Ali. I was so saddened by your mama's death and shocked. I did not realize she had been ill for so long. I am sorry I could not be there with you for the funeral. I'm certain it was a very difficult time for you. But now we shall heal together. Welcome home, my dear girl."

They walked up the orchard stone sidewalk to the stoop where Mr. Russell opened the door for them, setting Ali's carpetbag inside the door. He went back to the carriage for the large trunk, heaving it on his strong shoulder and steadying it with his other hand as he delivered it upstairs where Edy directed him.

"Ali, this is to be your room. I do so hope you like it. It has lots of sunlight in the mornings. It was our daughter Hannah's room, but please feel free to make it your own. I'm certain you and Hannah would have been fast friends as your mama and I were. She would be happy you are here with me as well. She was a lovely girl as you are."

The room was indeed lovely. Ali knew she would be comfortable here. Paper with pink roses and a faint touch of light blue in the background decorated the walls. The canopied bed was covered in a white lace coverlet and looked as if it had been slept in just the night before. Edy had kept the room immaculate just as her daughter had left it. Of course, Edy had removed the personal belongings before Ali arrived, carefully wrapping them in tissue paper and storing them in a cedar blanket chest in her own bedroom. Edy was comforted to have this touch of Hannah in her room with her.

Ali surmised Edy would treat her as her own daughter given how close she and Hannah would have been in age had she lived and given the sister-like relationship she had with Jo. She loved the thought that she would be here with Edy. It made leaving Wilmington and coming to a strange town in another state so much easier. Ali especially looked forward to exploring Savannah with Edy.

"Now," Edy began, pulling back the covers on the high canopied bed, "I am sure you'd like to freshen up and rest for a bit before luncheon is ready. Is there anything I may bring you to make you more comfortable, Ali? Some tea perhaps or orange juice? Anything at all?"

"Dear Edy, you have given me more than you know, and there is nothing else I need at the moment, but, yes, the bed looks so inviting to me after a night of sitting upright, bumping along. Please do not allow me to sleep past the time you normally have luncheon. I will be delighted to share it with you, and I will try to catch you up on Mama's life since you were last together—the happy moments."

"I will make certain to awaken you, and I look forward to chatting. Now rest," Edy said as she walked out, looking back once, in a brief melancholy moment, as Ali lay on the bed. It was good to have a girl in the house again, Edy thought, then quietly closed the door behind her as Ali fell fast asleep the minute her head hit the soft feather pillow.

Ali's deep sleep was troubled by memories.

"Wives!" the priest forcefully called from the pulpit, "submit to your husbands in all things!"

She saw herself walking into their home in Wilmington, holding fast to Mama's hand as her father loudly repeated the priest's admonitions to her mother, snarling out the words, and lording his control over Mama. Father was so domineering as he yelled at her, "Josephine, you are my property! You will obey me in all things, and if not we will see what the priest has to say!"

"Father!" Ali screamed in her sleep. "You treat Mama no better than the horses that pull your carriage! Please, Mama, let us go away from here," she said while pulling on her mother's arm, tears streaming down her cheeks. "Please, Mama, please. He will kill you eventually!"

Then Ali witnessed the most unexpected thing: She saw her mother smile at him.

"Of course, James," Jo said to her husband with a bright smile on her face.

Ali knew if Jo were to weep, it would be in private where no one would know so she would not diminish their father in his children's eyes. She was too strong to allow James to know he had hurt her and too thoughtful of others to complain, instead swallowing his cruel insults. *How do you do it, Mama?*

Anna and Marie were in her dreams as well, taunting her and laughing when she cried.

Her father snarled at her, "You, Ali, are not possessing of great beauty nor grace. Heaven help the man who has the misfortune of marrying you; he will either be blind or desperate, perhaps both."

Even in the dream, she felt ashamed. Ali heard her mother's soothing voice interrupting her discomfort as her soft hands reached Ali's cheek to wipe the tears away.

"My darling girl, your father does not realize what he says is cruel. And surely he cannot mean what he says, for you are so beautiful and clever and very intelligent! You will make some wonderful young man very happy one day as his wife and the mother of his children. Forget these things your father says when he is drinking or angry. It is not true, none of it," Mama said, tucking a lock of hair behind her ear. She lightly stroked Ali's ear as she sang her a lullaby.

In truth, her father's cruelty only served to embolden Ali. She was able to see what her father saw as lacking in her to be an advantage. Ali would not marry young if at all. She wanted to be free to pursue her own interests. Working, however, was out of the question. Ladies, her father would say, did not work. Not in his home, not his wife or daughters. This motivated Ali all the more to establish her own life. She admired the Suffragettes and followed their progress in the *Morning News*. She would prove to her father that having a pretty face and a rich husband as her sisters' did was not the only value a woman possessed. She had dreams and aspirations, and her father could not keep her from the accomplishment of them.

"You will not stop me, Father!" Ali shouted out in her sleep as Edy opened her door. She sat up in the bed, startled, not recognizing where she was.

Edy sat on the edge of her bed, softly rubbing her shoulder and arm, comforting her.

"Dear Ali, it is all right now. You are safe. Everything will be fine. It was just a bad dream," but Ali knew better as it had been her life for 28 years.

Looking around the room, hearing Edy's voice and appreciating her touch, so like Mama's, and remembering she was safely in Savannah now, Ali stood and splashed cold water on her face to douse the bad dream. While she had slept a full hour, it felt as if it had been merely minutes. Minutes of hard labor.

"Luncheon is ready, Ali. Please come down with me and let's enjoy some fresh chicken salad and biscuits from the oven."

On their way to luncheon, Edy took a few moments to show Ali the layout of her new home. Between Edy's room and Ali's, there was a shared bath that connected their rooms. The large white clawfoot tub looked so inviting—perhaps later today, she thought. Down at the end of the hall past Edy's room at the rear of the home, Edy opened French doors to the outdoor "sleeping porch," enclosed with screen to defend against the pesky gnats and ever-present mosquitoes. There were two daybeds covered in lovely floral fabric, and Ali knew this would be a welcome relief in the heat of the Savannah summer.

Two smaller rooms were located near the sleeping porch, one filled with her sewing and embroidery notions, the other a bedroom where her help, Mabel, stayed. Edy was happy to have Mabel in her home. She was such interesting company and a great support to Edy with the household chores and cooking, and Mabel had no family and needed a home and employment. It was a mutually beneficial relationship.

Together, arms locked, Edy and Ali descended the walnut stairs with carved newel posts to the landing, turned left and descended the final three steps into the inviting foyer with its large gilt mirror and grandfather clock. Immediately to her right was the parlor with lovely deep green mohair velvet chairs adorned with lace head doilies, a cabbage rose chintz-covered sofa, side tables, and a small game table in the far corner. Edy and Mabel occasionally challenged each other to a friendly chess match or played ladies' card games, which, of course, were quickly slipped into the drawer underneath if the priest or Ladies' Guild happened to call.

On the wall above the walnut mantle over the fireplace hung charcoal drawings of her loved ones. One of the three of them was a portrait of Able shoulder to shoulder with Edy, both holding Hannah between them. Another featured Hannah in her mother's arms, and the third picture was of Able in a dark suit and cravat, hand on a stack of books, looking very serious. On the mantle an oak clock stood, its pendulum swinging back and forth marking time. There were petite porcelain birds, a robin and a cardinal, and a large gilt mirror behind all of it. Ali noted there was not a speck of dust to be found anywhere. Everything was immaculate just as the upstairs. Ali absentmindedly fingered the delicate lace doily spread across the mantle. It felt like home here. She would be happy.

"Perhaps you would enjoy tea on the porch? It is so entertaining to watch the hummingbirds. I believe we will have a lush flower garden this summer. The hydrangea blooms look as if they will be enormous, and the roses are doing well. I do so love having fresh flowers throughout the house," Edy remarked as she wheeled the tea cart onto the covered back porch. It was a lovely, sunny day. They sat down on two dainty ladies' chairs at the small gate-leg table covered with a crisp white cotton tablecloth.

"This is so lovely and peaceful, Edy. A perfect place to enjoy our tea and get to know one another better. Thank you," Ail remarked.

More than two hours had passed, and the sun had dipped low in the sky when they finally ran out of conversation. Ali knew it was only a lull and that there would always be much they would share. She felt at home with Edy and felt she was a Godsend after losing her mother. They had discussed Ali's entire life with her mother and father, and Edy was saddened to know this kind girl had gone through such abuse. She felt tears forming in her eyes, thinking of what her dear cousin Jo had endured.

"Well, Ali, you are safe and here with me now and will never have to go through that type of horrible unpleasantness again. You will forge a new life here as Ali Thayer Malone, and your life will change in many wonderful and exciting ways. It will be a joy to watch the transformation. What time is your interview at the bank tomorrow?"

"I want to be there a bit before it opens at 8 o'clock. I will meet with Mr. John Meadows, the vice president of trusts & loans," Ali answered.

"Very well. I will ask Mabel to prepare a hearty breakfast for you so your tummy won't growl during your interview. That wouldn't do at all!" Edy and Ali laughed at the thought.

She and Edy had a cold supper and Ali turned in early as she was wearier than she had realized after her daring escape and long train ride. She slept soundly throughout the night.

Chapter 8
Counting Blessings

Dressed in a plum colored professional suit Jo had the dressmaker tailor for her—a skirt to just above her ankles and a short, fitted jacket with leg-o-mutton sleeves. Ali added her own crisp white shirtwaist and a smart black velvet ribbon tied in a bow with Mama's cameo centered on her long neck. Ali reached up and touched it, invoking her mother's care over her. She surveyed herself in the mirror and liked what she saw. "Very professional."

Today she would meet Mr. Meadows at the Atlantic Southern Merchants & Farmers Bank. If she was able to calm her nerves and interview well, she might be starting her first working position tomorrow. Her stomach was full of butterflies as she descended the stairs to breakfast.

"Oh, Ali, don't you look every bit the professional woman! What a pretty color on you with your auburn hair. You will dazzle them at the bank!"

"Thank you, Edy. Wish me luck!"

Ali quickly ate a piece of toast and drank a cup of coffee. Edy protested that she ate too little of Mabel's breakfast.

"Edy, I'm too nervous. I couldn't possibly eat another bite. Wish me luck; I'm off!"

Ali secured her matching hat with one of her mother's jewel-encrusted hatpins. It made her feel confident to have bits of her mother with her.

The bank was within four or five blocks of Edy's home, and the weather was beautiful and sunny, so Ali exited the front door and was on her way to her interview. As she walked she repeated the Rosary to herself. Today she needed the Blessed Mother Mary with her as well.

As she approached the rather austere red brick building no doubt made from Georgia clay, the sign above the entrance spelled out the bank's name in large brass letters. Ali reached to open the heavy wooden door when it swung open for her.

"Oh, my goodness! I'm terribly sorry," she said to the tall, handsome man now holding the door for her.

"Not at all. Miss Malone, I presume?" he said to her.

"Why, yes, thank you," Ali replied, somewhat startled, wondering how he knew her name.

Seeing her discomfort, the man said, "We have been expecting you, Miss Malone. I am John Meadows, but my friends call me Johnnie. During work hours, it is Mr. Meadows, but before and after I hope you'll call me Johnnie," he said with a bit of a flirtatious tone to his voice as he surveyed her hat to walking shoes.

Ali felt her cheeks flush at his obvious familiarity. "I hope we will be friends then, um, Mr. Meadows."

"Wonderful! Follow me and we will chat briefly, and I will then introduce you to Mr. Woodworth, our president, and the men with whom you will be working—provided our chat goes well and you want to join our bank," Johnnie said while whisking her into the bank.

It was still seven-thirty and the bank would not be open for account holders for another half hour. Ali assumed all of this attention from Mr. Meadows was not in his normal workday but time he had specifically allotted in his schedule for her interview. This gave her a bit more confidence, and she straightened her posture as she followed.

Ali sat across from Mr. Meadow's large banking desk made of mahogany with green leather inserts for writing. On his wall was a framed diploma from the University of South Carolina further north in Columbia.

"Tell me, Miss Malone …" he started when Ali interrupted him.

"Ali, please. My friends call me Ali."

"Very well, Ali, tell me how you came to be so proficient with numbers and accounting? It is quite unusual for a lady, I must say, but very admirable."

"I have always loved mathematics, Mr. Meadows, and found that I had a talent for formulas and such. Though I was certainly discouraged from pursuing this in school, because, as you pointed out, it is rather 'unusual for a lady' to enjoy sums and accounting, and my father forbade me from holding employment. I had seen an advertisement in the newspaper for a correspondence accounting course, so I surreptitiously, with help from my mother, applied and completed the course. As you may have noticed, the certification is in the name of William Davies. That is the name I used so I would be allowed to study the course. I quite enjoyed it. My mother passed only this past week, and I left my home to live with my mother's cousin on Lincoln Street here in Savannah. And here I am in need of employment," Ali explained.

"Well, I must say, I am quite impressed with your industry and creativity. Your skills are an exact fit for our needs in the loans & trust department. I would like to offer you the position if you would like to work with us," Mr. Meadows offered.

"Well, yes, of course, I would very much appreciate the position, and I can start today if you'd like," Ali answered.

"Excellent! Shall we meet your co-workers?"

He opened the door and motioned her into the outer office. She was introduced to many people until the names became a bit of a blur, but she was sure she would learn them soon enough.

"While you will be working with these gentlemen Will and Peter primarily. Your primary duties will include assisting me with special accounting for loans and trusts, preparing the financial documents for each transaction. And, of course, the first thing each morning, I enjoy a roll from Tinker's Bakery next door," he said, assuming she would be happy to also serve as his private secretary.

"Mr. Meadows," Ali began hesitantly, "It was my understanding that I was being offered the position of accounting assistant, not errand boy."

She felt certain this would be the death knell for her new position before it even drew its first breath as she was certain Mr. Meadows, as was the case with most men, did not care for the Suffragette movement.

He moved closer, close enough that Ali could smell the fresh scent of his shaving soap. She did not move nor retreat. If there were to be a problem, she might as well confront it now. She would find another position somewhere. He looked directly and deeply into her eyes, holding the connection just a bit too long. Ali felt her cheeks redden with discomfort, yet at the same time his gaze was mesmerizing.

"Ha!" He laughed. "Quite right! I admire your forthrightness. I don't see that much in the women I know, but I think it is grand. I respect you for standing up for your qualifications. I think we will get along famously." He laughed again and added, "Not only will I continue to fetch my roll, I will bring one for you as well. Is that fair?" he asked Ali and moved back to the prior close position before she could answer, relieved she hadn't overstepped his patience.

Her breath caught audibly in her throat, and he did not miss this telling sign that his charms had succeeded in affecting her. He was so close she could see the dark blue specks in his light green-blue eyes. *He has long eyelashes. Is he going to kiss me?* Mixed thoughts flooded her—masculine scent, beautiful eyes, danger—but she didn't back away. Instead she boldly allowed him this overtly familiar posture. What she didn't realize was that he was studying her eyes at the same time.

"What is in the depths of those dark eyes, Miss Malone, I wonder," he said cryptically. "I see great intellect and spunk. I believe you are a mystery I would enjoy solving."

Suddenly, he withdrew and quickly walked away as if she had bit him. Questions whirled in her mind. *What in the world is his game? Did I offend him? Did I say the wrong thing? Is he angry about fetching his own coffee? What in the heavens was that in response to?* At the same time, she noticed that her pulse was racing from the lingering effects of his closeness, and she decided she quite liked it. *Careful, my girl; he is a married man.* Even then, the danger was enticing to her. She was certain this would not be the end of his flirtation, but she was certainly confused about this encounter.

Did she want him to kiss her? *Stop, Ali Dav...er, Malone! You may not have this reaction to your employer! He has a wife and children.* Edy had mentioned this to her last evening along with a hint of warning about his reputation though nothing direct.

"Now I do not know for certain if his reputation is based on fact or gossip, still where there is smoke, there may well be fire. Guard yourself, Ali. I hear he can be quite charming," Edy warned, "and you are still quite vulnerable."

Today it became clear to Ali what Edy meant. He was indeed charismatic and *handsome.* She was captivated from their first meeting. Though it probably would never happen, if she ever found that he was available, she would definitely make herself available to him. After all, wives do pass away or sometimes they leave their husbands. Ali crossed herself quickly asking forgiveness. The likelihood was remote at best in any case. Sometimes wives were pressed to the point of leaving, though, just as her dear mama had been, and she had been planning her escape for many years and saving up. *But,* Ali reasoned, *if a wife left her husband due to infidelity, why would I want such a husband?* As happens, her hindsight was much clearer than her foresight.

Ali was able to control her infatuation with Mr. Meadows at work, though occasionally her mind would wander, wondering what it would be like to make love with this man—to be utterly possessed by such earthy masculinity.

It made her pulse race to think such thoughts, but then she would come to her senses. She couldn't fathom a time when he would choose her out of the bevy of beautiful women she was certain worshipped at his spit-polished fine leather boots.

Mama always said you could gauge the quality of a man's character by his shoes. If they weren't polished, it showed he didn't take care of things, was perhaps irresponsible or shiftless, or perhaps did not care about his appearance or reputation. It seemed a superficial adage to her, but she found it to be true more frequently than not. Because of this conditioning, the shoes were the first place her eyes went, and Mr. Meadows' were no exception. His shoes were so shiny she was certain she could see her reflection if she dared get that close.

His obviously finely tailored jacket and trousers made of the finest smooth wool, crisply starched white shirt and collar, cravat and matching pocket square peeking out of his breast pocket, were impeccable. Every single hair in place. And a smile like the sunshine itself that lit the room. Laughter that was infectious, and she suspected always kind, never at someone else's expense. He was intelligent, successful, and motivated and knew how to draw people in. Yes, Ali decided, Johnnie Meadows was the perfect man for her.

Ali again unconsciously pushed his reputation to the far back of her mind. So much good surely outweighed what little bad she had surmised from Edy's comments concerning him. He was perfect—for her. But that was as far as she dared go. He would have to remain a deeply buried heart crush, nothing more. If she looked hard enough, she might be able to find other more heinous faults in him, and she had no desire to see any, but she reminded herself to remain alert.

The romantic imaginary intimacy she thought they had exchanged at that moment ended abruptly as he bolted from the room. As she picked through every word, every inflection during their conversation, trying vainly to find fault with herself, she remembered what her mother told her, "Do not believe the things your father has said about you, Ali. You are a lovely, beautiful, and intelligent young woman; never sell yourself short. Men find you attractive. I've seen them looking."

"Thank you, Mama, for always being here for me just as you promised," Ali whispered softly to herself, remembering her words.

After Mr. Meadow's abrupt departure, she was summarily assigned to William Tyler, another accounting assistant, for the remainder of her training that day.

"Follow me, if you will, Miss Malone. Mr. Meadows has asked me to acquaint you with our operations and your responsibilities," Will Tyler said. Ali followed him to what was to be her desk, tightly fitted into Will's office along with the other accounting assistant, Peter Hoff.

"Pleased to meet you, Miss Malone. I hope you will be happy here. We have tried to squeeze your desk in here and give you as much room as possible. If I can be of any assistance, please do not hesitate to request my help," Peter offered.

"Thank you both, Will and Peter, for making me feel welcome and for making room in your office for me. I am certain we will get along very well," Ali offered.

Every now and then, she would catch the sight of Mr. Meadows throughout the office, and once to her embarrassment their eyes met. He looked away quickly, pretending to gaze past her. But she noticed. And she knew he had spotted her noticing him.

She spent the rest of the day going over the account logs Will had given her to study and arranging things on her desk to suit her. Johnnie returned at the end of the business day to inform her he would be out of town in Columbia for two weeks and she was to remain under the tutelage of Will and Peter. Trying not to allow him to see her disappointment, she looked down at her work, shuffled some papers, and said, "Have a safe and profitable trip, Mr. Meadows."

Johnnie did not miss the ever-so-slight tinge of regret in her voice.

Hmm, he thought, *she is a rare jewel indeed. I want to know everything about how she thinks and feels.* He was also beginning to experience regret at his two-week journey out of town.

Chapter 9
A Staunch Stance

Going to work each day was a newfound joy for Ali. She felt useful and competent and proud that she could fend for herself in a new locale. Of course, she reminded herself of all the help she had been given to come to this place—Mama's preparations and Edy's willingness to provide her with a home and, of course, Johnnie. There had been no word from her father just as Edy had anticipated. He did not know where she was now. Those who did were sworn to secrecy, and Ali trusted them quite literally with her life.

In the two weeks Johnnie had been away on business, Will and Peter had been more than kind in offering her some of their work to try and provided help when necessary, but Ali found she caught on quickly and rarely had to ask for assistance. There was also extra work that Will had given her on the instructions of Johnnie, which she was to do for him while he was away. She found she enjoyed the challenge. Her computation skills and correspondence course in accounting proved of great value to her. Her mother had been wise to encourage her to learn a skill "just in case."

Ali had shifted Johnnie to the back of her mind while he was away in Columbia, and, when she did think of him, she chided herself for her silliness. Her stomach no longer flip-flopped at the thought of him, and she was well settled into the daily office routine.

Because of the light drizzle, Ali opted to take the streetcar the short distance to work to spare her new working shoes. She stepped off the car just short of the bank, where it turned to proceed to the riverfront. Walking the half block to the bank, Ali was caught up in thoughts about the new day and the tasks that awaited her. She knew Johnnie would be back today, and with that thought her butterflies returned.

She felt a sense of pride and accomplishment stepping into the imposing building, knowing that her work was a small part in the bank's success. She felt a part of something important and valuable. She was a member of an exclusive group entrusted with fiduciary responsibility over the private finances of the people of Savannah, and she took this trust very seriously.

Stepping inside the heavy doors and past the Pinkerton officer guarding the bank, Ali quickly and discreetly scanned the lobby floor for any sign of Johnnie. She knew she shouldn't allow unprofessional thoughts to enter her mind in connection with him, but she was always able to justify them by reassuring herself that he was her employer and there was always work to think about in connection to him.

Ali had a pocketful of warning signs she continued to ignore, rather believing in the good that surely was in Johnnie's heart and that her intentions were honorable as well. She was there to use her skills to earn her way in the world. Nothing more. Nothing less. Johnnie was a married man and as such off-limits for her as she was for him. She would keep it professional. She tried to convince herself she could do this, but deep down she wasn't so confident and immediately felt a tad disappointed at not seeing him in the lobby area. She glanced upstairs at the wood-framed glass windows on the second floor where the accounting office was as well as Johnnie's. Still no sign of him.

When she arrived at her desk, she removed the pins from her straw hat with soft pink silk cabbage roses clustered on the brim and hung it on a small hall tree near the door. She sat down at her desk, straightened her pencils, and began looking through papers as if deeply engrossed in her work. She tried to focus on the task at hand, but her mind invariably wandered back to Johnnie and the day he had held her gaze for the most inappropriate length of time, then bolted away from her as if she had the plague. It made her heart skip a beat.

Surely he had intended to kiss me, she thought. *He must have or he would not have leaned in so close and so intently.* Ali had mixed emotions, not knowing if she was insulted because he took such liberties or insulted because he had not kissed her. *Where is he?* She was growing impatient to lay eyes on him again. *Stop! Stop! Stop!* She chided herself, lifted her pencil, and took up the fresh stack of accounts to be reconciled.

She had worked for nearly an hour when she had a strong impression someone was directly behind her. *Nonsense,* she thought, and continued her work. Still, she turned to look and there he stood, in all his handsome glory, wearing a beautiful suit and spit-polished shoes, smelling of shaving soap, and smiling at her.

"Miss me?" he asked nonchalantly leaning against the wall with that dazzling smile on his face and a confidence level that should have been illegal, knowing full-well just by looking at her flush that she had indeed missed him.

Startled, Ali jumped to her feet and stumbled back and away from Johnnie. "Oh! You startled me!" Regaining her composure, she said, "Well, of course, *we* missed you, Mr. Meadows. You are a large figure in this office."

"Hmm…am I now?" Then leaning in so only she could hear, "I would like to be large in, ah, your mind and other parts of you as well my dear," he said under his breath.

Before she could catch her breath from such a bold yet not wholly inappropriate statement if taken at face value, he was gone. She steadied herself and her cheeks flushed deeply because she knew what he said was not to be taken at face value but was a scandalous suggestion meant to arouse her imagination. And other parts. *Was it a scandalous suggestion? I'm not sure.* But she truly was sure. Johnnie's outrageous flirtation was quite transparent.

"Will and Peter, please come to my office and bring your ledgers," Johnnie called.

They quickly followed him to his office. Ali sat still stunned and somewhat hurt that he had not requested her presence as well as she had worked diligently on her ledgers in her best handwriting to record all transactions perfectly and accurately. Her mother always complimented her penmanship, and she hoped Johnnie too would be pleased with the quality of her work. But after his shocking comment to her, she was instead left feeling puzzled that Johnnie once again had quickly moved on to other business.

Oh, Johnnie Meadows, you are the Devil incarnate. She berated herself for ever giving in to the lust she felt for him and for the respect she had ascribed to him. *How could I have been so silly to think he wanted anything more than a quick romp in the hay with me? He desires anything in a skirt, and I guess I would fill the bill today.*

Her mind suddenly pictured Walter's sad old hound dog in a skirt and laughed aloud at the thought.

"Did something in that stack of papers amuse you, Miss Malone?" she heard Johnnie ask her, again, surprising her out of her musings.

"You do seem to enjoy sneaking up on a body don't you, Mr. Meadows?" Ali said, looking him square in his smiling eyes.

"I do when the body is yours, Miss Malone, though you do skate very near the line of insubordination, do you not?" he said quietly with a mischievous twinkle in his eyes. She recognized the question was more rhetorical, perhaps even a challenge.

If he expected an apology, he was disappointed, and actually, Johnnie would have felt an apology would be a letdown from such a spirited woman.

Ali was not one to grovel. *Johnnie has met his match,* she thought with some satisfaction. She sensed he was intrigued with her, and she was unwilling to give an inch. She knew men liked the hunt as much as the trophy. She would not be manipulated by another man.

"Not at all, Mr. Meadows. I am quite straightforward when I speak and always give respect to my superiors. How may I be of service, Mr. Meadows?" Ali said, never losing eye contact and stealing his thunder by ignoring his comment about her body.

"Well, I'll be damned," he said then immediately added, "I do apologize for my coarse speech, Miss Malone, but I don't believe I have ever met a woman quite so strong and so brave, and, ah, 'straightforward,' I believe you said." Recovering from his failure to provoke a response in her he continued, "I like a hardheaded woman who knows her mind and is not afraid to speak it. I have no patience for tears, theatrics, and cowering. Let this be confirmation that you may always speak your mind to me. I look forward to it. I've no use for simpering daylilies," he said and seemed utterly sincere.

"I am happy to hear that Mr. Meadows, but 'hardheaded' and 'strong' are different terms," she said, not quite ready to accept his partial surrender. "I do know my mind but if convinced logically that I am incorrect, I have no problem changing my mind without clinging tenaciously to a wrong thought." Ali had been caught off guard somewhat by his seemingly enlightened thinking but did feel the need to correct his verbiage as words were important and could mean so many different things.

She was proud of being a strong woman but could not abide by a person who was just illogically stubborn and entrenched in wrong thinking. She saw no reproach to femininity in being strong. If she had not been strong, she would have withered and died on the vine long ago with a father such as hers and losing her beloved mother. And she never would have had the courage to leave all she knew to come to a new city and state to start over.

Perhaps the world was changing thanks to the efforts of the women she admired most—Elizabeth Cady Stanton, the suffragette who had co-founded the National Woman Suffrage Association and International Council of Women, and Lucy Stone, her personal hero. Lucy was the first woman to retain her surname after her marriage, which Ali thought was deliciously rebellious, and she organized the first National Women's Rights Convention.

Ali was awed at the many brave and intelligent women who came before as well—all her heroines—Julia Ward Howe, the suffragist writer and organizer, among them. Ali and Jo had spent many conversations going over her writings that Ali surreptitiously smuggled into the house. There was Mary Livermore, a well-known suffragist and women's rights journalist. How she envied her for her career as well as that of Grace Greenwood, the first woman reporter for the *New York Times* newspaper, in which her articles advocated for women's rights and other social reforms. Others had picked up the torch and continued working for women's rights and especially voting rights. Ali reveled in the exciting events taking shape around the world for women, and she wanted to strike her own blow for equality, and perhaps she was doing just that.

In her own small way, Ali felt she had joined with these women, her sister Suffragettes. She had struck a blow for women's independence by being here in Savannah, hadn't she? And working at the bank in a position normally only held by men was quite an accomplishment, was it not? It was a small step but progress nonetheless. She was proud of this opportunity and intended to make the most of it.

Ali also was aware that had she married, her father's control of her would have passed to her husband—even if he abused her. In fact, Edy had been wise to change Ali's last name because as an unmarried woman who had been under his roof, her father had legal control of her even as a woman of twenty-nine! *One day I will vote and have the same rights as any man*, Ali promised herself.

"Miss Malone—Miss Malone? Are you with us; are you well?" she heard Mr. Meadows say, snapping her out of her suffragist musings.

"Oh, yes, I beg your pardon. Thank you, Mr. Meadows."

"You were far away in your thoughts, and again I am curious to know what lies behind those beautiful eyes of yours. I can see the gears are grinding in there and, if I were to venture a guess, not about your bank duties." He laughed at her discomfort and diffused her predicament, saying, "I assure you we will be great friends over time." He winked at her.

Blushing deeply, she replied, "I too shall look forward to frank and honest communication between us." However, she suspected this wasn't what Mr. Meadows had in mind. "Would you care to glance at my ledgers as well?" she asked, trying to remain professional though her heart was beating out of her chest and she realized that her question could be taken in a more risqué way than she meant. *Or perhaps I had meant it that way?*

Focusing again on the business at hand, Ali knew the two men she worked alongside more than likely made much more money than she though she was working at the same tasks and additionally on special files for Mr. Meadows. She wanted him to review her ledgers now so that he would be able to recognize the stark contrast between hers and the men's. She knew her ledgers were flawless.

Again, surprised by her boldness, Johnnie seized the opportunity to have her alone in his office to "look at her ledgers." Though his office was enclosed in glass so everyone could see him, it was quite soundproof.

"Of course, Miss Malone, I would like that very much. Would you please bring them to my office where we can go over them together?"

"Certainly, I won't be a minute," Ali said while turning to retrieve her ledgers from her desk. She did not see the smile cross Johnnie's face nor the sideways looks Will and Peter shot each other.

Gathering her things, she quickly moved to Johnnie's office.

"Like a lamb to the slaughter," Peter snickered to Will.

"Indeed," William agreed, and they placed odds on how long it would be before their boss had bedded his pretty little accounting assistant. They were unaccustomed to having a woman in the department and refused to acknowledge Ali's abilities. They were soon to realize their mistake in underestimating her though.

Inside the private space, Johnnie offered Ali a chair in front of his large desk. He knew he needed to sit down behind his desk or he might embarrass himself and this lovely woman sitting in front of him, feeling the pressure in his groin. *Damn, this woman has a way of completely captivating me even after having my way with Patrice in Columbia. I thought that would dampen my desire, but this, this woman… She is unlike any woman I have ever known.* And the pressure became almost unbearable.

Ali wasn't nearly as beautiful as the woman he frequently bedded nor those who caught his attention, but he suspected the auburn-haired temptress would not disappoint a man when it came to lovemaking. He wondered if she had been bedded before.

Johnnie resumed his lurid musings, pretending to examine her ledgers but unable to stem the growing fantasy in his brain and the growing girth in his breeches. Her intellect was the most sexually attractive attribute she possessed, and he wanted to plumb the depths of her brain—as well as other parts. Her exquisite form had definitely not escaped his notice in spite of the corset and bustle.

He longed to discuss everything with her—business, art, music, the newest literature, even her suffragist ideals which, try as she might, she had not disguised. He knew he would benefit tremendously just hearing her side of things and her opinions, though admitting this to her would weaken his position, he felt. What was it she had said—"clinging tenaciously to a wrong thought"? He might be persuaded and admitted to himself that it might not be a bad thing at all.

As a man with a hearty sexual appetite, he was also acutely aware that underneath those tailored tweeds and high, starched, stiff-necked and repellant collars, her luscious body was hidden away, and he wanted to be the man to liberate it from her constraining corset. *My God, I simply have to consume this woman!*

"Here is a list of my current accounts for reconciliation." She handed him her immaculate list she typed on the new Underwood she was just provided. She sat quietly as he perused the ledgers and ticked off her list with an occasional "hmm" and "yes."

After several minutes passed, Ali noticed he was merely staring at her work. "Now who is far away in his thoughts?" Ali teased and chuckled.

"Ah, caught in my own snare!" he laughed along with her. "I was just quite marveling at your figure, er, figures," he said, and again she saw that naughty, dangerous yet exciting side. Johnnie knew quite well the impact his carefully chosen words had on that soft secret place between her thighs—and Ali was well aware he knew. *This is torture,* she thought.

Trying to keep the conversation on track and professional, Ali replied, "I hope the ledgers are satisfactory, Mr. Meadows. If not, please give me whatever guidance you wish, and I will endeavor to correct any portion."

"No indeed, Miss Malone, I have never seen such truly beautifully constructed ledgers. They are flawless, clearly understood, and the best I have ever seen in this office. If you don't mind my inquiring, Miss Malone, how long have you been working with accounting ledgers, because I had assumed this was your first position?"

"This is my first formal position, Mr. Meadows. I first was taught by my mother so that I could assist her with the household accounts. I quite enjoyed it. She allowed me to do the accounts from the time I was very young, to give me practice. At times my father would bring home ledgers and allow me to look over them. Over time, looking at these, I learned. When my mother saw how much I enjoyed it and seemed to have a natural gift with numbers, she helped me obtain the correspondence course I mentioned to you."

"So your mother and father approved of you being an independent, working woman, eh?" he asked.

"Yes and no. My mother believed I needed to prepare myself for any circumstance I might encounter in life, and she encouraged me to learn a skill I could use if it ever became necessary. One that would use my mind and not my back. My father, on the other hand, felt I might be able to save him a dime by using my services at home. He felt I needed to earn my keep since I was no longer a debutante—a spinster, as he called me," she answered, realizing immediately she had said too much and revealed too much vulnerability. Instantly, the old feelings her father beat into her of being used and humiliated crept in. She feared Johnnie might take advantage of her as her father had. *He is too easy to talk with.* The words seemed to flow effortlessly out of her mouth before she could catch them. She chided herself.

"Please forgive me. I've said too much and taken up too much of your time."

"On the contrary, Miss Malone. I find our conversations fascinating and hope to enjoy more. And, of course," he added reassuringly, "everything we discuss will be held in the utmost confidence." *I hope this is true and that you don't throw this back in my face later.*

"All right, Miss Malone; thank you. I assure you, I quite admire women who feed and nurture their minds. I find you a breath of fresh air, and I am intrigued that you and your mother had the foresight to prepare for a different kind of life. One never knows what may happen from one day to the next as I know you are painfully aware with your current circumstances. I commend you and assure you I will let Mr. Woodworth know of your exemplary work. Thank you very much for your efforts, Miss Malone. You've made my return quite pleasant," he said genuinely and without a trace of the usual sexual innuendo.

She stood, knowing this was her cue to leave.

"Thank you, Mr. Meadows," Ali said while exiting his office.

Johnnie watched her every move as she walked back to her desk. He noted Peter and William watching her as well. They could never appreciate what was inside this woman, her qualities, her discretion, and her mind. He knew he saw her in a different light than the other men at the bank. Was he beginning to look at her as more than a potential playmate in his bed? Was she the woman he had hoped for all of his life? She gave him no easy exits in their conversations, and in fact, the manner she questioned his assertions and opinions was disconcerting to say the least. He was aware she did this not to question *him* or his authority, but he recognized this was how she learned and weighed things in that keen mind of hers. Any debate was carried on inside her own mind. How could he possibly resist a woman that seemed his equal match and so fiery at the same time? He had to have her.

When Ali got back to her desk, she placed the ledgers back into her "to-do" work box and sat down. She looked up just in time to see Johnnie staring at her, rubbing his chin and smiling. She smiled back, making eye contact, and driving him mad with her all-knowing gaze. He was unaccustomed to a woman with such depth of thought looking into his soul as she did.

Ali knew how to play the romance game. She had been courted by enough beaus to at least recognize the steps of the dance but certainly not master them, but this time was different—and dangerous. Johnnie was married with children. He was older than she and not given to boys' games.

She observed he was a master of the art of manipulation, not necessarily in an evil manner, but he knew the psychology of turning people to his way of thinking. He could easily persuade clients to deposit their money or borrow funds from the bank. His smile would light up the room whenever clients were about. She could recognize his talent just in the way he worked employees at the bank. He knew how to appeal to their vanity and self-esteem, thus inspiring them to greater diligence and productivity. He made them feel as if he truly cared about each of them and their families. Perhaps he did. She hoped this was genuine.

Ali didn't want to be skeptical or cynical, but she couldn't dismiss what Edy had told her about his reputation. If she allowed herself, Ali knew this obvious attraction between them could become serious, and she might well have her heart broken—again. *How many times can a heart be broken before the damage is irreparable?* If anything came of this flirtation, she would have to make certain she held her love back and kept her feelings superficial. *What harm could come from an innocent flirtation?*

But was it as innocent as she wanted to convince herself it was? Men had affairs all of the time without falling in love. *If they can do it, why shouldn't I?* she reasoned. Ali was able to justify every warning flag that flashed in front of her. Her heart was winning the war over her head, and she was running headlong towards the very trouble Edy had feared. She was not "innocent;" however, Edy had recognized Ali's vulnerability and had endeavored her best to protect her. But Ali was a hardheaded woman, and perhaps her "strength" was merely a misinterpretation of stubbornness, but she was blinded to this when Johnnie's sparkle gleamed so brightly and enveloped her thoughts and feelings.

Chapter 10
Risky Business

The weeks passed quickly and Ali continued to enjoy her position with the bank, growing ever more proficient in her duties. Before she knew it, spring had turned to a blistering scorcher of summer. The oppressive heat was abated somewhat in the evenings by throwing open the floor to ceiling windows so typical of the region's homes. The bank, however, was a different story as little breeze moved in the building. There were small windows to open, but it did little to provide relief from the stifling heat and humidity in the center of the business district of Savannah.

It wasn't so much the temperature that bothered Ali as she was certainly accustomed to the Southern summers of the Cape Fear region, but Wilmington had wonderful sea breezes that gently swept from the beaches across to the river on all but a few days of summer. Savannah, on the other hand, seemed to capture the heat, mix it with humidity, and suck the breath right out of a body.

For work, Ali dressed in the lighter cotton day dresses Jo had ordered for her, but she was still drenched to her undergarments with perspiration. As she sat working on her accounts and absent-mindedly fanning herself with a folder, she began to daydream about feeling her toes in the sand and the sun on her face, breathing deeply of the briny sea air. She longed to escape to the beach as she had in what now seemed like her "youth," though she was not yet thirty years of age. Her life in Wilmington almost seemed like a different person had lived it, and now very distant in her past. There was a tinge of sadness in this recognition. She had lost her beloved Mama yet was going on with her life and even experiencing joy. *Mama would be happy*, she thought, *but it feels so wrong to be happy when she is not here to enjoy it too. Oh, Mama, I do miss you so!*

When she was honest with herself, Ali knew her favorite part about her position was working with Johnnie. He was in and out of the office, taking trips to Columbia, Charleston, and even Augusta and Raleigh. She never knew when he would be in the office but appreciated when he told the three of them he would be out of town.

More and more, Ali noticed Will and Peter coming to her for assistance and advice with their work. Ali clearly was much more capable than they in accounting regardless of the fact that they had each completed courses in accounting. In Johnnie's absence, she became the de facto manager of the department.

When Johnnie returned from a trip, he would call each employee into his office and peruse their ledgers, which brought him up to speed on what had transpired while he was away. Early in July Johnnie asked Ali to have a seat in his office.

"Miss Malone, it has not escaped my attention that the work of both Will and Peter has improved markedly since you joined the bank. I have spoken with each of them, and both admit you have been instrumental in this improvement. I, too, am very impressed with your competence and growth in this position, and your natural leadership qualities have helped you rise to the top. It is for this reason that I am promoting you to head accountant of the loan department, effectively making you Will and Peter's superior. You have already earned my respect, and I have no doubt theirs will follow. I only caution you to tread lightly until they become accustomed to a woman managing them.

Ali was stunned and her mind was racing, making her incapable of uttering anything intelligible.

"Oh, Mr. Meadows. I am shocked but so very pleased. And honored. This was the last thing I expected. Thank you so much! I will do my best to live up to your trust in me and hope to never disappoint you for this vote of confidence."

"Of course, Ali," he said using a more familiar form of address that did not escape Ali's attention. "Do you have any questions? You may ask whatever you want."

Using his same familiar form of address, she began boldly yet humbly. "Johnnie, we have discussed my work and the promotion you have graciously given me, but we have not discussed an additional important point—my salary. While I am rather new to the bank, I was wondering if there would be any increase in my wages."

Though having an income now and being very frugal with the money her mother had given her, Ali wanted to do more to help Edy because she knew her cousin too had to watch her pennies.

"Now, Ali, you drive a very hard bargain for me to accept. Those two men have been here for five and seven years respectively, and they have wives and children to support. You do not. Is the honor of the promotion and title not enough for you?"

"Yes, sir," she said lapsing back to the formal mode of address, "and I understand all that you have said; yet I have only myself to rely on for income. I have no one else, and neither does my cousin with whom I reside. There are needs that we both have that require additional funds, and I had hoped…" She trailed off, not completing her thought.

"You are quite pushing the envelope now, Ali," Johnnie said, looking somewhat sternly at her. She ignored his annoyed reaction and pushed further.

"Also, if I may ask, does their work reflect the proficiency you would expect from their years of experience and education in comparison to what you have found in my work without the benefit of these advantages? If so, perhaps it would be wiser to promote either of the gentlemen over me."

Ali knew this was a brazen risk she was taking. Not only could she lose the promotion, but her job might be in jeopardy as well if Johnnie felt rebuffed or irritated, but to Ali this was just pure logic, and she stood her ground with no apology and no emotion for the request she had made as Johnnie had told her he did not care for tears or theatrics from women. She felt quite like a duck, appearing calm on the outside while under the water paddling as fast as possible to stay afloat.

"Well, I'll be damned! Let me see if I understand correctly what you are saying, Ali, because I want to make certain I am not misinterpreting your stance."

She felt the hairs on her neck stand up, knowing he was about to throw her words back at her and make her sound silly. He had used this same tactic before on Will and Peter. She cringed inwardly and braced for the impact but still intended to stand her ground. She would strike this blow for womankind. This was uncharted territory for her and for women in general, and she very much wanted to be strong and sensible, and, even more, respected by Johnnie. No matter how well she completed her work and regardless of his compliments, Ali still felt as if Johnnie condescended to her simply because she was a woman. As fair as he was, he still could not envision her as equal to the men.

She often wondered how this way of thinking had ever come about, knowing in her heart that she was as intelligent and capable as any man and willing to work just as hard to achieve excellence if just given an opportunity. Nonetheless, she still felt as if she must brace herself for what seemed was the inevitable consequence of standing firm against Johnnie.

He continued, "So you believe because you have been given this impressive, and generous I might add, promotion that you should also receive an increase in your salary. Am I correct? That the accolades bestowed upon you by not only myself but in consultation with the president of the bank as well are not enough to satisfy you?"

"Well, as I said, Mr. Meadows, I am very grateful..." she began, thinking to answer his question but was cut off when Johnnie continued.

"That was a rhetorical question, Miss Malone, just to affirm I had understood you correctly."

She recognized he had moved back to a sterner tone. Her stomach began to do flip-flops, imagining what was to come next and assuming she would be gathering her belongings within a few long moments to leave the bank and her position forever. *Oh, what have you done now, Ali?*

"You did not allow me to finish, Miss Malone. Please do not be in such a hurry to defend yourself as it is unnecessary. I was going to say that you have done more in the brief time you have been with us to understand our accounting system and our methods. Now most men would tar and feather me for what I am about to do, but I have been given the discretion and I am going to not only pay you what your co-workers are currently making but raise it another twenty-five percent due to your added responsibilities. How does that set with you? Am I being fair and upright with you?" There was a tone of sarcastic humor in his demeanor and voice.

Ali, prepared for a battle—a losing battle at that—could scarcely believe all she had just heard. She was unaccustomed to praise except from her mother. She never actually believed she would receive the additional income let alone twenty-five percent over Will and Peter!

"Oh my. I, I don't know what to say beyond thank you, sincerely. Thank you so much, Johnnie! I am most appreciative of the value you have placed on my work and your belief in me," she said blushing deeply.

She knew in a sense Johnnie was making fun of her for being direct, but she was still unapologetic about her request. Ali did not believe in false modesty any more than she sought to claim attributes she did not possess. She simply sought to do the best work she could and hoped to be rewarded in kind. Really, she thought, was this any different from what a man would expect? Hadn't Johnnie gone this same route in becoming the vice president of the bank's loan department? Hadn't he done his best work and received the justifiable recompense for it? Why should the rules be different for women? She simply could not accept this in her logical and thoughtful mind, but Johnnie had just gone a long way in restoring her faith in mankind.

Johnnie wasn't through yet. He lowered his voice to a tone near a whisper and said, "You have earned this, my dove, and I believe I have also earned something." He looked at her with that familiar intimate, eye-to-eye gaze that made her feel as if they were the only two people in the entire world. And his voice, that masculine deep whisper, made her imagine he was talking to her in the most private moments of her own bed. Ali had not missed the pet name he had called her either, and, though she surmised he said this to other women frequently, in her naivety she completely missed his unstated suggestion. She was to learn that courting boys was much different from understanding the passions and presumptions of men.

"Yes, of course, anything!" She nearly squealed. "How may I repay your kindness?" She started then abruptly stopped and looked into his eyes again. He was close to her now, having come from behind his desk to meet her. She found the scent of his shaving soap intoxicating in her already heady state.

"Have dinner with me, Ali. I want very much to see what lies behind those eyes, truly. I want to know you. I am utterly intrigued by you and your mind," he said in a quiet, almost pleading voice. This request took her aback.

"Wouldn't such an engagement appear scandalous and put you in jeopardy, being married with children? No one knows me in Savannah, but surely you have your reputation to consider? And I must think of my dear cousin's reputation as well as she has opened her home to me. I do, though, thank you for your invitation," she stammered out.

"I don't give a tinker's damn about gossips, Ali, and forgive me but I have never met a woman with such intelligence and tenacity. You are fearless, and I have to know everything about you," he said. "Please, indulge me this once. If it makes you more comfortable, we can go to a restaurant I know of on one of the islands, Tybee. It's not fancy, but it is somewhat remote, and we will be able to converse privately."

She knew she was taking a bold risk with her own reputation, and Edy would never agree, but she would make sure Edy never knew. Today was a day of bold risks, and she had promised herself on that first meeting with Johnnie to jump at any chance to be with him in any capacity, and she would. Perhaps this is what Mama had meant when she told Ali to take a risk on true love and something she wanted with all her heart. Right then, at that very moment, Ali knew Johnnie was what she truly wanted and quite possibly her true love.

Yes, she would allow herself this freedom. She believed in her heart she was meant to be with Johnnie. Everything about him was familiar to her and short of a seance at Madame Clarice's near the wharf, this was the path to the truth; she was certain.

"Well…yes. I would love to go to dinner with you then," she offered, trying not to appear overly anxious.

Her courage to claim what he was certain she wanted as much as he surprised Johnnie. His admiration for her grew even more in that moment.

Ali was aware if anyone saw them together at dinner it could ruin them both, socially and professionally. It could destroy his marriage and put her position and new promotion with the bank in jeopardy. Ali felt she had lived her entire life being safe and sequestered, and it was time to take this risk to be with a remarkable and desirable man. She felt certain her mother would understand and agree.

Ali also realized she might be imagining his feelings and misjudging his intentions. He could actually be planning just an innocent dinner to get to know his new head of the accounting department and nothing more, but she hoped it would be the beginning of much more. She had noted what Johnnie had said about his wife Beatrice. What was it? "Witless debutantes who do nothing to feed their minds, interested only in their social standing," a*nd he called me a "breath of fresh air."*

It certainly sounded as if he might be making a change in his life and perhaps one day make Ali his own. Johnnie Meadows. She wanted to slap herself at the same time for ignoring all Cousin Edy had told her about Johnnie. But she had to follow her heart in this. *I have to take this one chance on true love. Ali Meadows has a nice ring to it.* And in that moment, she lost all objectivity when it came to Johnnie Meadows. No amount of coaxing or coercing by anyone could shake her absolute belief in him. Ali could imagine nothing that might ever diminish her love for him.

"If we are going after work, perhaps I should go home and change into something more appropriate and let my cousin know I will be in late," Ali spoke her thoughts aloud.

"No need, sweet girl. I will send the messenger boy to your home to inform your cousin, and, my dear, you look lovely enough to befuddle any man. If fact, I venture to guess you would look loveliest in nothing at all. There is no need to change clothing for this restaurant. It is very informal," he assured her.

"I'll tell you what, you and I are going to leave now. Let's make it a day. No need to waste a beautiful, sunny afternoon in this stifling office."

"Oh my, we wouldn't dare Mr. —er, Johnnie. It would create too much suspicion. We couldn't possibly," Ali said in a panicked whisper.

"My dove, you are not looking at all well. In fact, I believe you are coming down with something—possibly the influenza. I shall escort you to your home immediately. Only a cad would leave an ill young woman to find her way home in such a sate. Shall we go immediately so as not to risk further distress?" he asked innocently.

"I, well, yes…I am feeling rather poorly, and, my goodness, I do appear to have a touch of fever. I feel rather flushed," Ali played along perfectly in tune with the ruse Johnnie was creating.

As she straightened the papers on her desk in preparation to leave, she added so that Will and Peter could hear, "Thank you, Mr. Meadows, for your kind consideration. I shall go home and straight to bed."

She retrieved her hat, secured it on her head, and walked slowly out the door as if feeling unwell. Deep inside her, Ali quite enjoyed this naughtiness. She failed to recognize this warning signal.

Johnnie followed her nonchalantly as if he had done this a hundred times previously.

Chapter 11
Stolen Moments

Johnnie pulled his shiny, dark green motor car in front of the bank and helped her in. He often visited Tybee Island just off the coast of Savannah, and soon turned the motor car onto McQueens Island Trail. Ali sat as far back and as inconspicuously as possible in Johnnie's motor car, tilting her hat with its wide brim to the side window to provide a further shield of her identity as they travelled the distance through Savannah to the ferry port. Johnnie spoke to the ferry master, whom he obviously knew well.

"Hello, Jack! Beautiful day for a little jaunt to Tybee. I can, as always, count on your discretion, I presume?"

"That you can, Mr. Johnnie, that you can. Haven't seen you," Jack said, tipping his hat and giving Johnnie a sly wink.

Johnnie turned to help Ali from the motor car so they could stand at the from of the ferry to catch the sea breeze as Tybee approached.

Ali immediately moved to the front of the ferry where she could take in every site on the journey. It was a short ride, but, as they set off, Ali began to breathe deeply of the ocean breeze as the spray splashed her face, leaving behind the taste of salt. She was immediately taken back in her memory to her walks on Wrightsville Beach. An unexpected wash of homesickness surprised her, and that familiar ache of losing her mother momentarily clouded her mind. These morose thoughts disappeared when she felt Johnnie's strong arm encircle her waist.

"Deep in thought again, Miss Malone?"

"Ali, Johnnie, please. Remember what you said—first names outside of the bank."

"Yes, of course, my little dove, whatever pleases you pleases me. Excited?" he asked.

"Yes, very excited." She hesitated a bit, concerned about allowing so much vulnerability to show too soon. She wasn't yet certain she could trust Johnnie. She thought of all the stories she had heard about the other women he had romanced over the years. She felt a bit like a lamb to the slaughter but quickly dismissed the thought. She was different. Their relationship, if there was to be one, would be different from the rest. Ali knew she could love Johnnie in a way the others including "B" could not, would not. She felt as if she could see into Johnnie's heart and perceive the loving, gentle and faithful man others were unaware of. *Yes, I will be the love of his life just as he will be mine.*

Johnnie drove his motor car off the ferry and parked it at the side of the street. Ali looked around in delight. "Oh, it is lovely, Johnnie! The sand is so pure and white, and just look at how turquoise the water is today! Not a cloud in sight and the seagulls are looking for supper as well! What is the name of the restaurant where we will be dining? Where is it? Is it a far walk? Will we have an early dinner, or may we walk on the beach for just a bit?"

In her excitement Ali shot questions at Johnnie in rapid-fire succession as if she were a Gatling gun. She was completely unaware that Johnnie was watching her and marveling at this bright and beautiful woman. *What a mind!* He had never met such an intelligent, deep-thinking woman.

Ali turned suddenly to Johnnie, realizing he had not said a word but was looking at her with that brilliant smile of his wide on his handsome face. "Oh, Johnnie, forgive me. I've said too much. I am so sorry for prattling on so. I'm just too excited, I guess."

"No, my dove, do not apologize for being so genuine and uninhibited. I love your enthusiasm for life. You utterly mesmerize me. How such a lovely, vibrant woman has managed to hold onto her childlike wonder is beyond me. Life so easily beats it out of most," Johnnie said, knowing he had lost much of his joie de vivre just by the inevitable sorrows of life. He brushed an errant hair from her face, tucking it behind her ear in a loving gesture that was not lost on Ali.

She smiled back at him, tilting her face up to meet his and without warning, Johnnie lost all control and took her in his arms and kissed her deeply. Ali remained tense in his arms, wondering what Jack must be thinking, but within seconds she forgot Jack and Edy, her father, her mother, "B" and anyone other than Johnnie. She leaned into his muscled chest and gave herself to his probing lips and tongue.

Johnnie slowly pulled back, lifted Ali's chin and asked, "Please tell me you enjoyed that kiss as much as I did and that you aren't offended, Ali, because I cannot bear the thought of offending you."

It was unlike Johnnie Meadows, suave, handsome, bold with the ladies, confident in his work, sure of himself, to ever plead or for that matter give a care that he might have offended a woman. But this woman was different.

While Ali ignored the alarms in her mind, Johnnie was well aware of those going off in him, telling him Ali was not just any woman. He almost physically felt her slipping into his soul.

Rather than answer his question directly, Ali leaned into his chest again, this time nuzzling his neck and kissing the soft, tender skin just behind and below his ear. This nearly drove Johnnie to complete abandon. Ali in her naivety did not notice his rising manhood.

"Darling girl, I fear if you continue on this path, I will not be able to control myself, and I remind you we are not alone nor in private," Johnnie teased her, leading her down the plank to the dock.

She whispered in answer, "I want more of you, Johnnie, much more. All of you. I want to 'mesmerize' every inch of your body. I want to experience all of you," now breathless with the anticipation, of what she was not quite certain.

Johnnie turned back to Jack. "We will be taking the final trip back tonight, Jack. Please do not leave without us."

"You can count on me, Johnnie boy!" Jack shouted back, already loading a couple of others and their wares to take back to the mainland. Johnnie waved in acknowledgment and took Ali by the elbow, helping her onto the walkway.

"Ali, I would like to share something with you and you alone. No one else is aware of this, including Beatrice, and no one else can know. Do you agree that this will remain our secret?"

"Yes, of course, Johnnie. You know, I hope, that you can trust me. I would never betray you," Ali answered, wondering what his secret could be.

He took her hand and began walking down the white sand beach, wide with the receding tide.

She turned to Johnnie and said, "Johnnie, would you do me one small favor, please? When we are together, would you please not mention her name? Please let this be our time without anyone else in the shadows. Ours alone."

"My dove, I prefer that as well," he responded, "We will call her "B" if this is agreeable with you, if she enters our conversations at all, and I prefer she not."

"I prefer she not as well, Johnnie. I know she is your wife and the mother of your children," she swallowed hard, disturbed by even admitting this aloud, "but when we are together, let us just pretend there is no one else outside of us."

"Agreed," he said, and they walked on.

They had gone quite a distance, perhaps half of a mile, when Ali leaned against Johnnie and slipped out of her shoes and hosiery. Without a word, she continued walking down the beach feeling the hot sand swish between her toes. Johnnie smiled at her lack of inhibition and anticipated what he hoped was to come. Ali had no idea where Johnnie was leading her, and truthfully she didn't give a care because she was relishing these private moments in the sun and surf. She was vacant of one care or concern for the first time in her memory. She was wholly present and immersed in bliss as she walked on the beach, a place she had always felt thoroughly free.

Johnnie remained silent and watchful beside her, experiencing his own bliss. After a time, he stopped, still holding her hand, her other palm full of shells.

"Doll baby," he softly said, grasping her shoulders and turning her to face a beautiful light blue-colored cottage, trimmed in white gingerbread, windows framed with long hurricane shutters. There was a wide porch with white rocking chairs and wisteria hanging from an arbor over the gate to the walkway.

"What a precious little home, Johnnie! It looks like a fairytale house," she said with a little girl's dreamy look in her eyes. "Who owns this?"

"This is our restaurant, darling girl," Johnnie drawled. "I hope you'll like it as much as I do."

But—it looks closed, Johnnie. Perhaps we are here at the wrong time or day?"

They went through the gated picket fence and walked to the steps. Johnnie reached into his vest pocket and withdrew a key then inserted it into the door lock. Ali heard the lock click and Johnnie swept the door wide to a completely decorated dollhouse of a cottage. Ali looked up at Johnnie, confusion showing on her face.

He closed the screen door behind them and latched it, allowing the sound of the surf and the breeze to flow freely through, airing out the cottage. He opened the windows to allow the fresh, salty sea air to fill the space.

"Johnnie…?" she began. "Is this your cottage?"

"Yes, my darling, and, Ali, you are the only other person I have ever shared this with, not even 'she' knows it exists. She knows nothing of it. This is my private piece of Heaven, and I want to share it with only you. Just your expressions of delight have made it even more special for me," he said genuinely.

"Oh, Johnnie, it is lovely. Thank you, thank you for sharing all this with me. It is perfect."

"I have a confession, Ali. I called ahead to the caretaker and asked him to deliver all we need for dinner, and I, my dear, will be your chef extraordinaire. Welcome to 'Chez Johnnie," he laughed.

Ali followed him to the kitchen where he opened the icebox to a chilled bottle of champagne as well as assorted delicacies he had ordered. On the counter were two exquisite stemmed Waterford crystal champagne glasses from Ireland. Johnnie expertly removed the cork with a loud pop and foaming champagne, pouring them both a glass, handing her one.

"A toast, Ali, to us. To the peace we find in this home, the rest from the sound of the surf, and the love I hope we find for one another in this place." He clinked her glass as she stood, speechless, scarcely believing what she had just heard. She sipped her champagne, blinking back tears of joy from his thoughtful toast.

"Thank you, Johnnie. All you have toasted to are my wishes as well. May I see the rest of the cottage?"

"Yes, yes. I will follow as you explore," and he grabbed the champagne bottle from the counter and carried it along with them on the short tour of the small cottage.

Ali walked slowly, trying to take in everything, memorizing each detail—every painting and trinket scattered about.

The gathering room had a small fireplace and comfortable furniture with white slipcovers. There were large conch shells on the tables and interesting pieces of driftwood. She could see that Johnnie loved the ocean as she did. A small table with two chairs sat under one window serving as the dining area as well as a game table as she saw cards and chips on a shelf nearby.

There was a bathroom complete with piped water and a flushable toilet! These were quite rare in all but the homes of the wealthy, having only come to use in the 1890s. To have one in a beach cottage was a surprise to her. A pleasant surprise. Next to it there was a small clawfoot bathing tub to be filled with heated water. She could imagine soaking in it listening to the roar of the surf outside. Johnnie had spared no expense in building and furnishing his little piece of seaside heaven. He had built it as if it were a full townhouse with all the amenities he had come to enjoy in his Savannah home.

Everything was awash in cool, gauzy white fabric. Ali grasped a glass door knob and opened the door into a dreamy white bedroom with a canopied bed, a crocheted white string canopy that allowed the breeze to blow freely through. Everything was pristine with touches of blue-green She stood frozen in the doorway—partly taking it all in, partly because of nerves. This felt like a forbidden room, one she should not be in alone with a gentleman. *I want this,* she told herself. *I want Johnnie. No matter what the consequences. I want to be his.*

"Ali, are you all right?" Johnnie felt her tension. To relieve the obvious conflict in her mind, Johnnie graciously asked, "May I pour you another glass of champagne before I begin preparing our dinner?"

He could imagine the thoughts racing through her mind, because when she opened the bedroom door, the same thoughts struck him afresh. He imagined what was happening inside her body, hopefully preparing her for what he hoped would be their intimacy.

"I, I, umm, well, I want to be with you, Johnnie. Here. In this room, in this bed," she said haltingly and aloud, not fully realizing she had just spoken her true desires to Johnnie.

She turned to him looking directly into his blue-green eyes, searching, wondering if he wanted the same. It still was inconceivable to her that this amazing man would desire her as she did him.

"Are you certain, my little dove? I never want to do anything that might harm you in any way. You are perfectly innocent and good. I'm afraid I might tarnish you somehow. You must be completely certain this is what you want," he said with tenderness, almost pleading. He gently stroked her soft cheek with the back of his hand sending a shiver through Ali.

"Johnnie, I have to be honest with you. I cannot be anything else," she said while at the same time unbuttoning her shirtwaist.

"Go on, love," Johnnie whispered, unmoving.

"The first time your eyes met mine, the day you came so very close to kissing me in the office—do you remember?"

"Yes, darlin', I do definitely remember."

"Why did you suddenly rush out of the office and leave me standing there?"

"Darlin," he drawled in his low voice, "I was about to embarrass myself and ruin your reputation. I had to leave to control my urge to take you in my arms," he admitted.

"Well, I thought I had said something wrong to anger or offend you."

"No, no, sweet girl; you were perfect. Just perfect. It was all on me."

He had been pouring their glasses of champagne, and, when he turned back to her, Ali stood at the side of the bed completely free of her clothing except for her chemise—exposed to Johnnie's approving and hungry gaze. She was exquisite. Everything he had imagined, and more—and she was willing. She wanted to be loved as much as he wanted to love her.

Love. Yes. I want to love her. She is nothing like the beautiful yet uninspiring women I have wasted so many nights on and all completely forgettable. I could never forget Ali.

This realization alone sent a shiver through him. He knew as much as he may want to leave Beatrice, he would never leave her. The best he could hope for would be that she would tire of his shenanigans and leave him. And then there were the children to consider. If they were grown with homes and families of their own, it would be so much easier to extricate himself without losing their affection.

The best he could hope for was Ali's patience and understanding and that she would grow to love him enough to settle for this relationship. He knew it was unfair to her, grossly unfair. Even wrong. But he could not deny himself this perfect fit, this woman. His conscience prickled him a tad, but he brushed it aside, which was his lifelong habit of doing when his conscience flared. He could justify most anything and even convince himself. Though he did not consider himself selfish, certainly the way he was conducting himself indeed was selfish.

He would live in the present whenever he could be with Ali and not consider the future. Wasn't that exactly the way she had described how she resolved to conduct herself with him? There. Her eyes were wide open to the dangers of this liaison. Johnny failed to consider there could be consequences not just for him but for Ali as well. Dire consequences for her. Again, he justified this by telling himself she was an intelligent, grown woman who was responsible for her own life, and she was willingly deciding to give her virtue to him and pursue this relationship. *Yes. She is as culpable as I.*

Turning to face her once more, he said, "You are the loveliest woman, just pure perfection. Ali, if you are certain you want this and acknowledge there could be consequences, I would dearly love to make love to you. I don't mean to put you on the spot, but is this your first time, precious girl?" he asked cautiously yet confidently. He was looking forward to bedding this virgin.

"You are my first and my only lover, Johnnie, and I never could have imagined or hoped for a more perfect man to claim my virginity nor a more beautiful setting. If you will have me, I am yours completely and without reservation. That is what I was trying to admit to you earlier. From the first moment we met, I promised myself if I ever had the opportunity to be with you under any circumstances, I would give myself that freedom. I have never been more certain of any choice."

She took the champagne glasses from his hands. Taking his hands in hers, she placed one on her breast. With his free arm, Johnny encircled her waist and captured her body, holding it tightly against his. A mutual moan escaped them both as this delicate dance of intimacy, this exquisite pas de deux, commenced. Little did either know this one moment in time would alter their lives forever.

Chapter 12
Perilous Passion

Ali's eyes fluttered open as the descending sun's rays streamed through the plantation shutters of the bedroom window and onto her face. She must have been asleep for quite some time as the sun was much higher in the sky when she walked down the beach with Johnnie. It took a moment for her to realize where she was. Then she closed her eyes again, drifting in and out of blissful dreams. *Mmm* escaped through her lips as she remembered the delicious love she had made with Johnnie.

It had been more than she expected—so much more. She giggled in embarrassment remembering all the secret places on her body Johnnie had explored with his hands, lips— and his tongue. *Oh my.* She hadn't known love could be so exquisite.

Rolling over, Ali came face to face with Johnnie who had been watching her sleep and heard her *mmm* and her bubbling giggle. He wondered what was going through her mind. It sounded as if she had enjoyed their lovemaking, and the initial thrust had not seemed to hurt her too much. He was certainly satisfied, so much so he joined her in their short nap, spent from their delightful activities. He smiled at her brushing back the loose hair from her face.

"You have the most beautiful smile, Johnnie. It lights up the room—lights up my life."

"I could do nothing else but smile considering what I have just experienced. I hope you enjoyed it as much as I, Ali, and I hope I was gentle enough so as not to hurt you too terribly."

He had been so thoughtful and gentle with her as he lifted her naked body and placed her gently on the soft feather bed, where she lay watching him as he slowly removed his clothes, allowing her to savor each new sight—bared broad chest covered with curly black hair, narrow hips and tight bottom, strong arms, and long legs. He had taken care of himself, obviously. She watched as he deliberately removed every article of clothing, carefully placing each on the over-stuffed chintz floral chair. He placed his pocket watch from his vest on the bedside table, turning it face down. Today there would be no time. No thought of anything but this moment they would capture and cherish.

Ali grew impatient to touch his body, yet he pulled just far enough away to frustrate her efforts. His hard, sculpted body was tan and covered with hair, and she could scarcely wait to entangle her fingers in it. When he allowed his breeches to drop to the floor, Ali's eyes grew large, not fathoming how he would be able to fit all of himself inside her. Yet, even though a bit fearful, she also welcomed his gift.

He stepped out of the trousers and folded them to join the rest on the chair. *He is precise.* She admired his tidiness and exacting personality. It was the impetus for his immaculate grooming, impeccable taste in clothing, and spit-polished boots. She found this utterly attractive. But more, this man, this body he now fully displayed to her, just beyond her reach, was beautiful. She wasn't sure if that was the appropriate word to use for a man, but surely in her eyes he was a beautiful man.

She flushed deeply wanting nothing more than to run her hands up and down his body, seeing, hearing, inhaling—and consuming him. She knew she was not quite as innocent as he thought, but her limited experience provided ways of delighting him. While her mother had not shared details with her in regard to the art of lovemaking, the few things she had imparted Ali felt certain would excite Johnnie. She was ready—ready to love this man. Ready to claim her womanhood. Her heart was beating out of her chest in anticipation.

"Don't be afraid, little dove," Johnnie told her noticing her slight shiver. "I will prepare you to accept me without all but a slight, sharp pain that will subside quickly. Trust me to take care of you."

"I trust you completely, Johnnie. Surely you know that by now."

She looked directly into his blue-green eyes without wavering. It nearly made Johnnie uncomfortable, and he struggled not to look away. There was an honesty and genuine love pouring from her eyes into his that almost burned in its intensity.

Momentarily he reconsidered his motives and intentions. He could see all the way into her soul, and there he saw something he now knew he had longed for all his life. There was a time when he and Beatrice had felt some modicum of love for each other, but this was something that was fathomless—and he wanted to drown in it.

Was he even deserving of such devotion as he saw reflected there? Was he capable of returning such love that would leave him naked and vulnerable to her? Could he dare lay bare all he was feeling? Could he trust what he saw, felt, from her? He did not know and the depth of introspection required for an answer was something he was unaccustomed to. He suddenly felt his nakedness exquisitely and in a way as never before.

He watched Ali lying like a stretched-out cat across the bed, unashamed of her body in front of him. No pretense. No layers of underclothes or nightgowns. *Dear God, help me. I am wholly captivated, consumed by this magnificent woman.* Johnnie was surprised by his own weakness when it came to Ali. He had known better than to ever bed any of his subordinates, but he somehow sensed that Ali would keep his confidence and never reveal their relationship to anyone. To reveal their secret would be ruinous for both. He suspected she would cherish this time as he would, never wanting to share it with anyone else. How long had it been since he had felt he could trust a woman—or man for that matter—as he was trusting Ali today? How long had it been since he was honest? *How long had it been since he loved? Never—that's how long.*

Ali was definitely different. He winced at the tragedies and abuses that had beaten her into the soft, open person she was today. He was sure her life had not been easy and, as such, expected her to be reticent to his seduction. Intelligent, lovely, honest and, as much as he loathed the responsibility, she was vulnerable. *I need to take care not to hurt her.*

Ali was an independent, strong, and capable young woman who did not surround herself with cackling hens gossiping over bridge parties and fashion, endlessly throwing money out the back door faster than their husbands could shovel it in the front door. She was irresistible. A once-in-a-lifetime woman to whom he was about to make love.

Johnnie had made sure to allow Ali the time to survey his body and prepare herself for what was to follow, and truthfully he was a bit of a peacock and enjoyed her obvious approval. He wanted her to cherish this memory of making love for the very first time. He certainly would. *Take your time!*

Ali was still taking in the sheer girth of his manhood. He detected admiration mixed with trepidation and a good dose of curiosity on her face. She ached to touch him. Anticipating her thoughts, Johnnie said, "I assure you my little dove, you have nothing to be afraid of. Your luscious body will accommodate all of me without issue. We will take our time and your body will ready itself."

And her body did respond to his touch in miraculous ways, lubricating itself in preparation for his penetration. They made love for over two hours. And still neither was fully sated.

As she lay on the bed looking into his eyes after their little catnap, the pleasure of their time washed over her again, and she found herself desiring him to start anew. He had treated her with a tenderness and respect, thoughtfulness and—though she hesitated to even think it—love such as she had never experienced from any man in her life.

"Johnnie," she spoke softly, "thank you for making love to me. Thank you for being so gentle and patient with me. I hope I didn't disappoint you. I wasn't quite certain what to do for you, but I so want to please you. I'm sure you have had other women who were so much more 'accomplished' than I, and I…"

Johnnie placed a finger on her lips to stop her talking. "My love, stop. You were perfect. I have never enjoyed what we shared with anyone else. Ever. You are precious and have a natural, open inclination for the sex act. And, I might add, it should be a regular part of your life. *Our life.*"

She caught his emphasis on "*our life*" and wondered what that could mean. "Well, Johnnie, that is not in my hands, I regret to say. When and how much we are together in the future will depend solely upon the decisions you make."

Johnnie knew instantly what or rather to whom she was referring—his wife. Beatrice. *Dammit, why are you always the gravel in my shoe, irritating me, always there?* That familiar tinge of guilt washed over him, and he couldn't discern if it was guilt from cheating on his wife or from making emotional promises to this guileless and vulnerable woman in his arms. Whichever it was, he felt it would prove to be a perilous path he had started down with Ali.

"No, darling. Never give your power away to any man. If we are to share this again, and I pray we will, it will be when you are willing to be with me. And I want you to have something, Ali," he said as he reached for his jacket. Reaching into his pocket, he withdrew a key and put it in Ali's hand.

"What is this for, Johnnie?"

"It is a key to this cottage, our beach heaven. You are free to use it at any time you choose. You do not have to inform me in advance or ask my permission. I am the only person who comes here, and now it is yours too. I want to share it with you. My only request is that you bring no one else here—that it remain our secret hideaway."

She wasn't sure if she should feel insulted or flattered. "What kind of woman do you think I am, Johnnie? There are no other lovers! You are my first and only lover, and I hope it will always be so!" She hissed, blinking back tears.

"My dove, I dare say you will have more, um, experiences in life. You are an unmarried, vibrant, brilliant, and very desirable young woman. I feel certain men will be lining up to court you, and, as I am a married man, you may certainly exercise your freedom in that circumstance. Just not here."

A coldness swept over the room instantly. He knew his words had cut deep, but he had to protect himself from falling in love with her and her with him, so he hurled his insult in a smiling, almost innocent way, made to convince her that she was in charge and responsible. In other words, Johnnie did not want to accept any responsibility for this situation.

"But, Johnnie, you indicated that you were through with your marriage. I would have never gone through with this…" she gulped and her voice cracked in anguish, "…if I had thought there was not some, uh, if we didn't have some, well…future. Are you now saying you are not leaving her?"

Tears now flowed down her cheeks.

Johnnie replied sternly as he got out of the bed and began dressing. "Ali, you know I do not appreciate tears and hysterics, and I thought you were logical enough not to use such tactics," he said in his office voice as if talking to his subordinate. He continued. "I made a holy covenant with my wife that I can never break. You know this as you too are Catholic. Divorce would be out of the question, impossible. I am sorry you are distressed."

Johnnie knew the impact his words were making on this vulnerable girl, but he had to somehow keep her at arm's distance and eliminate any expectations she might have of him, of them, of this. Still, he felt an ache in his heart. But he shut it down.

"Johnnie, may I ask you a question?"

"Of course. What would you like to know?" He replied with an uncharacteristic sharpness, feeling as if he was on the inquisition block.

Directly and bluntly as was her way, Ali asked, "Is your covenant any *less* broken simply because your wife is unaware that you broke it?"

He had underestimated her. She set forth the one, the only, logical argument against what he was saying. It wasn't emotional. Not a plea. No histrionics. No tears. In fact, with all the fawning he had received in his privileged life, he realized no one had ever spoken to him with such cold clarity. And intelligence. He knew Ali had bested him in this debate, and, as much as it angered him, it frightened him because he stood there in all his authority with no rebuttal. He had nothing to offer. So he did the only thing he could think of—he immediately bolted from the room.

Ali knew she had hit her mark, but she took no pleasure in it. She was admittedly stunned by his reaction. She expected some sort of push back, some pithy comment. He had told her he admired her straightforward communication with him. She sincerely wanted to understand how he was thinking about this covenant that he had so blithely broken so many times and all before he met her, according to cousin Edy, and each before today. He had told her several times she could ask him anything. Anything it seemed except about his 'sacred' marriage covenant.

Ali felt he was making a mockery of the marriage sacrament and abusing the confessional and the gift of absolution. If he wanted to talk of God, she was well prepared for it. Johnnie needed to acknowledge the reality of his actions. She knew he was now angry with her and assumed she should dress and prepare to leave as Johnnie would probably not waste time cooking dinner for her now. She climbed out of bed and began dressing, trying to pin her hair up as best she could.

Though her back was turned to the door, she could sense he was in the room again behind her. She turned to look into his eyes and she spoke first.

"You're angry with me, aren't you, Johnnie? I want to apologize and make it better, but I find I cannot. For that, I am sorry. I've always believed that actions speak louder than words. Your actions have indicated that you love me, but your words cut me like a knife."

"I was angry, yes, but not at you, Ali. At myself. You are, of course, correct in your logic, and I didn't want to face it. I find myself at war with myself. There is a dichotomy raging within my own mind. The marriage covenant *has* long been broken. You are right and well before I made love to you. As you can surmise, I am not quite the upstanding man you imagined I was. I am a scoundrel, and you have every right to be disappointed in me." He looked at the floor, then out the window at the surf. "I apologize, Ali—for disappointing you and for disappointing myself. I do love you."

"Dearest Johnnie, you are wrong—about my feelings for you. My heart is fragile. I am asking you now to promise that you will not hurt me. I have suffered such loss in my life, and especially with the passing of my mama recently, that I am not certain my heart can survive another break. If your intention is to stay with her, then let us end this now before either of us is invested in a doomed romance. I have a lifetime of scars upon my heart. My father demeaned and abused me. Others have as well. Please. Do not be like him. And never, ever lie to me. I beg you. I can handle the truth, but I cannot handle uncertainty. I do not intend to allow another man to crush the life from me as he did. So I am *begging* you, Johnnie, please do not hurt me. If you are staying with her, I beg you, walk away now," Ali pleaded through lashes heavy with tears, the ache nearly unbearable. "Listen to me very carefully, Johnnie, I would rather you be with her and miss me than be with me and miss her."

She indeed could see that Johnnie was in a battle within himself—the man he truly was, vital and exciting, versus the man he aspired to be and whom others assumed he was—faithful husband and loving father. He was discontented with who he was, never feeling quite "good enough." She loved him and couldn't understand why anyone wanted him to change. To Ali, he was perfect—perfect for her just as he was. But she would not beg him.

She surmised that being married to a woman he was not attracted to in any way other than as the mother of his children was unfulfilling to a man such as Johnnie. Beatrice did little to make herself attractive to Johnnie other than spending his money on lavish clothes. She felt certain that there was nothing stimulating in their conversation. If there was, why was he with her? She and Johnnie had deep conversations about so many different topics. Those conversations fed her and she suspected they fed him as well. Men need their women to polish them and make them shine so they can go out into the world each day feeling like a powerful knight capable of conquering any foe. Ali learned this from her mother during one of their afternoon confidences. But Ali also felt men could do the same for their women. She wanted a man who could do that for her.

Ali knew if given the chance Johnnie could find more than contentment with her. He would discover fulfillment and acceptance. And *joy*. The joy they had experienced this very day when they shared their bodies and hearts. She could meet his needs, support him to be the best version of himself, and love him in every way, just as she had always longed to be treated.

Her certainty lay in the knowledge that the two of them were so alike. No matter how great the accomplishment, each would think, *I could have done better*. Ali suspected the roots of this self-loathing went deep, but as adults she knew they had the power to overcome those debilitating whispers that always came back during those vulnerable and exposed times in life. She and Johnnie simply needed to change the silent dialog that was haunting them.

But Ali wasn't about to beg him to love her. Nothing good could ever come from any kind of coercion even if the coercion were merely tears. If he wanted her, Johnnie had to come to her on his own without reservation. Ali did not believe in the womanly wiles of manipulation so popular, especially among women of the South. Truth. Honesty. Trust. Respect. Those were the basis of a true and lasting pairing and especially marriage.

Johnnie had not said a word after she spoke. "Johnnie, sometimes no decision *is* a decision."

If he wouldn't make a decision, she would. She placed the cottage key in his hand, and it burned his flesh like a hot coal. He desperately wanted her to keep the key, but she walked past him and out the door to calm her mind with a stroll on the wet sand. She hoped the roar of the surf would drown the pain in her heart. She could not allow this to overcome her. This was one day, one experience, one man. She had to remember who she was and be realistic. She must clear her mind. She knew it was better to end things now than to drag out the pain until he ultimately destroyed her.

"Ali," Johnnie began, reaching out to touch her arm but not stop her from leaving. Johnnie knew she needed some time and space to consider all that had transpired that day. "I didn't mean to hurt your feelings or insult you. Take your walk and enjoy the beach. When you return, we will eat."

"I'm just going to breathe the salt air and enjoy the ocean while I may. I am fine." She lied and Johnnie was not convinced. And she did it with a smile plastered on her face like a simpering and manipulative fool, all the while trying to steady her voice and the shaking of her legs, summoning her courage as she walked out. The screen door slammed behind her.

Johnnie was resigned to letting her walk and have some alone time, yet the sound of the door slamming disturbed him much more than he thought it would. This door, in this special place, his haven, was not made to be slammed, and it somehow hurt his heart. He had meant for this to be a haven for them both. *Little Dove Cottage.*

"All right, I will get things started for our dinner at 'Chez Johnnie,' he laughingly called behind her. "It should be ready in an hour or so, so enjoy your walk, little dove." His endearment affected her deeply just as it always did, but this time it felt like a manipulation, which annoyed her. *I am so weak when it comes to him!* But she knew she did not want to be free of him. She knew she would always be available to him. For anything. This, Ali understood, was *real*. It was love, not the childhood crushes or teenage fantasies she had before. But she was uncertain if Johnnie's definition of love was the same as hers.

Ali could draw deep satisfaction in having Johnnie's heart if ever she did have it. But was that enough? Could she continue on in her spinster existence loving Johnnie in secret and from afar? Having only half a life, half of his heart, bits of his time and always his dirty little secret? "B" might wear his ring, and she might live in his luxurious home and enjoy spending his money as well as all the societal prestige that came with being his wife in public. Yes, she had what everyone thought was the fairytale come true. She had all the wifely advantages that Ali recognized would never be hers. But his heart? No. Ali knew she was the "wife of his heart." "B" had merely an empty shell of a marriage. All the trimmings and no content. Longevity without love. Ali had the reality of being in love with Johnnie and Johnnie loving her in return. Maybe it could be enough. Maybe she needed to lower her expectations a bit? Could she do that?

The moment she stepped out onto the beach, Ali was transformed and her cares faded in the face of the vast and ever-changing ocean. What she loved most about walking on the beach was how her mind cleared completely when she heard the sound of the waves and smelled the briny sea air. She didn't want to think. She didn't want to feel. She simply wanted the hot sand between her toes and the sun baking freckles on her unladylike tanned face. It was a glorious afternoon! Tybee was beautiful. She hadn't realized how much she missed the ocean. She felt young again.

She walked to the end of the island before turning back. She collected many shells on her trek, which she held in the raised skirt of her dress. *Even Mama wouldn't approve of this*, Ali thought, laughing aloud at her brash behavior. She neared the cottage and saw Johnnie on the sand working over the fire pit. Her stomach had those familiar butterflies she felt whenever she caught a glimpse of him. *I love him so*, she whispered into the sea wind, hoping for some miracle—from King Neptune or from God—whomever was listening—that Johnnie would one day be hers.

Johnnie had time to ruminate over their afternoon as well as he sat looking out over the ocean and waiting for the coals to receive the pot. He marveled that no matter how many times or how long he sat gazing at the same ocean in the same spot, it was always a different picture. A different perspective. Different skies, weather, waves, sounds. Always different yet always the same somehow. It was a breathtaking day.

He had planned everything for their afternoon at the cottage to the smallest detail. Seduction was a game to him and he was the master. This time was different, however, as was this woman. He knew his heart was starting to fall for her. This was no game, which delighted and terrified him at the same time.

Falling in love with Ali was a great personal risk. He was putting everything on the line just to love a woman, and this was completely foreign to him. He normally did not allow himself to go beyond a superficial and physical level, but Ali was a deep thinker, terribly analytical, and she simply would not be brushed off, redirected, or silenced. When she had a mind to know something to the minutest detail, there was no stopping her. That is what made her such an asset to the bank, and that is what made her so challenging to him on a personal level. That same mind that intrigued him could also provoke and often disarm him.

Johnnie Meadows was not accustomed to being pinned down or cornered, especially by a female, unless, of course, being pinned down was in the bedroom, and then he quite liked it. *I am insatiable when it comes to Ali. How does she do this to me?*

Johnnie had requested fresh clams, oysters, flounder, and crab along with andouille sausage, potatoes, corn on the cob, and a crock of freshly churned butter. As Ali was walking the beach picking up seashells, Johnnie prepared a sumptuous clam bake. He dug a pit in the sand and lined it with large, smooth stones. He stacked small kindling and larger fire wood on the rocks, making a sort of pyramid, and lighted the fire. It would take some time for the coals and rocks to heat to the red-hot temperature required.

He sat looking out at the ocean waiting for Ali. His stomach churned wondering what her thoughts and attitude would be when she returned. Why would he care so much about a woman? Normally he didn't. All the tears and angst and anger and accusations from other women he had bedded had little to no effect on him. But this woman? Ali? He felt like a neophyte when it came to matters of the heart in relation to her.

He desperately did not want to be responsible for any hurt she may experience because of their affair. One tactic he employed quite frequently was encouraging the woman to deeply examine why she wanted to be in a sexual affair with him and then making sure she acknowledged she was deciding of her own free will. This absolved him of all responsibility and spared him from the confessional. This way he could throw up his hands in innocence, saying the woman was willing and chose this herself, so he was merely acting as a man does when presented with a beautiful and willing woman. Who could fault him for taking advantage of the "opportunity?" He was, after all, *only* a man and unable to control manly urges. Normally he would smile at his artifice, but somehow Ali challenging him to be honest worked on his conscience.

When he stirred the coals and saw the rocks were ready, Ali still wasn't back and the sun was slipping closer to the horizon. He was not terribly concerned though still a bit trepidatious about what her mood would be when she did return. He suspected the longer she walked, the more solemn the mood. In his usual assured manner, however, he continued with the preparations as if nothing was amiss. He raked off the coals and moved the four stones to the corners to hold the large pot of the clambake fixings that he had prepared and set the pan on the rocks. He hoped Ali would enjoy this informal dinner on the beach and that she would forget the unpleasantness earlier. If they were to have only this one day together, he wanted her to have a memory to cherish. And again he wondered why he cared so much.

She's just a woman! And your assistant at that! Snap out of it, Johnnie! You've never lost your head over a woman yet, and now is not the time to start. Johnnie was accustomed to women doing for him, waiting on him, begging for his attention. Even Beatrice acted more like his mother, always "doing" for him, except where it mattered most, in the bedroom. That ship had sailed long ago, and she had only herself to blame if his attention was pulled elsewhere to fulfill his needs.

But not Ali. No, not this woman. Ali would beg for no man's attention, and she was made for the bedroom.

The abuses of the past had caused her many scars—enough to weave a tight shell around her heart. After all she had said earlier today, he was aware that she would not give her heart away to just any man, but then again he had never considered himself just any man, and he felt quite certain her heart was already his for the taking. He had worked hard from the time he was a teenager, married young and had a baby and family responsibilities from an early age. He built a good life for himself—one any woman would be happy to share. Beatrice certainly enjoyed spending his hard-earned wealth. But Ali was not just any woman either.

Hmm, perhaps she is the woman I need. She arouses me like no other woman has. And her mind, my God, I love her mind. Could he find a way to be free of his marriage that somehow wouldn't destroy him and all he had worked for? He didn't know. It wasn't like him to be indecisive. What he knew for certain was that this woman reached into him and claimed his heart, which was quite unexpected. The jury was still out on whether he believed this was a good thing. The thought of their earlier exquisite lovemaking today caused a rise in his breeches, and he found himself wanting Ali again—her creamy white skin, beautiful breasts, and that luscious mound between her legs. *Ah, I want to taste her sweetness again!*

"Oh, Ali, what is this spell you have put on me?" he verbalized aloud.

"No spell, precious man. Just me. I never want there to be lies or unpleasantness between us. We will always be the best of friends no matter your decision; I know it," Ali said softly as if reading his mind, stooping beside him where he sat on the sand near the fire. She put her arms around his shoulders, and she too wanted more lovemaking immediately when she smelled his scent, though neither spoke their desire.

"So, my sweet, what has Chef Johnnie prepared for our dinner? You are a man of many talents, I see—even outside the bedroom," she teased, looking at him quite innocently.

"Oh, my dove," he groaned, "If you say those things to me, we may have dinner in bed." He touched her cheek and pulled her to him for a passionate kiss. "My God, you beautiful creature, I cannot resist you! When you come near me, I simply have to touch you. It will be even more delicious to see you in the bank working now, knowing what is beneath those tailored tweeds you wear and those reading spectacles. I must find a small apartment nearby where we can be together," he said and waited to read her reaction.

"Mmm, Mr. Meadows, another round of lovemaking in your bed somehow makes me lose my appetite—for all except this," as she reached down to boldly touch the growing manhood between his legs.

"Ah, my little virago! You would make me your sexual slave? As it will be a bit yet before the coals and rocks cook our dinner, perhaps we can find a pleasurable way to pass the time. I am yours to command, my love." He took her hand and led her to the bedroom once again.

Thoughtful of her only recent loss of virginity, Johnnie tilted her chin up to look into her eyes and whispered, "My sweet, are you sure you aren't too sore for this once more? There will be more times we can be together. I don't want to hurt you. I could just hold you."

"There is no physical pain that your touch cannot assuage and no thirst your love cannot quench. Our moments will be few, so let us drink deeply of this day of passion," Ali said as she shed her clothes once more.

And drink deeply they did. Johnnie so tenderly brought her to her bliss, and the new skill he taught her—her soft kisses around his manhood and her warm mouth consuming him nearly caused him to reach his climax too soon.

"My love, I can wait no longer to be inside your soft, creamy, womanly delights." With that, he wrapped his strong arms around her and barrel-rolled her none too gently onto her back. "I must have you, darling—now, please now!" He thrust into her softness again and again until he could hold back no longer.

A low guttural sound came from him as he climaxed, still thrusting into her, not wanting to stop. "Oh, Ali, Ali," he whispered to her hoarsely, "God help me, I love you. I love you, my little dove."

With that he lay still atop her for several minutes savoring this unfamiliar sensation he was experiencing. An emotion he had never associated with the sexual act. Johnnie realized at that moment he had never truly made love to a woman. Always before it was nothing more than physical gratification and then, in the case of his wife, procreation. Johnny had never wanted to please a woman the way he did now with Ali.

"Oh, Johnnie," Ali began, looking at him seriously, "my Mama told me to never trust what a man told me in bed," so if you'd like to withdraw what you said while you were, um, well you know," she stuttered, "you can. I'll understand. But if you mean it, please get out of bed and say it to me again."

Johnnie looked puzzled then laughed. "When I climaxed, my sweet, just as you did. I knew exactly what I was saying, and I do not want to take back one word of what I said. I believe I do love you, Ali, in a way I have never experienced before in my life. And now I know I will always love you," he said as he pulled her close, stroking her hair, kissing her softly on her lips.

She lay silently in his arms, willing the moment to last forever. His chest hairs were tickling her nose. She had longed to hear those words of love from him, yet Ali was not ready to reciprocate. He had indicated earlier that she would never be with him as a wife. And she somehow felt it would cheapen this precious moment if she merely regurgitated his words.

She was consuming every breath, scent, touch, and sound of this moment. In her heart she knew nothing in her life would ever compare to this again, and she wanted to stop time and savor it.

Disappointed the response he expected was not coming, Johnnie said nonchalantly, "My love, much as I would like to stay here in our little love nest with you longer, the sun will be setting soon, and I'm sure the rocks and coals have done their job, and our supper-in-a-pot will be ready. So release me and allow me to feed you more than merely love today," he chuckled and rolled to sit on the side of the bed, pulling on his drawers and pants, then his shirt which he left open revealing his strong chest. Ali enjoyed the sight of his chest a little longer.

"Johnnie, please explain to me what supper-in-a-pot is," she said and laughed. "Are you referring to a clambake? That's what we call it in Wilmington."

"Oh, it's not just a clambake, little dove, it is a Chez Johnnie specialty! I think you will enjoy it. I must warn you, however, we are at the beach and things are much less formal here. We will be eating primarily with our hands out of one pot."

"Yes, of course, Johnnie! We will be Bohemians tonight. We are beach gypsies!" She could hardly wait to see what he had managed to pull together for the clambake.

Johnnie had a blanket for her spread on the sand near the fire, where she stretched out to dig her toes in the sand as they watched the sun set on this most amazing day. It was a *momentous* day. She lost her virginity to a man she adored. It was perfect. He was perfect. She smiled and watched the sun slip below the horizon. *Mama, you would be happy for me.*

"Dinner is served, my darling," Johnnie proclaimed as he removed the lid from the pot and the pot from the rocks. He drained the water into the sand and added a large spoonful of the fresh butter. "Be careful," he cautioned, "it is very hot."

They sat side by side on the blanket, eating from the large metal pot in front of them, and drinking cup-fulls from a pail of beer from the small brewery in the village, watching the sun set and the night sky fill with stars. Ali felt one of the twinkling wonders must be her mother's. Her back to his chest, his arms around her, they listened as the waves crashed onto the beach, the tide coming back in.

"Johnnie," Ali said softly, turning to meet his eyes, "this has been the most wonderful day of my life. Thank you for everything—the cottage, champagne, the beach, delicious dinner, and most of all, for making me a complete woman today. I will never forget this day, and I will cherish it—and you—for the rest of my life." She paused then whispered, "And, Johnnie, I love you too."

With that, Johnnie knew he had accomplished all he had hoped for—a precious memory for Ali, a wonderful day, and a new love he felt sure would feed his soul for many years.

"Oh dear, I must look a fright, and my hair must be wild by now after walking on the beach!"

Johnnie stroked her long auburn hair that fell about her shoulders. He loved to see her hair unpinned and in its natural state. He loved that she was so comfortable in her own skin and unpretentious.

"Darling, if you will go into the cottage, you will find all you need for your toilette on the dressing table in the bedroom. If there is anything I have neglected to provide for you, please let me know and I will see to it that you have it from this day on. You will make yourself presentable to the world and especially Cousin Edy. Please do hurry along now as we must catch the last ferry to the mainland."

As Johnnie had said, she found all she needed to repair the day's damage from lovemaking and the wind and sea mist on her beach walk. Ali marveled again at his thoughtfulness of her needs. Looking around as if to memorize every inch of the cottage, she stepped onto the porch where Johnnie waited for her.

"You look beautiful as always, my dove," Johnnie said as he kissed her forehead. He took the key from his pocket and locked the door behind them.

"Now you have your key and will feel free to use the cottage as your own whenever you choose, yes?"

"Yes, my dear sweet man, I understand and thank you for all of your kindnesses to me this day. It has been lovely," she whispered into his ear as her breasts brushed his arm. He turned and hugged her one last time in this private world they had made for themselves.

They set off to walk the half a mile back to the ferry. It was already boarded and ready to depart. "Jack!" Johnnie called to the ferry master, "Do you have room for one more vehicle?"

"Indeed, I do, Mr. Johnnie! I've been watching for you and was prepared to wait if necessary, but ye nearly missed 'er tonight. Would hate to think ye'd be stranded all the way out here," and he shot a sly glance at Ali, winking at Johnnie knowingly.

Johnnie reached to shake the old man's hand and thank him for his discretion as he tucked a crisp five-dollar bill into his hand.

"Thank you for your discretion, Jack May I introduce you to Miss Malone? She will be coming out here on her own occasionally, and I would appreciate you showing her the same kind consideration you have always afforded me, my brother," Johnnie said, looking directly into Jack's eyes and knowing that calling him "my brother" ingratiated him even more in the old man's eyes. Johnnie was proud of his prowess in bending people to his will, not always in manipulation but sometimes kindness. Still, he could use this skill well in business and certain sordid affairs of the past. There was no end to what he could accomplish with a few carefully chosen words, and he quite enjoyed it.

Jack nodded and smiled, "I take yer meanin', Mr. Johnnie, and I'd be happy to take a care after 'er."

"I'm sure you will, Jack, and thank you again."

Once on shore, Johnnie drove his car down the ramp to take Ali home. It was nearly ten o'clock at night and past the time proper young ladies, especially single ladies, were safely at home. She was also unchaperoned and in the company of a married man. Ali was filled with trepidation about how she would be received coming in at this late hour. Her best hope was that Edy had received the note from Johnnie and had gone along to bed, leaving the foyer lamp burning for Ali. She knew this was a highly unlikely scenario, but still she could hold out hope, be it slim.

Aware that her emotions often betrayed her through her eyes alone, Ali prayed Edy was not yet adept at reading her the way her mama always could. Johnnie had certainly picked up on this rather quickly. While they sat talking on the beach earlier, he told her that he had detected a momentary flash of her eyes and an upraised left eyebrow and sensed this was Ali's temper, which she normally kept so well hidden. This happened when they discussed her salary in comparison to the men she would now be supervising. Ali laughed at his skillful perception. Johnnie asked her if she had been angry with him.

He assured her, "If you are ever angry with me, Ali, you have only to speak to me so that I no longer have to read your, uh, eyes. We will calmly discuss any issues you have."

On hearing this and in a barely audible whisper, Ali said, "Johnnie, of course, I was not angry with you. I was only seeking information from you and requesting that you see the logic of paying me a higher salary than the men whom I would be supervising and training. To pay me less simply because I am a woman seemed illogical, demeaning, and grossly unfair, wouldn't you agree?"

Johnnie did not want to enter into this discussion again after he had lost the first time. *Damn, this woman has a way of completely captivating me even when we argue.* Her intellect was sexually stimulating to him, in fact, the most attractive attribute she possessed, or so he thought at the time. He had suspected then that underneath those tailored work suits and high collars, her body must be as irresistible. He could barely conceal his absolute desire to consume her completely. He didn't give a damn if her eyes flashed throughout their lovemaking, but he wanted to possess her. And later in the day he had confirmed his suspicions about her body and had indeed consumed her completely.

As much as Johnnie admired and respected her fiery determination and independent bent, he reckoned that deep down Ali needed and desired to be loved more than anything else.

As Johnnie pulled up in front of Edy's home, he leaned over, taking her in his arms one final time on this perfect night, and kissed her one last time. She melted into his chest. "Goodnight, doll-baby," he whispered. "Pleasant dreams."

"Goodnight, Johnnie. I love you," Ali whispered back. "You are my pleasant dream."

Before he could get to the door to give her his hand, Ali was on the step and heading up the walkway to the house. She glanced back one more time, hoping to see his face again, but the carriage had already turned onto the next street, taking Johnnie home to *her*. Try as she might not to despise her, Ali loved Johnnie so much that anyone who did not treat him the way she wanted and hoped to was an enemy to her. *God, forgive me, but she doesn't deserve a man like Johnnie.* It was obvious to her that Johnnie was a man who needed to have his sexual and intellectual needs met, and, from all he had told her, "B" did not even make a stab at fulfilling him. As much as it made her sad for Johnnie, it was a comfort for her to know he had no desire to touch "B." *Johnnie is mine. I will love him in a way he has never experienced. I will fulfill him.*

Ali tiptoed into the house after gingerly opening the heavy oak door and closing it behind her. She was relieved that Edy had left the lamp burning for her and gone to bed. Taking the lamp, she quietly and carefully walked up the stairs. She undressed and not at all characteristic of her, slept totally naked that night, feeling the fresh pressed sheets on her skin, reminding her of the bed she had shared earlier next to Johnnie. There was a soreness in her private parts from the lovemaking, but, as Johnnie had predicted, it was a precious pain.

Ali remembered her half-sisters talking about intercourse as if it were a horrible burden. They were unaware that Ali was listening and were astonishingly candid in their conversation. They called it a "wife's duty." Ali suspected it was quite wonderful after experiencing what she now knew had been her first orgasm one night as she was thinking about kissing Collier. She lay alone in her bed and rubbed herself when suddenly she felt this indescribable pleasure moving upward from her toes to her head.

The next morning she told her mother what Anne and Marie had been talking about and then what she had experienced. Her mother smiled knowingly and hugged Ali telling her she was becoming a woman. She told Ali that when two people are deeply in love, the sex act could be blissful. Ali guessed her mother must have had this kind of relationship with someone other than father. She could see that dreamy, faraway look in her eyes once again. She had seen it before on rare occasions. There was a mystery about her mother and, though Ali knew they shared a close confidence, she also perceived that her mother held something back. As Ali grew, she wondered if it were a treasured memory only she and someone special shared. Ali never pressed her to tell. Some things are best kept in the heart, things such as she and Johnnie had just shared. Somehow that made it even more precious.

She slept soundly that night, knowing that tomorrow was Saturday and she did not have to rise early to go to the bank. Quite unlike her normal behavior, Ali slept until nine o'clock and realized upon waking this was not a wise thing to do if she hoped to keep her activities of yesterday out of the topic of conversation. She would rush to ready herself and descend for a late cup of tea and toast, hoping she could convince Edy that her stomach was upset due to something she ate last evening. She also hoped beyond hope that Edy was about other business and unaware of the time.

This was a tipping point, a watershed moment. She instantly felt it. For the first time and as it turned out the first of many times, Ali would lie to Edy to cover her sinful and disgraceful behavior. The fact that she did not feel terribly guilty was the signal she was losing her good conscience. Sunday school had taught her that. She resigned herself to doing whatever was necessary to be able to spend those stolen moments with Johnnie. Ali couldn't have known at the time that her minor deceptions were weaving an intricate and dangerous web in her life that one day might ensnare her.

Ali trusted Johnnie implicitly, ignoring all the signs and cautionary tales from others who had known him for many years, including Edy. They believed he was a snake in the grass, ready to strike and never to be trusted fully. Oh, he had made some kind and generous donations to the needy over the years and lent a hand whenever possible to help neighbors. These all provided Johnnie and Beatrice with a certain respect in society, and, of course, continued business success for Johnnie. These same people who cast shadows his way felt that little of his altruistic behavior was due to true concern and empathy. He was shrewd and knew exactly how to manipulate for his benefit.

She despised these people for their unfair judgments. *How can anyone read the true heart motives of another? They are just jealous of his success and want to demonize him for it. It is nothing but idle and vicious gossip, and I will not listen to it!* Ali determined to continue believing that Johnnie was a good man until something happened that proved her wrong. This, she thought, was a much more Christian approach to any acquaintance. She ignored the possibility that, if she were proven wrong, it could be at the expense of her broken heart and shattered life.

A light knocking on her bedroom door brought her out of her musings. "Yes, come in," she said with as much weakness in her voice as she thought appropriate for a digestive issue. Mabel, Edy's housekeeper, cook, and confidant, opened the door carrying a breakfast tray.

"Oh, Mabel, you dear! This is not necessary. I was just on my way down to breakfast but thank you."

"Miss Ali, there ain't no breakfast to come down to. We've been up since the crack of dawn, and Miss Edy feared you was sick and asked me to bring you a tray. So here it is and I hopes yer feeling well this mo'nin.' If there's anything I kin hep you wit, jez holla."

"Well, thank you again, Mabel, but my goodness, you've already done more than necessary. My stomach was a bit unsettled, possibly from something I ate yesterday, so I stayed in my room a bit longer than usual. I shall eat a bite and attend to my toilette and dress for the day. Do you know what Cousin Edy is about this morning, Mabel?" Ali hoped Mabel would betray some sense of Edy's state of mind.

"Yes, miss, Miss Edy dressed and said she needs to go to the bank to see about some bidness, then was stoppin' by the market to fetch some butter and taters."

"Thank you, Mabel. Please close my door as you leave. I will bring my tray to the kitchen when I come down."

She knew there could be disaster around the corner if Edy suspected something and was going to the bank to confront Johnnie. She prayed he would be at home with his family this Saturday morning and not catching up on work at the bank. Suddenly Ali did feel a sickness in her stomach, that panicky feeling of one about to be tried in court. She ate little of the breakfast.

Moments later Mabel knocked again on her door. "Yes, come in, Mabel."

Mabel stepped in, barely visible behind a large crystal vase filled with three dozen exquisite roses and feather ferns.

"These come fer ye, Miss Ali. Ain't they purty? Someone is sweet on ye, I reckon!"

"Whatever in the world!" Ali exclaimed.

"Deliv'ry boy just brung 'em by for you. There's a card there, Miss Ali," Mabel said plucking the note from the bouquet and handing it to Ali. Mabel lingered as if waiting for her to read the message.

"Excuse me, please, Mabel, may I have a bit of privacy?"

"Oh, yes'm," a very curious Mabel said, exiting and closing the door behind her.

Ali set the flowers on the side table and dropped into the chair to open the card. Her heart was pounding. She had never received such an elaborate vase of flowers from anyone let alone a man. She carefully lifted the enveloped flap and extracted the delicate card of paper lace. It read, "I am falling in love with you, my little dove. Yesterday was exquisite—*you* are exquisite. Affectionately, JM."

She felt that tingle between her legs again, recalling his touch and his manhood thrusting into her, bringing her to climax. *Oh, Johnnie, where is all this leading? Will I be your wife one day?*

Chapter 13
Revelations

During the oppressive summer heat, Ali and Edy had taken to evening walks to enjoy the cooler air. There were many small parks in Savannah that offered lovely areas to walk, Columbia Square to the East and Oglethorpe Square to the West of their home. Edy was not nearly as judgmental as Ali's father, and never complained when their strolls inevitably included the riverfront. This was Ali's concession for having given up her home and all things familiar to move to Savannah. She took an extra portion of delight in knowing her father would disapprove.

Ali also enjoyed these walks because of the "scheduled" time with Edy, which was hard to come by when she worked all day and now spent time with Johnnie as well, though Edy was unaware of this. Ali felt guilty about withholding this confidence from Edy and had determined to speak with her about it on their walk that day.

It was a tender subject because Ali knew Edy looked at her as a daughter, and she felt this same close bond with Edy, who had eased Ali's heartache at losing her own mother and her only known way of life. Ali was aware she could never take Hannah's place as Edy knew she was not Ali's mother, but Ali relished the feelings of motherly love from Edy as much as Edy enjoyed giving this gift to Ali.

For her part, Edy was all too aware of Ali's pain and believed together she and Ali were making the best of the undesirable cards life had dealt them. In fact, perhaps they were both thriving. Edy knew it was nearly impossible for Ali to admit she was happy with her sense of loss still so raw, but Edy had seen a change in her and a lightening of her mood that indicated she was finding enjoyment in her new life. This pleased Edy. She wanted to do all she could to help her cousin, and she had to admit Ali was easy to love. Edy hadn't realized she still had love to give and found joy in that revelation.

The evening was pleasantly and thankfully cooler than most, and perhaps autumn was not far off. The summer had seemed interminable to Ali, yet she had delighted in the lovely times she had spent at the cottage—with and without Johnnie. Sure that Edy had wondered where she had gone on those occasions, Ali felt it only right that she open up to her at last. Edy also had a right to know because if she and Johnnie were ever discovered, it would have grave consequences for Edy as well since she was Ali's "guardian." In reality, Ali was too old for a guardian, but Edy had become her social chaperone, assuring no one could cast aspersions on her conduct.

She felt the guilt prickle up her body from her toes to her neck. "Edy, there is something I need to tell you. Please, dear cousin, hear me out and I beg you not to judge me too harshly."

Edy stopped and faced Ali.

"Ali, I always want you to feel free to talk to me about anything. You are as dear to me as my own daughter."

She reached out to take Ali's hands in her own, nodding to encourage her to speak.

"I am in love and in a relationship with Johnnie Meadows. I'm sorry, Edy, but he is so perfect for me, and there is simply no doubt we were meant to be together. He loves me too and wants to marry me. I just felt you had a right to know."

Ali felt as if she had vomited this information all over Edy and immediately regretted her impulsive outburst. Now it was out and there was no taking it back.

"Oh, my dear." Edy exhaled as if struck in the chest. She certainly had no idea this was coming but chided herself for not seeing or thinking of it sooner when she had witnessed such a change in Ali's demeanor. *Of course, she is in love! How did I miss all of the signs?*

Edy did her best to recover from her first reaction, but the news was, for obvious reasons, quite startling yet inevitable. She had been worried about this very possibility and for that reason had warned Ali sternly to tread carefully at the bank. And wasn't it just like Mr. Meadows to take advantage of this vulnerable girl? Edy knew enough about him to know Mr. Meadows would be irresistible to Ali as he seemed to be to all women with whom he came into contact. He met her every emotional need, she was certain, and she prayed to God, not her physical needs as well.

Edy was nothing if not pragmatic. She had known that one day Ali would come to her with just such news. Her mother's marriage situation certainly foretold Ali's fate. Edy had surmised that if Ali worked for Johnnie she might well become involved with him. Edy could definitely see the attraction. Johnnie was every woman's fantasy. Now Ali, Jo's precious daughter and her oath-sworn responsibility, was running headlong into the abyss with the very dangerous Johnnie Meadows. This same pragmatism was now screaming at her: this relationship will only end in heartbreak for Ali.

Could she interfere with fate? She had tried once before many years ago to talk Ali's mother out of marrying James Davies, but, with Ali in her womb, Jo had few acceptable options and only one that wouldn't ruin her socially. Jo hadn't been interested in saving her reputation, only the life of the unborn child that she cherished, and a relationship with her as her mother. Giving away her child during an "extended trip" was unthinkable to Jo.

Once married to the brute, Jo lost the will to fight back and accepted James' abuse and coarse behavior. Divorce was out of the question, and, because of her strong Catholic faith, Jo would not have considered it. She had made her bed or rather her father, General Thayer, had made it for her, and she would make the most of it. Her grief was unfathomable, and Jo simply did not have the strength to resist.

The same Catholic faith was the fountain of Jo's strength, giving her the grace to be his wife with dignity and a happy countenance. Admittedly, Edy could not recall ever seeing Jo despondent except for that one horrible moment in her life when her beloved Robert was murdered. Edy had never seen a heart so rent. Beyond that, she could never decipher what Grandfather Thayer had said to Jo to push her forward out of her "slough of despond" and into the hell that was her marriage to James Davies.

All Edy could be assured of was the joy Jo experienced in the birth of Ali, her sole remaining piece of her love for Robert Malone. Bearing their child, the perfect manifestation of their immeasurable love, and being able to raise Ali herself was the only catalyst or incentive that could have propelled Jo into such a disappointing coupling as was her marriage to James Davies, but because of Jo's deep faith and commitment to giving her daughter a stable home, the marriage lasted twenty-nine years.

Edy's solace came from seeing that Ali was indeed a product of a deep mother's love and from something Ali had mentioned to her. She told Edy that even in death there seemed to be a smile on Jo's face. Edy comforted herself that perhaps Jo was at this very moment resting in the arms of her beloved Robert in Heaven. Perhaps her Hannah was being held by her papa Able. Edy's faith told her this was so. Now, what to do and how to advise Jo's daughter if asked. Edy hadn't a single idea.

"I am sorry to startle you so with this news," Ali added. "I know how you feel about Johnnie and your thoughts on his reputation."

Edy said a quick, silent prayer for the Lord's guidance. "My dear, as I have said, my thoughts on Mr. Meadows' reputation are shared by many upstanding people in Savannah who are much wiser and more in the know than I. These are people whom I respect and trust. I have imparted this information to you, not as a gossip but because I hoped to spare your reputation and inevitable heartache. You must believe me when I say I want only the very best for you, Ali, and to spare you from the same heartache your moth—well, never mind that. I just hope you will hear what I am saying because I love you. I think perhaps we should take the short path home and continue this discussion in private. Neither of us wants tongues wagging about this." They walked on silently as Edy prayed for wisdom. Her nerves were in turmoil.

They climbed the steps of the quaint brick rowhouse that was their Lincoln Street home. In the foyer, Ali reached to unpin her hat, then turned to Edy who motioned for Ali to join her in the parlor. They sat beneath the gaze of her husband's portrait, and Edy hoped he would somehow give her the wisdom to direct her precious cousin.

"Do you mind my asking how far things have progressed and what your intentions are regarding Mr. Meadows? May I ask this?" Edy was treading softly so as not to alienate Ali when there was any sliver of a possibility she might still be able to dissuade her from what Edy was certain would turn out to be a calamity at best if she went forward with this disastrous liaison."

"Dear cousin," Ali began also sensing the need for tact and calm, "you may, of course, ask me anything."

Edy immediately caught Ali's use of "cousin" when addressing her. Certainly not incorrect, but still it somehow wounded her. Was Ali making a point that she was not her mother? Edy wondered. She had begun to feel much more like a mother than a cousin. She also wondered if perhaps Ali had *chosen* this particular word or if it signified no special meaning. Edy shook her head. *No, this child hasn't a hint of guile in her.*

"To answer your question, Edy, Johnnie loves me, and I believe he is struggling right now with leaving his wife to be with me. I know he wants to be with me, but as you know he is also Catholic, so this presents a bit of a challenge. But he does want to marry me."

Edy listened patiently and politely, hoping that by telling her story aloud Ali might discover the error of her ways on her own, but shortly Edy knew this situation was solidly in Johnnie's grasp and he was, like Excalibur and the stone, irretrievably in her heart. A dark foreboding caused Edy to shiver on this warm evening. *This will not end well. Nothing good could ever come from another's heartbreak.* And Edy assumed if Johnnie divorced Beatrice, she would be heartbroken or at the very least act the part of the wronged wife and mother.

Edy saw the excitement in Ali's flushed cheeks as she regaled Edy with the fairytale romance in which she was involved.

"Oh, Edy, you should see the darling dollhouse of a cottage Johnnie has on Tybee Island! The eaves and the porch all have a delicate gingerbread trim, and the house is painted a lovely sky blue color, and the inside is just pristine white—everywhere. It is like being in Heaven. And Johnnie fixes us clam bakes. Can you imagine? Right on the beach where we sit on blankets and eat from the pot as the sun sets.

"Edy, you would love it, and I'm sure you would love Johnnie too if you only had an opportunity to *really* know him as I do! He is a good man, Edy, trapped in a loveless marriage from which he cannot extricate himself presently. But one day, one day we will be together. I know it. Johnnie has promised me. Edy, he even got down on one knee, took my hand, and asked me to be his wife! Of course, I said, 'Yes!' He has even spoken to his solicitor to begin the process of providing for his family financially after we marry. We could be married by the end of the year, Johnnie says. And we will go to Ireland for our wedding trip. Oh, Edy, isn't it all too thrilling?"

Ali finally took a breath and allowed Edy to answer, but Edy was still trying to collect her thoughts so she could handle this properly. She was taken aback by Ali's outward show of exuberance. It seemed out of character for the normally level-headed and composed young woman. *Oh my, has it gone too far already? Will she hear what I have to tell her?*

"Dear heart, of course it makes me exceedingly happy to see you so happy and full of excitement and life again. I know losing your mother and coming to a new home—beginning a new life—have all been overwhelming and difficult. You must feel as if you are an orphaned refugee. I have tried to make your transition as easy as possible, but, of course, I can never replace your mother and home, but you have assimilated quite well in just a very few months. Such a short time ago that your dear mama passed, and the heart is a tender and fragile thing that requires much time and peace to heal from such a traumatic loss.

"What I am trying to say, Ali, and perhaps ineffectively, is that you have suffered a great loss. You have been here in your new and unfamiliar home a scant two months, and more importantly you have known Mr. Meadows for that same terribly short period. Just as it requires time to heal from such a loss, the heart takes as long to develop true love. My precious girl, real love does not grow over a few minutes; it forms after months and sometimes years of getting to know the person.

"Please allow for the 'tincture of time' to heal your heart that has been rent from your loss. It is exposed to every catalyst of emotion that enters your life presently. You lost the physical love of your mother's presence, and it is only natural that you would need and want to fill that void with another love."

Ali remained silent. Edy continued hoping what she was trying to say was not falling on deaf ears. "This next year will be a period of extreme vulnerability for you, which is why, I believe, society expects a year of mourning after a loved one has passed. Not only is it our respectful duty, but it is a time to mend the wounds left by death. You must protect your heart from ill-advised liaisons and harmful emotional expressions. Your mind has not yet processed what your heart is feeling, and I believe that if you would only give yourself some time to grieve your loss, you might see things differently. Please promise me you won't make any major decisions for at least a year, my dear. I am afraid it would be very unwise not to mention you have your reputation to protect as well."

"My reputation be damned!" Ali said. "I am happy—truly *happy*! Perhaps for the first time in my entire life, I have joy. Why can't anyone ever allow me just a modicum of joy?" Now on her feet and pacing the parlor carpet, Ali nearly screeched at Edy.

"Ali, I believe you have just perfectly demonstrated that you do not have the proper control of your emotions right now," Edy replied calmly.

Immediately Ali realized her mistake. She had behaved unkindly and childishly towards this dear cousin who had taken her in and treated her as her own daughter, loving her without question from the first day. But Ali remained firm in her love for Johnnie and would not be dissuaded. She would not give up the love of her life no matter how her reputation suffered or how angry her decision would make Edy. In not considering what might happen to Edy's reputation in this, her home of Savannah, Ali was aware of how selfish her behavior was. Edy had maintained a spotless character throughout the years since the loss of her husband and child.

"Forgive me, Edy," Ali said as she grasped her cousin's hand. "You didn't deserve that, and, of course, I was not referring to you. You have given me back much joy since coming to Savannah. And you have been like a second mother to me. I care deeply about your thoughts on this. I know that if we were to be found out it would bring shame down upon you as well, and I would never want to see anything happen to you because of me."

"My dear girl, shame upon me is the very least of my concerns, though it is a concern, but not the primary one. I…I must…I feel it is even my obligation to be very bold in speaking with you. I realize what I am going to say is not what you hope to hear, but please indulge an old woman who loves you very much, and allow me to advise you as I believe your own mother would. And, Ali, please take this with all the love with which it is imparted."

"Of course, Edy, please go on. I will listen to all you have to say," Ali said as she sat down.

"Again, just let me reiterate that your heart has not yet healed from your dear mama's death enough to make such a major lifelong commitment. It would be unwise to do so, and no good will come from channeling your grief into this relationship. It will not bring your mother back nor make you feel whole again. You must work through the grief. I tell you this as a person who has experienced overwhelming grief.

"After my Able and precious Hannah passed, I wanted nothing to do with the business Able had worked so hard to build for our security. Had I gone forward with what I wanted to do at that time of deep sorrow, I would not have my home nor the financial support I now receive from the business. Though it is not much, it has kept me comfortably in my own home and will for the remainder of my life. I do not know what would have happened to me had I followed what my heart wanted. A heart can tell you lies that your mind desperately wants to hear. You simply cannot deceive yourself. That is why it is best to wait, have patience, feel your grief, and give yourself time to heal without making decisions.

"To protect you, I shared with you all I had heard regarding Johnnie because I have only seen him occasionally at mass. I am told he is a very charismatic and smooth-talking man, which is probably why he has been so successful in his business career. I had heard that his words could melt butter in January. Allow me to interject that the Bible tells us in Proverbs to beware of a flattering tongue and a man who winks.

"Ali, given your upbringing with your father and his constant demeaning and cruel behavior towards you, it is only natural that such an attentive and charming man could easily sweep you off of your feet. I can imagine his words must sing like music in your wounded ears, and that is so understandable, and it makes a part of me happy to know you have that joy.

"When your mother passed and you were forced to flee your home, you gave up every smidgen of support you have ever had—your mother, who was also your best friend, the only home you had ever known, and your friends. Your entire life! Everything you knew and all that made you feel secure. Once your mother died, your father obliterated all of that.

"These circumstances you have found yourself in placed a large target on you, Ali. You are in a very vulnerable state and your heart is raw. I realize Johnnie provides you with the comfort and security you are craving, but please trust me when I tell you this is cold comfort and false security.

"Johnnie is married, Ali, and the Savannah society views them as a strong and solid couple, recognized as leaders in the community and church. He has three children. He appears to be very happy and satisfied with his family and the lifestyle they enjoy. Hear me, dear, no possible long-term good or happiness can come from this liaison. You simply cannot base your happiness on another's misery.

"Think, Ali, please. Just see the reality of all this. Johnnie must go through what I am sure his wife will make a very public and very nasty divorce if for no other reason than pure spite. She may indeed not want her husband, but I will guarantee you she certainly doesn't want anyone else, especially a younger and prettier woman to have him. She is afforded a very luxurious and socially high lifestyle here in Savannah. She will not give that up without a vicious fight, and she will definitely not relish losing face and carrying the reputation as a divorcee.

"Right now, the entire society of Savannah believes their marriage is strong and happy. Beatrice will vehemently oppose anyone who threatens her hearth and home—and husband. And you will be left a social pariah. Regardless of whether he leaves his family, you will lose your fine reputation.

"And, dear Ali, please consider the Church. You, Johnnie, and Beatrice all are Catholic. He will not be granted an annulment unless he accuses her of some wrongdoing. And the Church expressly forbids divorce. You will be excommunicated. Are you prepared for this certainty? If your affair were found out now, regardless of whether Johnnie seeks a divorce, you will be excommunicated for consorting with a married man. I know your faith is very important to you—as it should be. Beatrice will emerge as the wounded saint in all of this regardless of what she may or may have not done or what the truth of their marriage actually may be. Marriage is sacred. No matter how deep, pure, or sincere your love for Johnnie may be, over time these slings and arrows will wear on your relationship until it will destroy you. It would take a very strong love to overcome these issues if indeed Johnnie is ever granted a divorce.

"There is also the enormous obstacle of his children. It will be several years before they are grown and have families of their own. They will need their father and mother as they mature."

Ali had been listening silently to all Edy had said. In her head she knew Edy was correct, but her heart would not listen. For all she had said, Edy was still unfinished.

"You quite simply would be known as a scarlet woman, a homewrecker, and would never, ever again be welcomed into any respectable home in Savannah. Make no mistake, this reputation will follow you wherever you go. People are unforgiving, and gossips' tongues will 'make hay while the sun shines' with this juicy tidbit."

At last Edy finished her monologue and paused for Ali to take it all in. *Please, Heavenly Father, let her garner some sense of what I have said,* Edy silently prayed.

"But, Edy, I did not wreck his home. It was already wrecked before he met me! Beatrice is the one who withdrew her love from him. Did she really think a man as vital and virile as Johnnie would not find his comfort elsewhere? I assure you, Edy, the fault does not lay with Johnnie nor with me," Ali protested.

"Allison! Listen to what you are saying! No gentleman would ever betray the intimacy and sanctity of his marriage to another. I understand what you are saying; however, the outside world, God willing, will never know of the, umm, intimate relations in their marriage, and it is certainly not a defense for your adultery. I must interject as well that your view of Johnnie's marriage is one-sided—only his side of things.

"This life you imagine you will have with him has dominated all other considerations—even your own good sense and normally sound logic. You must stop and give yourself the time to see the reality of what you are planning. It is folly—a relationship doomed straight out of the gate. It will not bring you the ultimate happiness you envision or deserve. Think, Ali, think! Number one: He is married. Number two: He has children at home. Number three: You are both Catholic. Number four: Beatrice will ferociously fight this divorce. Number five: Both of your names will be gossip fodder for years to come and a media scandal—dragged through the mire.

"And, finally, if Johnnie is unable or unwilling to divorce Beatrice, what will become of you? If he finds he simply must go back to her and attempt to rekindle their love, saving their marriage, where will you be? *Ruined.* You certainly will lose your position at the bank and your means of financial support. Of course, I would never cast you out of my home, but you may find yourself forced to board yet another train to another town to start over yet again.

"My dear, the end is inevitable if you pursue this disastrous course of action for the sake of fleeting joy. If you cannot break things off with Mr. Meadows, then please at least give yourself a year to see if your feelings for him are the same—and if they indeed are mutual. Mr. Meadows has a reputation as a ladies' man, and you do not want to end up as just one of 'Johnnie's girls.'

"I beg you to hear these words as if coming directly from your dear mama's lips, for I know she would tell you the same things. Better to nurse a bruised heart now than a broken heart—and life—later. There is not one decent man who will give you a second glance, and you'll be forced to marry some scoundrel like your m….," Edy's voice trailed off, and again she hoped Ali hadn't noticed.

Ali was stunned. She felt as if she had been struck full force across the face, scolded like a naughty child, and chastised as if by a fire and brimstone Baptist revival preacher throwing hellfire and calling down demons on her head. Her skin prickled and she was not sure if it was a result of anger at Edy's words or the particles of truth in what she had said.

I trust her with my life. But I love Johnnie. If she truly loved me, she would know that she is putting me in an impossible position. Ali could not come up with an answer or appropriate comment. She said a soft and defeated "good night," then slowly climbed the steps to her room in silence. Ali was uncomfortable with this uneasy and unfamiliar tension between them. On the third step, she turned and said, "Edy, I love you very much, and I never want to do anything to hurt you in any way; truly, I do not. I also deeply love Johnnie. I promise I will consider all you have said, but I cannot guarantee I will make the choice you hope for. But thank you for your honesty and courage to say these things to me. As hard as they were to hear, I feel certain they were terribly difficult for you to deliver. I love you for that." She came back down the three steps to hug Edy and kiss her cheek, now wet with tears.   "Good night, dearest," Ali whispered, "and please do not cry. All will be well, I am sure. Please do not worry so."

"Tomorrow let us talk again, Ali. There are things I must tell you, but we are both much too weary to speak further tonight. Please," she added, almost pleading. The time had come for Ali to learn the full truth of her mother's past.

"Of course. Now pleasant dreams. I think we should both retire for the night. Our walk quite tired me."

"Good night, my sweet girl," Edy replied.

Ali saw for the first time how tired Edy sounded, how despondent. Her conscience was tinged but not because of her relationship with Johnnie, as she was sure Edy had hoped for, but because she hated herself for disappointing Edy, for actually hurting her, it seemed. *Edy will come around once she can see how blissfully happy Johnnie and I are. And even more when she begins to help me plan our wedding! How can she resist?*

December, the date Johnnie had said they were to be married, would come soon, and she had much to plan. With these dreams dancing in her mind, Ali fell asleep soundly.

Chapter 14
Confrontation

Ali and Johnnie shared many stolen moments when they were able to slip away. It had become difficult to meet frequently at the cottage because of the distance and time involved, and Johnnie was impatient when he wanted to be with Ali. He had secured a standing reservation at the local Marshall Hotel under the pretext of needing a quick retreat for evenings when he was required to entertain bank clients and unable to get home without great unrest to his family. Here he and Ali enjoyed afternoon trysts, lying next to each other spent from lovemaking, the large windows open and breeze and street noise from below flowing in. This was perhaps where they shared their happiest moments, often napping in each other's arms until the gas streetlights flickered below. They would dress, say their goodbyes, and discreetly leave several minutes apart by different doors and taking different routes. No one was the wiser.

Whenever Ali knew she would be with him, she worked through the day with butterflies in her stomach from the anticipation of yet again feeling Johnnie's skin on hers, his lips kissing hers, his strong arms holding her and making her feel small and protected, delicate and beautiful. The smell of his shaving soap stayed with her even when she left. Ali secretly kept one of his undershirts in a drawer at home. She took it out at night and slept with it across her pillow just to smell his scent as she drifted off to sleep. This kept her from missing him too badly while he was away on frequent business trips.

At times Johnnie would be gone anywhere from a week to over a month. He always let her know where he was going, and it never occurred to her that perhaps he had someone just like her waiting in another town—Atlanta, Columbia, perhaps Charleston. She sometimes heard rumors and hushed whispers when she walked by but ignored the gossip. It never occurred to her that every person in the bank guessed Johnnie was having an affair with her. Ali was always discreet and betrayed nothing or so she thought. She was careful of her dress and her behavior in the office always, not just to protect herself but to guard Johnnie's reputation, career, and by extension his marriage.

Ali felt like the noble and long-suffering lover, shielding Johnnie until he determined the time was right to leave his wife and marry her. Until that time, so they could have a good start in their marriage to come and the respect of the community, Ali did nothing to give away their affair and besmirch Johnnie's good reputation.

She had convinced herself that none of this was Johnnie's fault anyway. She reasoned that he was simply a physical, virile man with sexual needs his wife would not or could not meet. She denied him what was his right to expect in marriage.

On the other hand, Ali was happy to give the comfort of her body whenever he needed her. Ali was certain Johnnie loved her for more than just the sexual side of their relationship. It never occurred to her that by providing for his needs he was able to go home to his wife and family quite contented with no further reason to "rock the boat" of their marriage.

Johnnie and Ali would talk for hours about everything—politics, religion, women's suffrage, finance, world events—and she knew he enjoyed this intellectual stimulation as much as she. He had shared with her that his wife was anything but intellectual, preferring to talk endlessly about her needlework, children, and garden club. He found this boring and Ali enthralling. He treated her as an equal during these conversations and sometimes even asked her advice about topics. Ali was convinced of Johnnie's love and that he desired a life with her as much as she with him. In Ali's mind, they were a perfect match.

Johnnie had been on a business trip for about a week with three or four more weeks before he would be home. Ali took the ferry to Tybee to enjoy the cottage that Saturday. Each time she arrived there, she found fresh flowers and groceries Johnnie had sent ahead to be delivered. This time there was also a post waiting for her.

He always sent a letter when he knew she would be there during his trips out of town. He told her about business and dinners with clients. He never blatantly talked about any other women but sometimes he would slip in a comment here or there. She knew Johnnie was an outrageous flirt and so brilliant and charismatic that women were naturally drawn to him. Ali felt lucky that he had chosen her from all those other women. Many she knew were more beautiful than she, but somehow Johnnie always made her feel like the most beautiful woman in the world and the love of his life.

Ali looked around the cottage always left just as it was their first day there together. Gorgeous flowers sat on the table, this time lilacs, peonies, and roses that smelled glorious. A new block of ice was in the icebox and an assortment of her favorite delicacies awaited her for the weekend. She unpacked her things and found Johnnie's post beside the flowers as always. After opening the tall windows for the sea breeze to blow through and air out the cottage, she eagerly sat down to read the letter. She could smell his scent on the paper and breathed it in. It had been so long since she was in his arms! Sliding her finger under the flap, she opened it and pulled out the letter, unfolded it and began to read his words of love.

My Darling,

How desperately I miss seeing your face and sitting around the dinner table with our beautiful little family. My business will not be concluded for at least three more weeks. Oh, my dearest, how I long to hold you in my arms and make love to you.

Soon, my precious, soon! Kiss my babies for me and tell them Papa will be home soon.

Your adoring husband,

J

Ali sat on the bed—their bed—numb, disbelieving, devastated. It wasn't just what he had said obviously to Beatrice that cut like a knife. Terror struck through her heart when she realized Johnnie had obviously mixed up the letters in the envelopes! Had he put the letter intended for her into his wife's envelope? If he had, she may be reading it right now and would know everything! What should she do? What *could* she do? Johnnie wouldn't be home for several more weeks. How would she handle this? She couldn't just drop by his home and exchange letters.

"Oh, hello, Beatrice. I'm Allison Malone. I think Johnnie mixed up our letters. Could we exchange, please?"

Then the worst occurred to her: What if Beatrice went to the bank looking for her and caused a scene? She could lose her position! Johnnie wouldn't be there to protect her or head off his wife before she went to the president demanding her dismissal. Perhaps she could feign illness and stay at home until Johnnie's return.

What if she came to Cousin Edy's home and vomited the entire tale all over dear Edy? What then? This was the very thing Edy had warned her about, and she had so blithely told Edy everything was going to work out beautifully.

Suddenly Ali remembered Johnnie's promise to divorce his wife and marry her. Perhaps this was the catalyst he needed. Perhaps Beatrice would divorce him now instead! Though this wasn't the way she had hoped things would be resolved, at least maybe now Johnnie would move ahead. He had told her only recently his solicitor had already drawn up all the papers and was making financial arrangements to care for his family.

Oh dear, this will scandalize Edy. She will throw me out and never forgive me. Johnnie, Johnnie, how could you have been so careless! Ali had been so discreet, so careful to protect everyone involved. *If Johnnie had just acted on this when he made the decision, none of this would have to come out now! Oh, Jesus, Mary and Joseph, what will happen now?* Ali crossed herself twice, hoping for providential intervention to spirit her away.

It had never occurred to Ali that Johnnie may have sent her Beatrice's letter deliberately. She never could imagine anything bad about Johnnie. She was deaf to negative comments about him. Ali loved him unconditionally and felt it was her duty to always assume the best of him, and he had treated her like a queen, she reasoned. He had given her no reason not to trust him.

Except he had delayed telling his wife he wanted a divorce. They were still meeting in secret.

Gathering her belongings and closing up the cottage, Ali took the ferry back immediately. Jack looked at her quizzically given the brevity of her visit.

"Not feeling well today, Miss Ali?" he inquired.

"No, Jack, I am not; thank you for asking." He noted the stress in her voice and on her face.

What's ole Mr. Johnnie done now, he wondered with a smile, casting off.

Ali took the streetcar to Cousin Edy's block and walked the short distance quickly to her home. Once there, she changed clothes, had a quick bite of cold fried chicken and collards, then walked to the cathedral for evening mass. Edy would already be there by this time.

The cathedral of St. John the Baptist was breathtaking inside, rivaling anything in Europe, she was sure. It made her think of her mother in Heaven. The ceiling was painted a dark sky blue like nighttime with gold-leaf stars scattered about. It was framed by huge timer arches carved with Biblical figures and saints. Ali touched the holy water in the vestibule as she entered and dabbed a bit on her forehead, chest and shoulders as she crossed herself with it. She lightly placed her black mantilla veil over her hair, walked up the aisle to the pew where Edy was already kneeling, bowed, crossed herself, and knelt next to Edy in prayer.

"I thought you weren't going to make it in time," Edy whispered but was obviously pleased to see Ali.

"I left a bit later than usual," Ali whispered back, "but I'm here now." She squeezed Edy's hand and looked cautiously around the cathedral for any sight of Beatrice, silently praying that God would mercifully absent her from mass tonight.

"Indeed, you are my sweet girl, and I am happy to see you."

Now at long last, Ali began to feel the heat of a pricked conscience flaring up in her and enflaming her cheeks.

While Edy was engrossed in the Rosary, Ali continued to scan the area for Beatrice. As large donors, the Meadows family always sat in the same pew, but, in her kneeling position, the sight was blocked by other parishioners. As the processional began, Ali and the others rose and at that moment she spotted Beatrice and her three children. Beside her sat a man. *No! It couldn't be! Johnnie? But he is out of town!* Ali was torn between elation and terror.

He told Ali he wouldn't be back for several weeks, and yet here he was. She could scarcely believe her eyes and barely contain her excitement at seeing him home early. She momentarily completely forgot about the circumstances of the letter. She only wanted to throw her arms around him and kiss him full on the mouth. Of course, that was impossible but perhaps soon. Maybe tomorrow after he had cleared up this misunderstanding, he would arrange to meet her at the hotel.

The rest of mass, even the Eucharist, her favorite part, flashed by with Ali almost in a trance.

As mass ended, Edy turned to her and asked, "My dear, where on earth are you? And don't tell me you paid any attention at all to Father's homily. You were staring in the direction of Mr. Meadows and his wife the entire time." Edy pointed in their direction. Ali quickly swatted her hand down.

"Edy, please!" she hissed. "You're drawing attention. Let us leave *now.*"

But it was too late. Johnnie had turned around and was now looking directly at Ali, but the look on his face betrayed nothing—no warmth, no love—just a cold, hard stare. Ali didn't understand but, in the unlikely event Beatrice had received the letter Johnnie had intended for Ali, there would be nothing gained by a face-to-face meeting with her—with them, the whole family, at this time.

The more Ali tried to push Edy along, the more impediments came into her path. Heart pounding, mouth dry, hands shaking, Ali dropped her purse. She stooped to pick it up and looked directly into Johnnie's face. He was not smiling nor did he even act as if he recognized her. He blankly handed her the purse. Ali slowly rose and stood looking at Beatrice.

"Oh, uh, Mr. Meadows, thank you. I didn't expect to see you for several more weeks," Ali managed to stutter out. She linked her hand through the crook of Edy's arm, hoping to steer her in the opposite direction.

"Yes, well, I have some, hmm, family business to attend to." With that, he took Beatrice's arm to move along as well toward the door.

"Why, John, don't be rude. Introduce me to your, uh, friend." Dripping with lethal Southern charm, Beatrice purred like a cat ready to pounce on a defenseless mouse.

Instantly Ali was aware Beatrice had indeed received the letter intended for her. This was the "family business" to which Johnnie had referred and rushed home to handle.

"Certainly, forgive me, dear, this is Miss Malone, the accounting assistant I hired at the bank. Miss Malone, my lovely wife, Mrs. Meadows," Johnnie said with a bit too much arrogance.

Ali held out her hand to Beatrice as Johnnie looked her up and down with an amused smirk. Beatrice's obvious dismissal was written on her face, and Ali could detect her temper simmering just under her strained smile. Ali withdrew her hand, proffered and rebuffed by Beatrice Meadows.

"Ah, so this, this is the—how did you put it—the 'little dove' who seems to be adequate at sums?" she said still looking directly at Ali with icy contempt.

"Oh, my stars, it is getting late! Come along, Ali; we must hurry home before darkness overcomes us," Edy said as she put her hand on Ali's back while she pushed her young cousin toward the side door. From over her shoulder, she smiled brightly calling out, "Lovely to see you again, Mr. Meadows, Beatrice. Good evening."

Before Ali could recover, Edy had her out the exit of the cathedral and on their way home.

Turning slightly, Ali could see Johnnie leaving with Beatrice and his children. She could not read his expression in the shadows, but she would never forget the coldness and detachment on his face when he looked at her. It as if he didn't know her. It frightened her. This was not her Johnnie, not the man she loved or who loved her. What was happening? While her feelings were bruised and her heart still racing, Ali surmised this was all just a ruse Johnnie was using to dissipate Beatrice's suspicions. Somehow Ali did not think it was working. Perhaps he had told her he was leaving her. That might explain everything.

After walking nearly home, Edy turned to Ali and said, "Are you going to tell me what that was all about, Ali, or should I venture a guess?"

"Oh, Edy, wise as you are, I'm not sure even you could imagine all that has happened." As they walked, Ali related to Edy what had transpired with the letter. Edy resisted the urge to tell her she had told her something of this nature would happen. After all, Ali was well aware.

"Can you ever forgive me, Edy? I do not know where this is all going or how it will turn out, but I fear I may yet bring shame upon your house."

"Sweet girl, it isn't a matter of my forgiving you. It is a matter of these desperate circumstances in which you now find yourself that concern me. This indicates an even more serious relationship than I had imagined. I had hoped that after we last spoke of this perhaps things had cooled off a bit. Instead, it seems things have grown more complicated. And now I fear it may become public. If it does, this could ruin you, Ali. And, Ali, if looks could kill, Beatrice would have strangled you with her bare hands tonight. What have you entangled yourself in to produce such reactions? Oh, my dear. While Mr. Meadows may be a blackguard, I am afraid his wife has quite a vicious tongue. She will not let this go until she sees you ruined."

They walked the rest of the way home silently, then sat in the darkness on the small back porch swing together. "You know, Ali, your precious mama sent you to me for a reason. She and I were so close we were sisters. We confided in each other about everything. I even knew about your father's treatment of her. And I knew of you before you were born. Jo entrusted you to my care knowing that she and I were alike in so many ways and, knowing her history, hoping I could stand in her stead if ever you needed me. She vowed to do the same for my daughter. We made that promise to one another decades ago—both of us hoping such a thing would never be necessary yet preparing for the worst.

"I am not your beloved mama, but I love you as she did, and I do so want to help you out of this difficulty if you will allow me. Please trust me, my darling, not to judge you or speak harshly. Trust me to say only those things your mama would say. Let us prepare for bed now. When you are ready, please come to my room. There are many things I need to tell you."

They went inside together, climbed the stairs to their separate rooms to prepare to retire.

Chapter 15
Origins Revealed

Ali knocked lightly on Edy's bedroom door, then let herself in to find her cousin already in bed, reading her Bible.

"Come in, darling, and come sit next to me." Edy pulled back the covers beside her in the large bed and patted the place for Ali. She climbed in just as she always had with her mama. It felt good and natural to her. She instantly experienced a longing for her mother and more innocent days.

"Edy, I would not blame you at all if you want me to leave, knowing all I have done and the now very real possibility that this could all come down on your head as well as mine. I can pack tomorrow and catch a train back to Wilmington."

"Do not be silly, Ali. Your home is here. There is nothing left for you in Wilmington but heartache. Whatever happens here, we will face together. I appreciate you holding my reputation in such high regard, but you must know I have had my own dalliances and degradation in life. I didn't give a fig what people thought of me then nor do I now. I only want to protect you from some of the pain your mama and I both suffered as a result. I am too old now, frankly, to give a tinker's damn what the neighbors say about me. But you, you are young and we must consider what is best for you now."

"You, Mama, scandals? I don't understand, Edy. Whatever could you or Mama have done that could in any way compare to all this? Mama was always so well-regarded in the community as you are. Surely neither your sins nor hers could come near what I have done." Ali sat there in disbelief, and she wanted to know more.

"Well, to begin, Ali, I didn't say your mama 'sinned.' I'm only telling you how society reacted. But your mama was strong and very intelligent. She knew when she was defeated and needed help. Let me ask you, Ali, have you never done the arithmetic from the time you were born and your parent's anniversary? Have you never wondered why your father treated your mother and you so dreadfully? Think, Ali."

Edy gave her a few moments to let this sink in and contemplate what she had just insinuated. Ali did not want to believe it, but as she mulled it over the sense of it began to become clear to her.

"Mama and Father were married in July of 1877. I was born in March 1878." She used her fingers to calculate what she already knew, somehow needing the tangible evidence. "August, September, October, November, December, January, February, March…Edy? Eight months! Mama was with child when she and Father were married! But how? Why? What did Mama see in him to make her do such a thing? Is this why he hated me? Because he was forced to marry Mama?" Ali's questions flew out in rapid-fire succession.

"Forced?!" Edy sarcastically laughed. "Indeed not! It was your poor mama who was the pawn in this match! *She* was forced to take that brute as her husband just to save face and to be able to keep you!"

"Edy, you must start at the very beginning and tell me everything. Every detail! I must understand why Mama made these choices!"

Edy grasped Ali's hands in hers. "I will tell you everything now, Ali. It is time and your mother gave me her permission to tell you all when I felt the time was right. Now is that time.

"As you know, your mama came from a very prosperous family at the top of New Hanover County society. She was very beautiful and never more so than at her coming-out ball. She was a vision of Heaven in her beautiful white gown, and her dance-card was always full. The boys felt very lucky when she accepted their dance. She and I were debutantes at the same time in the Thalian Club, but I tell you with no guile there was not a girl present who could come near your mother's beauty. And she was radiant on the inside too, Ali. Just a lovely lady. Josephine Marie Thayer was the catch of the season. She could choose a husband from any of those beaus and would have lived a life of social ease and standing."

"But, Edy, if that is so, and I believe you, and this is the reason I have always been bewildered by her choice of my father. Why on God's green earth did she marry him—a man who treated her so cruelly? Surely there were others among the socially acceptable young men who wanted to marry Mama! I know she came with a sizable dowry and a home from her father in Wilmington, a home in which my father is now living in with his new bride, that whore Rebecca Bard!" Ali nearly spat the words out, becoming more agitated by the moment.

Edy patted her hand and said, "Ali, Ali, let me tell you all, please. To answer your question, yes, indeed there were many young men who would have loved to be a husband to your mama, but to one in particular she gave her heart. And he absolutely and completely adored Jo. In fact, they were betrothed just after she was introduced at the ball. Your Grandfather Thayer made the announcement the month after the ball much to the disappointment of many a young beau. Their banns were published at the church the following Sunday, and they were planning a traditional June wedding. I have never seen your mother so glowing. She was truly, completely in love and happy, Ali, like never before and certainly never since except on the day you were born."

Edy could see Ali was bursting with questions.

"But, Edy, if that is true, why did she stoop to marry Father? His parents were poor dirt farmers in the hills of Southern Ohio. Father always said they 'didn't have a pot to pee in,' usually when he was bragging how he was a self-made man who had 'pulled himself up by the bootstraps.' How many times did Mama and I have to hear that lie! Why then? Why did she marry Father and why did she lie with him and conceive his child when she loved another and planned to marry? I do not understand any of this. But, if nothing else, at least I know Mama did have some love in her life at some brief moment."

"The tragedy, I am afraid, will be compounded by what I tell you next," Edy warned. "Your mama as I said was very much in love with a wonderful young man named Robert Malone. Perhaps you are beginning to understand our choice of Malone for your new name. I'm sure you remember your

Grandfather Thayer's friend, General Malone, who used to visit your mama occasionally? Robert was his son and he and your mother fell deeply in love. Robert was a student of the law at the University of North Carolina in Chapel Hill. He and your mother were to be married in June 1877 as soon as he read for his degree. Oh, Ali, he was a lovely gentleman and the perfect match for your mother. They were such a lovely couple, and I was so happy for them. On his way home to Wilmington, Robert decided to stop in Raleigh to purchase a wedding ring for your mother at Bailey's Jewelers. He had ordered a special band to be made for her, the one your mother gave you that you wear now on your right hand."

Ali looked down at the gold ring on her finger, still trying to make a connection and understand how she fit in. "Go on, Edy, please."

"When Robert came out of Bailey's with the ring he had purchased for your mother, he had to walk past an alley to get to his horse. There he was accosted by two robbers."

Edy heard a sharp intake of breath from Ali and knew the next revelation would be extremely difficult for her to hear. "Ali, they murdered Robert in broad daylight and left him to die in the alley." Tears were flowing from both their eyes.

"What no one but Jo and her dear Robert knew at the time was that she was with child. You, Ali. The man you have always called 'Father' is not your father. Your papa was Robert Malone, the love of your mother's life."

Edy stopped and let Ali work this through her mind a bit, but she knew it would take much more time to grasp the enormity of it all. She went on.

"With your mother attending the funeral of her beloved Robert rather than beginning a new life with him and their child, Jo had no alternative but to go to her own dear father and tell him of her condition. I am certain you can understand that your mother desperately wanted to keep you. You were the very embodiment of their love, and you were all she had left of dear Robert. But she was bound for certain disgrace if she did not go away for a year abroad, give birth to you secretly, and return home alone. You would have been adopted, and no one would have been the wiser. Jo could have picked up with her social calendar after the year as if nothing had happened other than her grieving. That was the only viable solution for a pregnancy out of wedlock in those days. Believe me when I say, the old bastion of gossiping pariahs would have made her life a living hell otherwise and brought shame down on both the Thayer and Malone families.

"Your Grandfather Thayer was a compassionate man, and God knows he loved his daughter. Jo told him she would rather die herself than give you away. Seeing how broken she was, he said he would find a way for her to keep her child. And he did. He instructed Jo to tell no one about the pregnancy, especially your grandmother, who, forgive me, was an icy cold and snobbish woman. She would have turned Jo out if she had known. Of course, so close we were, Jo had already told me of her happy news, but she knew I would take it to my grave. So Jo waited as her father devised a plan.

"Ali, I cannot tell you how strong and remarkable and resilient your mother was at the worst possible moment in her life. But she was resolute in her unwillingness to adopt you off never to see you again. Her papa knew his daughter and her strong will, so he devised a plan though it turned out to be more tragedy for Jo. At least, though, she had you and you do look so much like your dear papa.

"Jo's father told her of the arrangements he had made so that she could keep her child and her reputation. It did cause a bit of a scandal, but she could keep her baby, so she held her head high and did what she must. Forrest made a deal with your fath—with James—who was a laborer on his plantation. James was recently widowed and left with two baby daughters to raise, Anna and Marie. Your grandfather approached him in private and told him of the entire tragedy. Forrest was a good, wise, and honest man. It simply would have been unthinkable to have not told James that your mother was with child. There was no trickery involved. James knew a good deal when he saw one and so agreed on the spot to marry your mother to save her from disgrace.

"Your grandfather offered him a beautiful home in Wilmington and a suitable allowance, but that wasn't enough for that greedy man. Knowing Forrest and your mama were in an untenable predicament, James felt emboldened to demand more. He wanted a position that would guarantee his rightful place in society as Forrest's son-in-law. That is how your father, uneducated and inexperienced, became the president of your grandfather's cotton business. Forrest instantly elevated James to a high and privileged society life—from being no more than a sweaty and ill-bred field laborer.

"Your mama was willing to do just about anything her father directed to keep you, so she married James one month to the day after her Robert's funeral. She even wore the same dress down the aisle that she had purchased from Paris for her wedding to Robert, but she had dyed it black for his funeral. And she determined to wear it for her wedding to James. It was beautiful, yes, but she let James know from the start that he would never be first in her heart. I don't think he ever forgave her for this. The gossips, of course, wagged their tongues in shock over the quick turn of the tables and the fact that Jo had not respected the acceptable mourning time of one year, but, of course, as you know, she couldn't wait—not even two months. The dress in part compensated for this a bit. The wedding was small, family only, and down-played in the society papers with just a small "at-home" announcement.

"Your mama made a deal with the very Devil himself, and do not think for one second James didn't lord it over her. He put on airs and dressed like a dandy, had women all over town, it was said, and even when he went out of town. Your mama turned her head the other way, and frankly, Ali, I don't suppose she cared what James did or didn't do as long as she had you. You were the greatest joy of her life."

Tears were flowing down both their cheeks now. "Edy, so my papa's name was Robert Malone? Where is he buried?"

"His name was Robert Malone, yes, and now you know the significance of the name we chose for you in your new life here. It was time for you to claim your birthright. Robert is buried in the Oakdale Cemetery in Wilmington.

"Oh, Ali, he was a fine, kind, and generous young man. If his murderers had simply asked him for the ring, he would have given it to them. As it was, you have it today because he had slipped it out of its box and into his vest pocket to present to your mama that very evening. The thieves made off with a box and nothing else. They killed him for absolutely nothing, but, of course, today you have the ring on your finger. Your dear papa would have given it to them and money for supper if they had told him of their need. That's just the kind of man he was—always giving to others. He and Jo were the loveliest couple I have ever seen together. Even to this day. I know she would have wanted the same love for you, Ali."

This revelation had changed all of Ali's perceptions about her life. James, for she could never again think of him as "Father," hated her and her mother because he had never wanted either of them—only the money and lifestyle they represented. He could have that as long as he kept them. In a sense, he had locked himself in a gilded cage. She was sure that was at least part of the root of his constant ill-humor.

Now she understood why Grandfather Thayer visited so often; he was bringing the monthly stipend to James and checking up on the welfare of his daughter and granddaughter. What James was unaware of was that Grandfather Thayer also brought a stipend to Jo—to use as she saw fit but also as a cushion in the event she ever chose to throw aside the ogre he had wed her to. But Mama honored her vow and stayed with him for nearly thirty years until she died and had given all that she had to be certain Ali would never be left to his control.

"There is one more thing I need to tell you, Ali," Edy said.

"Oh my, Edy, more? Really?" She braced herself for a final blow.

"When your dear mother passed away, all of her inheritance passed to you. Not only will you inherit from Grandfather Thayer, but you are also the only heir of General Malone. Your Grandfather Malone has stated that you will receive the inheritance that would have rightly gone to your papa had he lived.

"Additionally, Ali, the house in Wilmington—it belongs to you. It always has since your mother passed. Your grandfather felt it was best at that time not to tell you this as the primary concern was to get you away from that abusive James and not heap more coals on the fire. Forrest wrote the deed so that the ownership reverted to you exclusively on the death of your mother. James arrogantly and stupidly assumed it all came to him at her death. He may have moved his harlot into your home, but, I assure you, eviction proceedings have already begun by your grandfather's solicitors. James' stipend has been cut off, and he is no longer working at your grandfather's enterprise. In a word, James is out on his ear. From dirt he sprang and to dirt he has returned. As you can surmise, however, it is even more important that he is unaware of your whereabouts now in the event he might seek you out for funds or revenge."

Ali sat on Edy's bed trying to digest all she had just learned. Stunned, she was unable to speak or think. Edy patted her hand and said gently, "My sweet girl, your mother left you in my care because, other than Jo, there were only four people who knew of your origins—your grandfathers

Thayer and Malone, James Davies, and, of course, I, and only your grandfathers and I were aware of this plan.

"Trustees have been retained to manage your financial interests and property once your grandfathers have passed because, as you know, only men or widows may own property outright. Grandfather Thayer has everything in hand for now. My darling girl, you will always be well cared for, and you will be a very wealthy woman one day in your own right.

"Now, I know you must be filled with many questions, but I think this is enough to absorb at one time. Go along now and get some sleep. I realize some of this news is very upsetting, but I hope you will be able to see the vast number of blessings you have been given as well. Please don't be angry at your dear mama. She was doing what she thought was best at the time, and I am certain Grandfather Thayer was doing the same. Treat all I've shared with you with a tincture of mercy and kindness for them, won't you? Your grandfathers will be visiting within the next two weeks, and they will discuss everything with you."

"Yes, of course, Edy, and I am so looking forward to getting to know Grandfather Malone better. I want to know as much as possible about my papa. I am very tired, Edy, and I think I'd like to go to bed now. May we talk again about all of this?"

"Of course, my dear. Any questions you have, as much as you need, I am here for you."

"Edy, I haven't appreciated you enough and all you have done for me and borne in secret for all these years for my benefit. It must have been very difficult. I hope I can repay all of your kindnesses to me," Ali said as she bade goodnight to her guardian.

"Sweet dreams, Ali."

Chapter 16
Starting Over Again

The sun streamed through the white ruffled curtains into Ali's bedroom and directly on her face. She felt the warmth, smiled, and began turning things over in her mind once again. She was still shocked at all she had learned from Edy last night, but the elements that were the most important to her were cause for joy—she had a wonderful papa who loved her without ever meeting her, a precious mother who was willing to go to any lengths to keep her child, a legacy of their love, and she no longer had to feel any connection whatsoever to James Davies, his daughters who were no longer her "half-sisters," nor their entire dreary pasts.

Today was the first day of her new life. Again. Hadn't she thought the same thing when she arrived in Savannah what seemed now like years ago? *Allison Edyth Malone! That is who I AM!* She was finally starting to feel comfortable and at home in her own skin for the first time in her life. *Thank you, God. I know I don't deserve this great gift you have given me, but thank you for your mercy.* Ali crossed herself and touched the small gold crucifix that always hung around her neck, a confirmation gift from her mother so many years ago.

Ali dressed and went downstairs to have a light breakfast with Edy, who was already drinking her morning coffee when Ali came into the dining room.

"Good morning, Ali, I do hope you slept well and did not toss and turn all night due to our discussion last night."

"I slept very well. Thank you for your concern, Edy. And I awoke happy, Edy, happy and no longer homesick for something I could never put my finger on. None of the restlessness that had been there since I was a child, always trying to understand where I belonged. I am Allison Edyth Malone, daughter of Josephine Thayer and Robert Malone, granddaughter of Forrest Thayer and General Robert Malone Senior. And Edith Thayer Leonard is my very dear cousin who has shouldered a great burden most of her life to spare and care for me. How can I ever thank you enough, Edy? I hope you have also found some relief that this well-guarded and important secret is now out in the open so you no longer have to worry about spilling the beans," Ali said as she hugged her cousin and chuckled.

"Well now, Ali, there is no need for you to thank me or feel obligated in any way. Your mother was in truth my sister, and I would have done anything for her. She entrusted me with the wellbeing of her dearest possession—you. That is thanks enough. I do have one final obligation to fulfill." Edy reached into her skirt pocket and withdrew an envelope. She fingered it as if it were a delicate treasure, remembering the day it was placed in her hand so long ago.

"Ali, this is for you. From your mama. She gave this to me many years ago in the event anything should happen to her.

I know she desperately wanted to tell you everything herself and had hoped that one day the two of you would be free of James Davies together and she could deliver the news face to face. Because she was unable to do this and keep you safe, she gave this letter to me to keep for you. Today, I put it in your safekeeping."

"Have some breakfast; then take some private time to read the letter. Again, darling, I am here if you have need to discuss anything at all with me." With this, Edy gently placed the letter written on faded pink stationery, still lightly scented from being so long in Edy's dresser drawer, into Ali's hands.

Ali looked down at the delicate packet. It felt heavy in one way yet light as a feather in another. These messages she had received all had very different yet significant ramifications in her life. As much as she wanted to take the first train to Wilmington and throw that brute and his whore out of *her* house herself, she sensed that now was an especially crucial time for her to proceed cautiously. Thankfully, her mother had instilled in her good sense and the absence of avarice and vengeance.

Although her financial station in life had changed, she did not intend this to allow her to become the type of person she had always felt the wealthy to be—selfish, unconcerned with those less fortunate, and greedy. She would be grateful this windfall would provide her with a comfortable living and perhaps a bit left over to help others too. Sharing good fortune multiplied it, at least that is what her mama had taught her.

However, James had placed himself in an entirely different category with his behavior. Still, Ali felt her mother would not want her to exact her pound of flesh no matter how much he deserved it. She tried hard not to laugh inwardly though when she thought of the look on James' face when he and Miss Bard were tossed out on their ears. She'd have to go to confession for that one because as sorry as she was for gloating, she still took satisfaction in it. *Lord, help me to be the better person in the midst of all these blessings you have poured out on my head.* She crossed herself as she stood with the letter to go to her room. Edy did not miss her motion and wondered but smiled. She knew the mixed emotions all of this caused for Ali.

Ali lay down on her bed, her stomach fighting off butterflies as she carefully opened the letter from her mother as if it were the most precious, delicate bone china. She withdrew the folded letter from the envelope, made herself more comfortable, and began to absorb her mother's words as if she were sitting next to her saying them.

> *My dearest Ali,*
>
> *I will assume as I write this that I am no longer with you in body, but know, my darling girl, I will never leave you in spirit.*
>
> *You have been the single most cherished blessing of my life. I am also writing this under the assumption that you are now safe in Edy's care. See her just as you see me, for she will now be your mother in my stead. I have trusted her with your life since before you were born, and you may do the same. If you are with her in Savannah now, then you are safe and out of the clutches of James. It is also my assumption that Edy has revealed all to you.*

Lovely girl, I wanted to be the one to tell you what a precious papa you truly had and how he loved you even unborn and how he loved me. He cherished us both. He was an eminently good man, and it almost breaks my heart to think of how different our lives would have been if he had lived to share his with us. But that was not to be.

When your dear papa died, my sole objective was to protect you, still in the womb, and give life to the love Robert and I shared. Know this, Ali, no two parents have ever loved a child or desired a child more than yours.

How I wish I could have told you all of this from the day you were born, and I know the heartbreak it would have spared you all these years under the abusive treatment at the hands of James Davies. But I realized that if you knew, especially as a child, it could only put your wellbeing in jeopardy. Forgive me, my love, for withholding such crucial information from you. Truly, it was done because of my vow to protect you always.

Forgive me for not sharing the fact that you were the beloved daughter of a beloved man, Robert Malone. I can only hope that you can find some understanding in your heart for the difficult decisions I had to make in the midst of my youth and thrust into sorrow. There were few options available to me, and I felt I made the best of it.

I want to say just one thing about James, and I hope you will indulge this one request. Do not hate him. Do not allow him to have the final victory over your heart and soul by seeking vengeance or expressing hatred. With what he was given in life, I suppose he made the best of it, and, despite his multitude of shortcomings and brutality, he remained faithful to the extent he could to the bargain he struck with your grandfather and me so many years ago. If you can, just let it end there. He is not worth more of your time.

Oh my, Ali, he was such a handsome and intelligent man! He looked splendid in his tails and white tie, and he asked me to dance. Though my dance card was full, I ignored it and cleared it just for him. We danced every dance together from that first dance on. When I first told him I had promised all my dances to other beaus, he said to me, "You are the loveliest creature I have ever seen, and, if you will cast off your dance card now, I will fill it and we will dance together for the rest of your life."

It was love at first sight for us both, and I did cast off my card, and I danced exclusively for the remainder of the ball and would have happily danced through the rest of my life with Robert. That we were so in love, no one could deny. It was written in the stars and all over our faces.

We were perfectly suited for one another. We were so happy that words cannot begin to describe it. That joy, that devoted love, led to your conception. Robert had already requested my hand in marriage, and Father, seeing the love we had for each other and knowing Robert and his good family since he was a little boy, was certain Robert would always give me the love and care that a father wants for his daughter. He gave his consent without question or hesitation.

Robert and I initially had not wanted the usual long engagement and year of festivities leading up to a society wedding. We didn't need to wait; we knew in our hearts we were meant to be husband and wife and we wanted to begin our lives as quickly as possible. When I discovered that I was with child— you—it made our plan to marry soon even more important and certainly even more joyful.

Edy has told you, I'm certain, how Robert met his demise. Murdered. My beautiful Robert murdered because he stopped to buy a wedding ring for me. To his dying breath, he was kind, your precious papa. Desiring to give me the perfect ring, he insisted on stopping at Bailey's Jewelers in Raleigh on his way home from Chapel Hill. He felt only Bailey's could produce the vision of the ring he wanted me to have, and his family had used this jeweler for years and had become close friends.

I told Robert I didn't need anything more than a plain gold band because he was my treasure and all I needed, but, like you, Robert was quite determined once he made up his mind about something. So I was in Wilmington readying for our wedding when that devastating news came that he had been murdered just outside the jewelers by two thieves. He had secured the ring in his vest where it was not readily found, and it was given to me.

It goes without saying that I too died a bit that day. My wedding dress was dyed black for the funeral and my veil as well. I have little recollection of those days, which in itself is a mercy. I couldn't think or eat or breathe except as it was done without my will.

My father, God bless him forever for this, knew that I would never agree, nor would he ask me, to give away the only part of Robert I had left… you, Ali. I had only confided in my father and Edy about the pregnancy, and, because of what happened to Robert, I thanked God every day that I had kept my blessed secret to those two. Of course, things being what they were, no decent man of society would have married me then because I was with child, and, if he wasn't told before the marriage, could legally divorce me and send the two of us packing, you and me, on the street So Father devised a plan, one that solved the immediate problem but foreshadowed an unhappy life for us. I hasten to say, however, my father did his best without many options.

My mother's solution would have been to send me on a "grand tour" of Europe until you were born, leave you orphaned at a convent, and come home as if nothing had happened. I could have never turned you over to the nuns or anyone else. You were the very manifestation of the love Robert and I shared, and, because of his death, having you became even more precious if that is possible.

Robert and I were to have been married in a month. The hardest part of marrying James was that I felt as if I had to betray your papa's and my love to marry James on the very same day I had planned to marry my Robert. I got through it by knowing you were inside me, and you and Robert were with me always. I'm quite certain everyone was astounded by the events, and gossiping tongues will wag, but it was the only acceptable solution at the time.

Father approached James Davies in one of his cotton warehouses at the wharf. Father knew he had recently been widowed and left with two young daughters to raise and predicted he would be amenable to this solution for himself and daughters, and it would take care of me and the child I was bearing.

Father saw that glint of greed and social ambition in him to raise himself up from dirt poor to society, and he played on it. Father was certain he would accept his proposition out of greed if not for his daughters. Father made him a very good proposition as well and one he could not have refused. So James and I were married one month after your papa died, and six months later you were born "prematurely and quite unexpectedly."

Father let the word out that James was a well-to-do businessman from "up North," whose wife had recently passed and left him with daughters to raise with no mother. He "confided" with those who listened that this was a good alternative to my heartbreak as well. Ali, I never set eyes on James until I met him at the altar. I was so heartbroken and in a fog. I did not even ask Father about him. I simply agreed, knowing that Father loved me and would do what was best. Father was not unaware of James' more detestable proclivities, but he made certain if ever I could not take any more humiliation, I had funds to leave. That, my love, is the money I saved for you to go to Savannah. How I wish we could have gone together.

Father knew that his daughter deserved more than the coarse and greedy man he was marrying her off to, but he set his plan in motion to save his granddaughter and his daughter from a life of degradation and humiliation. Little did any of us know James would provide a plethora of both. What Father did he did out of love and allowed me to keep the most precious part of Robert and all that I had left—you, Ali. What James could not have understood with his limited capacity was that the papers Father had him sign cut off his stipend, his yacht club membership, his position, and the Wilmington house—everything—in the event I left him or died. The house was owned by a trust Father created for you. James was in such a hurry and so greedy that he didn't even bother reading the agreement or consulting an attorney.

Father had James followed everywhere all the time, and every dalliance of his, which could fill a volume, have all been entered into a ledger to assure he had no opportunity for appeal to the courts. All his misdeeds invalidated the agreement with my Father.

I'm certain that you wondered many times why I stayed with him rather than take you and run. I hope I may explain adequately. I knew in my heart there would never be another love after my precious Robert died. I had no desire to be alone in the world trying to raise you and no desire to have the world label you a bastard when you were anything but. By staying with James, I allowed you to grow up in a social position that you would not have enjoyed otherwise, not because of anything James did to attain this but because your grandfather had assured it in his plan. No matter how much money Father could have thrown at the situation, nothing could erase the stigma that would have been attached to you. I honored my vow to James for the sake of my Father and you. I was comfortable enough, knew if it became unbearable I had the means to leave, and with you we made a world that was beautiful just for the two of us. Many times, Father begged me to leave, but, as long as we were together, I could bear anything. I was able to spend so many days and hours and minutes with you, sweet Ali, and, looking so much like your dear papa, those were blissful times, and I would not trade one for anything. It also gave me time to prepare you to leave when I passed.

You are the embodiment of the love Robert and I shared. He would be so proud of you as I am. Now live, Ali, for us both.

My dear cousin and I were closer than sisters, nearly identical twins in our personalities and thinking. She is the woman to turn to when I am gone. She will speak for me because she is the same. Please heed her guidance just as you always have mine. She too has loved you since before you were born and has pledged her life to care for you if ever needed. She will encircle you with all the love you will need now, Ali, and I hope you will give her the same.

Your dear grandfather, if he is able, will meet with you in the next few months to explain all the details of your trust and eventual inheritance and properties. He will deal with the unpleasantness of cutting James off from the sugar-teat he has enjoyed. My strong feeling is that you should never go back to Wilmington for your own safety. James will no doubt be humiliated and desperate. There is no limit to what he may do in retaliation. Please let your grandfather deal with him. Allow your grandfather to sell the home and establish yourself in Savannah. No tears, my darling Ali.

I want you to be happy and live a wonderful life. Everything is new and renewed for you. You have a precious papa to be so proud of and he loved you. My only regret is that he never had the honor to know our extraordinary daughter as I had as your mother. While I rejoice that I will now see my darling Robert once again, I know that I shall miss you terribly until one day a long time from now, God willing, we are reunited. God bless you, my precious daughter.

With all of my love
forever,
Mama

Ali folded the pages now damp with her tears and tucked the letter back into its envelope. She splashed some tepid water on her face, dabbed it dry with a hand cloth, and, straightening her dress, descended the stairs once again that morning to speak with Edy.

Edy looked up as Ali entered the parlor, trying to read her face and mood. She knew Ali had just been forced to absorb more than could be imagined. Taking Edy's hand, Ali knelt down to sit at her feet.

"Oh, Edy, Edy—this is all too much! I feel as if I have lost Mama all over again, and yet I am elated to know of my true and wonderful papa. It explains so much, answers so many questions I have had since I was a child. Now all the pieces of the way James treated Mama and me are coming together to solve the puzzle. He was *paid* to be with us, but that didn't mean he had to *love* us. He provided exactly what he was paid for and not another thing, namely, social respectability. What a dear price my mama paid for that. She is a better woman than I and stronger. I cannot imagine how she survived such a heartbreak as losing my papa, then so soon afterwards having to marry *him,* a man whom she made wealthy and socially acceptable who otherwise wouldn't have been fit to lick my papa's boots.

"Edy, I *must* travel to my Grandfather Malone's home before it is too late. I want to know him and, through him, know my papa. Mama described him as such a fine man of character."

"No need, my dear, I've received a letter from your Grandfather Thayer this morning, and next month both your grandfathers will be traveling to Savannah to meet with you. Hopefully by then they will have word that James Davies is in the past and all is well. You will have time to get to know your Grandfather Malone then, and I think you will love him instantly. He is much like your dear papa. He is in frail health, but I believe he has lived this long with the hope that one day all would be revealed and he could claim his granddaughter. Unfortunately, your grandmother passed before you were born, but she was a lovely lady.

"You have met your Grandfather Malone several times over the years, I believe, but you probably paid no mind because you were unaware of who he was to you. I know that he visited your mother in Wilmington yearly just to see how she and you were. Accepting the necessity of the ruse, he seemed content just to be able to see you as you grew. You do look so much like Robert, and I'm sure it was a comfort to him. After a time, it became too risky for him to visit directly. You were growing old enough to recognize him, and there was the possibility that unknowingly you might mention his visit to James. He always had to visit when James was away.

"He and your Grandfather Thayer worked together over the years, quietly and secretly, with only their solicitors' knowledge, to plan for your future in the event your mother passed away. They hoped, of course, to never see that day; still they accepted the labor of love. Your mother was always so frail after Robert's death and your birth. She was never the same though she found great joy and contentment in you, dear, and I'm sure this infuriated James even more.

One thing, Ali—what you decide to do with this knowledge you have been given is up to you. You may purchase a full-page advertisement in the *Star-News* and announce it to all society if you please, but I would not recommend it. As your mother believed, I think it might be best to continue living and building a life here in Savannah, continue to use Malone as your last name, allow the attorneys to catch any dirt James may try to fling your way, and be happy. And you have much to be happy for—a good name, a wonderful mama and papa who loved you more than life, people here who love you, and the financial means to live out your life in comfort regardless of if you marry.

"Which brings me to another subject—your financial means and the attention it could bring. Your grandfathers will be coming to Savannah, as I told you, but they will be staying at the Marshall Hotel so as not to draw undue attention to you or our home. They will be meeting with representatives at your bank, and possibly Mr. Meadows will be involved. You will be included in this meeting so that you are fully apprised of every detail of the estates you will be inheriting one day and your support during the interim.

"Ali, money changes people, which I know you are aware of, but it bears repeating. I'm not worried about you, because you have always been level headed and not given to extravagance. Even if Mr. Meadows is not a party to this meeting as an officer of the company, he will certainly know the details of your financial portfolio's worth. I am assuming, because I have purposely not inquired, that you have broken things off with him. This pertains either way.

"You may expect to see a wholly different side of Mr. Meadows once he realizes your wealth. He is well-to-do himself, I know, but, Ali, we are speaking of the combining of two large estates and one heir—you. At the same time, he may have access to the trust agreement and learn that no man may ever touch a penny of your money unless God gives you a son one day, in which case he may inherit from you. You are well aware of the inheritance laws and property laws surrounding marriage, and this is why your grandfathers have elected to capture your holdings in a trust intended only for you, irrevocable and unbreakable by anyone. What this means, Ali, is that you are truly *free*. No man will ever rule over you unless you allow it. You have the freedom to make your own decisions. Now how that would affect a marriage will be up to you and your husband to decide, but, as far as this trust goes, it is exclusively yours.

"There is, however, a stipulation that your grandfathers have included in the trust agreement. If you are to die childless, the trust will be bequeathed to finance a chair in the law school at the University of North Carolina in honor of your papa."

Ali's mind was racing again, taking in this information and synthesizing it to a manageable concept. Her stomach was in knots, and her heart felt as if it were in her throat, beating so hard. Ali had intended to speak with Edy about her relationship with Johnnie well before any of this was brought to light. Things had indeed changed in their relationship or were about to, and Ali felt the need and fear to confide to Edy all that was happening. *But now, knowing what Mama went through—in love, unmarried, and with child—what will I do? What will it mean in regard to my relationship with Johnnie and our child? He can leave "B" now and not worry about her money. Johnnie can marry me now. Her entire future depended on it—and their child's.*

While the money she would receive would definitely make a difference in her life and eliminate much of the fear she lived with as a spinster having to earn her way in life, it did not change society's expectations, public opinion, nor the strict laws of the Church. All she could do now was hope that Johnnie would understand and do the right thing. He had asked her to marry him, and now his promise would be tested—in a beautiful way. She was carrying his child inside her. She fully trusted his word and excitedly began imagining their life, home, nursery, but, in the back of her mind, was that ever so minuscule doubt, probably exacerbated by her mother's story. *But I won't think about that now.*

Chapter 17
Predicament

Sleeping fitfully that night, Ali awoke early, wondering if the letter from her mother and all Edy had told her and the letter from her mother were just a dream. She was still trying to grasp that a wonderful man named Robert Malone was her true papa and that he and his father loved *her* very much. Also, clearly present in her thoughts was that, with Edy's involvement, her grandfathers had devised a plan to care for her for the rest of her life. Never in her most cherished dreams could she have imagined such a revelation. And now there was a new life borne of love growing inside her. She rubbed her stomach gently as she contemplated that life.

Dear God, if you are listening, I'm sorry for doubting you, and thank you for all of this. She thought of a Bible verse she had heard long ago that went something like, *man makes his plans, but God directs his steps.* She was ashamed that in her arrogance she believed she was in control of her life. She had always been in God's hands, living by His plan, and she should have anticipated good things from Him. But given her present condition, her Catholic faith was, as much as she hated to even think it, a potential looming hazard. Illegitimate pregnancies were not tolerated.

She attended to her morning toilette, looking at her belly in the mirror. She would not be able to hide her growing waist forever, but hopefully with this latest news that she could replace any money Johnnie might lose in a divorce, he would look differently on her and leave Beatrice. She was acutely aware that time was measured, and every day that Johnnie stayed in his marriage to Beatrice was a day that was lost to them forever. It was also a day closer to her ostracism if anyone discovered or even guessed she was with child before she and Johnny were married. As her mother before her, she did not want her beloved child labeled a bastard. So far she had been able to hide her morning sickness, but soon Edy or Mabel would notice.

Ali knew that if she spent every minute with Johnnie for the rest of her life it would never be enough time to love him as much as she wanted to. Now he would have to make a move because he loved her and this child was his and he would naturally want to build a home with her and their family together. She knew that she could never face the choice her mother had made—to marry a man whom she knew she could never love to save her reputation. There simply was no alternate solution. Johnnie must marry her.

Relieved that she had not told Edy of the pregnancy, she resolved to make plans with Johnnie and marry first. She donned the loveliest dress her mother had given her, a pale blue with white lace at the color and sleeves, and even added some lovely sapphire earbobs that had belonged to Jo.

She sent a message to Johnnie yesterday asking him to take her to the Tybee cottage as there was important information she needed to share with him. If they were to be married and claim their child as a full-term baby, time was of the essence. Everything had turned around so beautifully in her life, and she could not remember ever experiencing the kind of joy she now felt. *Is it possible, Allison Malone, that all of your dreams are about to come true?* This morning, she was convinced it was indeed possible. Nothing would go wrong now.

Walking the short distance to Columbia Square where Johnnie would pick her up in his motor car, Ali found herself humming and smiling. It felt good, really good, to be happy. Johnnie pulled to a stop so she could get in, and they were off to Little Dove cottage. The ferry ride was short, and even Jack noticed the obvious change in her.

"Ye certainly do seem on top of the world today, Miss," Jack said.

"Yes, Jack I am. Thank you!" Johnnie parked the car and helped her out for the short walk down the beach to Little Dove cottage. They held hands, but walked most of the way in thier own silent musings. Johnnie would no doubt prepare a clam bake for them. She closed her eyes and smiled, feeling the sea breeze and the warmth of the sun on her face. She gazed at Johnnie after she put her things inside the cottage. Something about the way he was holding his jaw with the small muscle just in front of his ear flexing repeatedly gave her pause. Unlike Ali, Johnnie did not look happy. He was sitting on the porch rocking and waiting for her.

She smiled and said, "Well, hello, handsome man!"

Johnnie seemed deep in thought and had missed her compliment. "Oh, hello, Ali. How are you?" he said trying to cover for himself.

He had not spoken to Ali after their disastrous meeting at mass a few days ago. He had been busy trying with every trick he knew to placate his angry wife after coming face to face with his lover. Beatrice behaved haughtily and rudely to Ali and her cousin, but it was an especially inopportune time for the two of them to meet after the unfortunate letter mix-up debacle.

Johnnie wondered to himself if somewhere in the back of his mind he had mixed up the letters intentionally? Did he want to get caught? He knew if Beatrice caught him blatantly cheating on her, in Savannah no less, his affair with Ali would either be over, Beatrice would become more attached to him and make his life miserable by never allowing him out of her sight, or she would take the children and leave. Beatrice tolerated his nefarious behavior as long as it was far outside the city limits, but she would never abide his entertaining a mistress in her home town right under her nose. She would not be made a fool of, he knew for certain.

Johnnie realized that many wives of powerful husbands just accepted there would be mistresses and turned a blind eye—as long as there was no public humiliation. To add insult to injury, Ali and her cousin attended the same Catholic Church as he and Beatrice did. Sadly, he felt a twinge of freedom in either direction. Trying to keep two women satisfied was more than he bargained for, but, of course, he had never allowed himself to fall in love with one of his "ladies" before. This was a wholly different level of complication and intrigue. *Have I ever loved any woman?* This thought disturbed him momentarily.

Perhaps the most wounding to Beatrice and obvious to Johnnie as he watched Ali looking out to sea was that Ali was young, ambitious, beautiful, vibrant, and intelligent. And childless. Everything Beatrice was not. Time and childbirth had not been kind to Beatrice. But Ali, she fed his soul in a way Beatrice could never even imagine doing.

He congratulated himself on choosing Ali as his latest conquest. He knew she loved him, and he counted on that to keep her from ever causing any embarrassing issues for him at home, church, socially, or professionally. She would preserve their dirty little secret as long as he wanted to keep her on the line. He realized she could, if she was that type of woman, bring his life down in ruins around him and destroy everything he had worked so hard to put in place as well as his family. He still wasn't out of the woods though. Good as Ali was, somehow he had to tell her it was over and remain in her good graces.

Beatrice had given him an ultimatum—fire Ali immediately and stop seeing her or don't come home until you do. Ali was a particular threat to Beatrice, possibly because he had told her that he loved Ali. He never loved any of his sporadic lovers and she knew that. This was different and a distinct threat to her way of life. Confessing this to her was a misstep. One of several. Since then, he had been staying at the hotel suite in town he regularly shared with Ali. It made him uncomfortable that Beatrice had the power to decide if and when he could come into his own home and see his own children, but she controlled the purse strings as their wealth came from her inheritance. Legally it was now as much his as hers, but he did not want to go down that road publicly.

Johnnie contemplated having one last tryst with Ali at the Tybee cottage before he had to dismiss her, in the event Ali decided to break off their relationship altogether. As much as he did not want to admit it, he had fallen in love—hard—with this girl. After Ali, even the idea of sex with Beatrice was repugnant to him. He didn't want to give Ali up, but, on the other hand, he didn't want to divorce either. Beatrice was tolerable as long as he stayed in his lane and didn't get caught.

The letter mess was entirely his fault for being careless. He thought Ali more than likely had been hurt by what he wrote to Beatrice, but he did what he had to do to keep both women happy. Who could blame him? Confrontation was not something he relished, but he was having to do some fancy dancing to manage both.

Yes, telling Ali it was over was not something he wanted to do, so he had to exercise extreme caution. He might just want to share some intimacy with her from time to time if she would allow that kind of relationship. But Beatrice could never get wind that he hadn't completely ended the affair. It would take all his charisma and manipulative prowess to convince Ali to settle for just a part of him. No question, Ali loved him, adored him even, and it was a great confidence boost for him.

Some time ago Beatrice had stopped noticing his body, his clothes, his intelligence, his jokes—everything. She didn't want him, but he knew they would be rolling snowballs in hell before she ever stepped aside for another woman to love him. He was her toy. On the shelf, shiny and pretty, impressing her friends, and taken down to dust rather than play with. Which was exactly the way he treated Ali.

The sexual part of their marriage was dead never to be resurrected. Any intimacy between them died at the birth of their last son, Michael. But that did not mean his desires were dead—far from it. That part of him was perhaps even stronger thanks to Ali. She was definitely useful to Johnny meeting his physical needs, and he could tolerate going home to his cold fish of a wife at the end of the day if he knew he would be holding Ali's delicious body again soon. In this way at least, Ali strengthened his marriage, poor girl. He felt a twinge of guilt, but it passed soon enough. He knew Ali enjoyed their physical relationship as much as he, so she was as much to blame as he.

Beatrice would stay with him as long as he respected the boundaries and provided her with an acceptable lifestyle of luxury and social standing. Whispers could be endured, but he had to make more of an effort to keep his philandering pecker in its place. While it would sting a bit to tell Ali it was over, he would wait until after their lovemaking. No reason to ruin a good fuck; they were here together in privacy on a beautiful day. Why waste the opportunity? He'd be under Beatrice's thumb soon enough.

"And so, my little dove, you needed to desperately see me? May I inquire if it is because of some physical need I may meet for you?"

Ali realized immediately she had read Johnnie's mood wrong. He was his usual happy-go-lucky, delicious self.

"Oh, Johnnie, there is so much to tell you I hardly know where to begin! So much has happened since I last saw you."

Though Johnnie fancied himself a good listener, in truth, his own world was exciting enough to keep him stimulated, and the stories and struggles of this girl couldn't compare. She challenged him intellectually, but that could grow wearisome after a time. He pretended to be listening to her, but Ali was quick and, when she sensed he had tuned her out, she would ask him to repeat what she had just said. So he learned the art of half-listening so he had *just* enough of an idea what she was talking about to satisfy her of his attention.

For her part, Ali was aware that Johnnie was at war with himself, with two armies raging constantly in his brain—the man he wanted to be versus the man he actually was. He could not accept flaws in himself and, worse, couldn't accept other people seeing flaws in him. His image was all important to him, and he was utterly impressed with his own importance. She also knew there was another battle within him as well— being married to a woman he was in no way attracted to and had no feelings for other than as the mother of his children. He had found his true fulfillment with her in every way— physically, spiritually, intellectually.

They discussed his leaving Beatrice nearly every time they were together. It was the one constant dark cloud that hung over them. He had told her, "Ali, I wouldn't miss her, not as I would miss you. I would miss your laughter—our laughter together—and your quick wit and sharp mind, and those breasts, oh my God, those breasts. Yes, I would definitely miss the breasts."

They laughed together and the subject was again swept under the rug. This was how Johnnie dealt with unpleasantness—he didn't. If things got too close or he didn't want to answer a question, he would redirect the conversation. He was a master of redirection, but Ali always picked up on it. If he truly did not want to discuss something or answer her question, there was no use cajoling. He was immovable.

Johnnie rose to meet her with a hug and deep kiss. "My lovely, perhaps we should make love first and talk later. Would you mind terribly?"

"Oh, Johnnie, I do have very important information to give you, but you know I cannot resist you. Make love to me, you rake!" Johnnie lifted her up in his arms and, laughing, carried her to the bedroom.

There was a sweetness to their lovemaking this time that caught them both off guard. Johnnie thought perhaps it was because he knew this might be the last time he ever made love to her. Ali thought it was because his child was growing inside her, and she had a "family" feel about her. Neither was prepared for the truth of the other, but, as with any heartbreak, there was no good time for it.

As they lay together holding hands, looking at nothing in particular, they began to talk. "All right, my darlin' doll baby, tell me all that is on your mind, and we will plumb the depths together," Johnnie said with a smile and a tweak of her nipple. "I am all yours."

"Umm, yes, you are and if you talk about plumbing depths anymore there will be no conversation. I could love you over and over and over again and never tire. I love you, Johnnie, very much; you know that. What I am about to tell you are things that have altered my life significantly in just one day. I hope that they do not have any adverse effect on 'us,' and that being said…"

Ali spent the next hour telling Johnnie the entire story from her conception onward. She vacillated between tears of joy, tears of sorrow, tears of anger, and tears of thankfulness. The story was overwhelming to her, and she felt it might overwhelm Johnnie too. She stopped short of telling him she was with child. She wanted to give Johnnie an opportunity to marry her and not add that extra burden. If he didn't want her for herself, she didn't want him. She didn't want any man to marry her for the money or because she was pregnant.

"Well, doll baby, it appears you have won the day, hit the jackpot, and your ship has come in all at the same time. It is wonderful to know that you will never have any financial hardship, and for that I am very thankful. I worried about you sometimes, supporting yourself on just what you make at the bank, but I also admired you for it.

"I am thrilled for you that your chosen name of Malone is your rightful and legitimate name and one of which you can be proud. It sounds as if your father was a fine man. Congratulations! I know that is very important for you to know what kind of stock you are made of. I always knew it must be strong."

"As important and exciting as all of this is, Johnnie, something wonderful has happened—is happening—that makes the rest pale in comparison."

"Do tell! You have my full attention," Johnnie said as he raised up on one elbow, looking into her eyes. Ali, still holding his hand, softly placed it on her belly.

"Johnnie, the most wonderful news of all…I am carrying our child—yours and mine. Oh, Johnnie, I have never been happier and cannot wait for us to begin our life together as a family."

Stunned, Johnnie dropped flat and stared at the ceiling without saying a word. Ali raised up on her elbow and looked down at his face, concerned.

"Johnnie, aren't you happy? Say something. Please."

Suddenly their fun morning of lovemaking had taken an ominous turn. Johnnie sat up and began to dress, saying nothing. When he finally spoke, it was with a cold, sharp voice that slapped her down.

"Ali, I came to meet you today to tell you that I have decided that our relationship is at an end. I can no longer be with you. I wanted this to be a lovely memory, a friendly way to part. Because of the letter, Beatrice is now aware of our relationship, and she has thrown me from my own home until I fire you from your job and promise to never see you again. I know her, Ali. She will make me account for every second of my day until she is convinced I have no time for anything but work and home. She will make my life a living hell."

"Johnnie, as much as I love my position at the bank, I can live without the income now. I no longer have to work as I told you. My grandfathers have seen to my financial support. And anything you would lose in the divorce, my trust will more than make up for. I'm not certain how much is in it to the penny, but I have been assured it is very substantial. You will know more about it very soon as my grandfathers intend to meet with your bank to control the trust. That will include your input."

Ali was trembling now. This was not the response she expected. She imagined that Johnnie would be as happy as she to share this child. How had her mama described it? *The manifestation of their love.*

"We have discussed this, Ali, and I told you I made my decision. I will not break my covenant with my wife. I will not divorce her and destroy my family. I cannot be any more transparent and truthful than that."

"But, Johnnie, that is not what you have been telling me. You even got on one knee and proposed marriage to me. You told me we would be married by the new year. You discussed our honeymoon to Europe. You told me to plan our wedding and have my dress made. And you have continued to see me and make love to me! *Even just now!* Where in any of that would I get the message that we were not going to be married? Where, Johnnie? If I am missing something, you'll need to point it out to me because I am very clear about what you have told me."

Ali was sobbing now in disbelief that her life had just taken yet another sharp turn, and she was desperate to hold onto Johnnie. "Look into my eyes, Johnnie, and tell me to my face that you do not love me."

"I cannot do that, Ali. I do; l…care for you. But I have made up my mind, Ali. I will not change it; you know that. As far as the, uh, this predicament goes…"

"*Predicament?* Is that how you are referring to *our child,* Johnnie?"

"…I have had occasion, through a friend, naturally, to be privy to certain people who can, uh, resolve this condition in which you find yourself," Johnnie nearly spat it out, trying to say it to her face but obviously uncomfortable. He was unaccustomed to being called to task, especially by a woman. He tolerated enough of this from Beatrice.

Ali surmised from what he said that he had used the services of an abortionist for a pregnant lover before. She wondered how long ago. She read as much as possible about this practice in her support of the Suffragist Movement. While Ali supported a woman's right to receive proper medical care if her condition supported the need for such surgery, she was appalled to think Johnnie could ever even imagine she would abort their beloved child.

"Hmm, all right, so your child is now a 'predicament,' a 'condition,' that you have to 'handle.' How utterly coarse and unkind you are, especially considering what just happened in this bed not fifteen minutes ago. Can you actually stand there and think for one second that I would even consider killing our child? A child that is the product of our love, because I know you love me, Johnnie. I have trusted every word you have said to me. And you cannot deny it to my face."

Johnnie finished tying his cravat and turned to her. "Ali, I have to be a better man to be able to live with myself. I have to be a better husband and father—the kind of husband and father God expects me to be. I have sinned by loving you. I have broken my marriage covenant. I talked with Bishop Flanagan, and he has advised me that there is no alternative in the Church but that I return to Beatrice, ask her forgiveness, and try to repair my marriage. I am sorry that you have to be hurt, and I will, of course, pay for you to, uh, resolve this problem, but there can be no further discussion about divorce."

As if shot in the heart, Ali folded over and screamed her sobs, then became deathly still. *No, this isn't happening. No, God, you won't let this happen to me after just yesterday bringing me such joy. Please, God, take the money, take everything back, but don't take Johnnie and our child from me,* Ali begged and bargained with God in her mind.

Uncomfortable with her hysterical outburst and subsequent eerie silence, Johnnie said, "Please try to understand how unfair I have been to Beatrice. And you, of course. It just simply can't go on."

In truth, seeing Ali's reaction, knowing that she was carrying his child, gutted Johnnie too. He wanted to cry, scream, hold Ali and tell her everything would be all right, but someone had to keep a level head.

"You *dare* speak to me of *fairness?*" Each word was punctuated with a sharp pause. "Johnnie, I have not *imagined* our relationship. This has not just been a little fantasy I have dreamt alone. You told me you loved me *first*. I have not made up a fairy tale of my own about us getting married. I have not given my body to you lightly. And I do not carry your child without loving it as I love you. Fair? To *Beatrice?* You cannot be serious! She cares nothing for you; you told me this yourself! If you are going back to *her* and leaving *me* and your child, could you please explain to me how fairness reckons into this arrangement for me because I cannot fathom it. I would have never entered into a relationship with you if I had not been convinced you were leaving her!"

Johnnie could sense he was entering into a conversation that he could not win, and that was uncomfortable and unfamiliar territory for him. His mind sounded the retreat call, but Ali could be tenacious when she wanted answers, and he was certain this time she would not be dissuaded or redirected.

Ali continued as he anticipated. "I love you—God help me, Johnnie, with every breath in me, I love you. I am carrying your child. A child that I already love, who, if you return to Beatrice, will grow up a *bastard*. We will both be ruined! I will not make the choice my mother had to make. Are you prepared to accept that fate for your child? To never have a father? Never have the opportunities that your children with Beatrice have—to grow up in a family? To feel unloved and abandoned as I have always felt? Is that a 'fair' resolution, Johnnie? Tell me, please, how does 'fair' play into that?" Ali was on her feet now and presenting quite a formidable resistance to Johnnie's plan.

"Of course, you know that is not what I would ever want for one of my children. Or yours," he said, cutting her deeply by not claiming the child she was carrying.

Ali saw the cold reality of Johnnie Meadows at that moment. He spoke with such detachment. Such cold-heartedness. He did not consider their child growing inside of her to be "one of his children." He felt no connection to their child, a child she thought had been conceived in deep love.

Quietly she began, almost a whisper. "Has it all been a lie, Johnnie? Has every word out of your mouth been tainted with deceit? Were you playing a game that I was unaware of? Did you take advantage of my love for you for your own gratification? For your ego? Did you ever love me, even a little?"

"Of course, I loved you, Ali. I do...*care* for you. But I love my wife and family too. Please try to understand it from my point of view. I cannot desert my family. I have to try to rekindle the love I once had for my wife." Johnnie had said the words, but Ali saw he could not look her in the eye. She knew he was lying to her.

"Well, Johnnie, this is the first time I have ever heard from your mouth that you love Beatrice. Is this something new you've just discovered after all these years?"

"No, Ali, Beatrice and I have just these past few days committed to rekindling our love, and I intend to give this second chance my all. Once I move back into the house. It is a little too soon for her."

"So Beatrice is willing to just overlook this 'indiscretion' with me and forgive you and go on as if nothing has changed?

When did the two of you decide all of this? It has only been a week since we were last together. What do you think she will do when she finds out about our child?" Ali stood tight-lipped and incredulous. She felt as if the past six months were all a dream, and she was just now waking to this shattering reality. Who was this man standing before her and where was her Johnnie?

"Ali, Beatrice and I had a long discussion about this one night in bed this week," he began, and Ali instantly knew he had lied to her once more. He wasn't staying in his hotel suite as he said, but she didn't interrupt.

"On the priest's counsel, I told her everything—every last one of my sins—and she even revealed to me that, because of my behavior and neglect of her, she had contemplated having an affair herself! I cannot believe I drove Beatrice to those lengths. We cried together. We prayed together. And we recommitted to each other. That is all I can say in my defense. Now, obviously, I have to see you through the resolution of your predicament, and I assure you I will arrange as well as pay for everything, but that is the extent to which I can be involved. And you will not be able to come back to the bank to work. You must never reveal this to anyone. You have the power to ruin me, but I am trusting in your love that you will not do that. And Beatrice has done nothing to deserve this being made public. How can I even be certain this child is mine?"

"Surely you cannot believe that I have been with anyone other than you. I was a virgin when you first loved me, and I have been with no other man. *How dare you!*

And predicament? *My* predicament. You are standing there after having just made the most tender love to me, calling *our* child, the manifestation of *our* love, a *predicament?* Please, God, wake me up because this cannot be real. How *could* you? How *dare* you? *Who are you?* Even the most practiced narcissist cannot argue with pure biology. This is your child! Did you just use me to meet your needs so you could tolerate staying in your marriage to *her?* And you are staying with her even though you claim to love me? Why? To save face in the community? What about my reputation? What will it be as an unwed mother? And *our* child, Johnnie, have you thought of anyone but yourself?

"The biggest heartbreak for me is that I so completely, totally misjudged you. I defended you to Edy! I argued and told her what a good man you are in spite of your womanizing reputation. How could I have been so foolish? I have been taken advantage of in the worst possible way while you have gone on with your life, never missing a beat. No, I see clearly now that nothing ever changed in your life as a result of loving me. And now I am to be left with a...a... bastard child. *Everything* has changed for me, and nothing, nothing has touched you in the least." At this she collapsed onto the bed and began sobbing.

"Well now, honey," he said in his slow southern Georgia drawl that had always been so irresistible to Ali. "My life has indeed changed, Sugar, because now I love you and I can't be with you anymore. It hurts me to the bone; you just cannot see it."

"No, you're correct, Johnnie, I see nothing of the kind. All I see is you trying to get out of a 'predicament' of your own making and leave me to pay the price for your sport."

"Can't you go home to Wilmington? You told me earlier the home is yours now."

At this, Ali's voice dropped to a hissing whisper. "Have you not listened to anything I have told you about my life in Wilmington? I have *nothing* and *no one* there anymore, and certainly if I did they would not welcome an unwed mother with open arms. All I have left of home is the memory of my precious mama. And she is gone. I have no one and nowhere to go. Edy will certainly expect me to find another home. All I have, Johnnie, is your child growing inside me but no idea how I will make a life for him. Or her. So you will not do the right thing and marry me? Is that correct? You will not be a part of your child's life?"

"Now, honey, you and I disagree on what is right and what is wrong in this situation, and I guess we will have to agree to disagree because I see no obvious resolution if you demand to keep this unfortunate child. We were both adults when we entered into this relationship; we knew the risks. You are as much responsible as I. You knew the possibilities of our relationship."

"Knew the risks? You cannot be serious. You told me you were going to leave your wife within the year! Do you not remember you said those words to me? You made promises to me, Johnnie, important promises, binding promises. And I *trusted* you. Do you have any idea how hard that was for me—to actually trust a man after what I had been through?"

She snickered to herself, "No, of course you don't because you can't think further than your own cares and concerns."

"Ali, that's not fair. You're being ugly and rude now and it is unbecoming. I do care deeply for you." Ali winced when he used the word "care" rather than the "love" he had used earlier.

"I'm deeply disappointed in you, Ali. I didn't expect such behavior from you."

"*You! You?* You are disappointed in *me?* You are completely oblivious of your responsibility in this, aren't you?"

"All right, Ali, this is going downhill quickly and I do not want to end our relationship on a sour note. We have enjoyed it so much. The simple fact is I cannot have further contact with you or your child, and given the situation it would be best for all of us if you would listen to me and have the pregnancy terminated. Beatrice would never stand for it if you lived in Savannah and went about with a child that everyone would suspect was mine. She would be humiliated if word ever got out, and I cannot even fathom how Ginny and my boys would react to an illegitimate half-brother or sister. I cannot do that to my family. I love Beatrice. I love my children. I love my life as it is."

Again, Ali reeled as if struck by another blow. "You *love her? Tell* me, Johnnie, when was it that you had this message from God?"

"Yes, I love Beatrice. I have determined, set my mind on falling in love with her again. It is my Christian duty to honor my vow to her."

"Oh, you mean the vow you had already broken repeatedly before me—with countless women—and the vow you continued to be unconcerned with when you became involved with me? In fact, you indicated then that the vow was already broken beyond repair. You *promised* me, Johnny!"

Her head hung down and she was just beginning to realize the full impact and implications of what he said to her. "You are not a man of your word, John Meadows. Was it also your Christian duty to spread your seed far and wide and then leave me alone to raise your child? Because you claim to be a much stronger Christian than I, why don't you explain to me how that reckons with Christ-like behavior? And 'duty' and 'vow' and 'love.' Please, Johnnie, enlighten me. I am obviously confused."

"I cannot explain this to you when you are hysterical."

"I believe my emotions are perfectly fit for this situation. I am behaving exactly as a terrified, unmarried pregnant woman without a father for her child would be expected to behave. I am behaving as a woman who has just had her heart ripped from her chest and shattered to pieces—all of her dreams stolen—and as a human being who feels that the person she trusted with her life has just played a very cruel joke on her, and rather than being the good man she believed he was, he is nothing but a handsome, charismatic, manipulative, and opportunistic cad. Under the circumstances, I think my behavior is exceptionally appropriate and as to be expected."

"No, honey, there is no need for us to ruin the lovely relationship we have enjoyed together. You must have known it could never be permanent. You knew I was married and devoted to my family."

"Pardon me, Johnnie, but you are also a bare-faced liar. What in that scenario—that very real relationship we enjoyed—would have ever made me doubt that you were anything but honest and completely moral?"

"Darlin', there was nothing honorable in what we were doing. Either of us. You aren't innocent in this. You were having relations with a married man. It was wrong. And I apologize if you feel I have disrespected you in any way. I hope you can forgive me one day and come to understand this was the only right decision."

"You want me to forgive you as Beatrice has? There is a big difference, Johnnie. She will feel you next to her when she goes to bed at night. She will be given your kiss as her good morning. She can forgive you because she has children who have a father. She can forgive you because she must in order to have the life with you she desires. She will forgive you because all of what is important to her depends upon her husband not bringing scandal to her doorstep.

"Let me tell you a secret: she will never truly forgive you. No, she will remind you in a thousand subtle ways every single day for the rest of your miserable life that you are indebted to her. Mark my word. Remember I said this. This will not be swept under the rug as if it didn't happen. You will never be free of this.

"Tell me, Johnnie, should I forgive you the day I labor to birth your child alone? Or maybe when Father Maloney secretly christens our bastard child with only his disgraced mother to witness? Perhaps I shall forgive you while I lie in bed alone at night, imagining your touch—*on Beatrice.* Perhaps one day when I can once again bear the shame of going back to mass, if permitted, I will be able to confess my sinful affair, as you pointed out, with my child's father, and perhaps throw myself on the mercy seat of the Lord and receive the charity of forgiveness."

Ali noticed Johnnie shuddered visibly when she mentioned making love to Beatrice. Ali knew he preferred her physically.

She was aware he had reached his saturation point with this conversation. Why was he being so obstinate? He could afford to divorce Beatrice, and marry her, knowing she now possessed ample funds to support them, not unlike his arrangement with Beatrice. She would give up anything for him and may well be doing so.

It appeared Johnnie lacked the strength of character to follow through with his promise and desire to be with her, hiding instead behind the guise that he was honoring his marriage vows to Beatrice as he had never done since their wedding day. She knew he had made this choice to abandon her and their baby because he wasn't willing to face possible ostracism from his friends and colleagues. This wasn't about Ali or the baby. It wasn't about him loving Beatrice or even his children. It certainly wasn't about God. This was all about his *image*—what people would think of him. Why had her birth and then the birth of her child been determined by what someone else might think? How could human life be reduced to the opinions of people who really didn't matter anyway—most of whom might not even be known to him?

Ali knew that those in the higher social strata could be the most vicious, especially when they got the scent of blood in the water, especially one of their own. Oh, how the mighty fall. And now she must face the same music. *And Edy, oh, dear Edy. She has done nothing to deserve this, and yet it will bring her down through her association with me.* Ali's next thought was of her grandfathers who were due to visit her in Savannah in the very near future. How could she possibly face them and tell them she was unmarried and with child? How could she ask either of these dear men to go through this same scenario with her that they so painfully experienced with her mother, to relive the horror of Robert's death and Jo's clandestine marriage because of her pregnancy with Ali? *How can this be happening to me? How could I have so misjudged Johnnie? And what do I do now?*

"Ali, I am surprised that you are turning on me like this after all I have done for you—given you a position in the bank, given you an unprecedented promotion and pay raise. No other man would have done such for you, nor have the power to do so. I took great personal risk for your benefit. I have to admit I never would have expected you of all people to be ungracious."

Johnnie was purposely laying it on thick, trying desperately to absolve himself of any culpability that could possibly besmirch him should this become public. Ali suddenly saw it all so clearly as if she had burrowed deeply into his mind and heart and soul. He was completely naked in front of her but this time she derived no pleasure from it. She was disgusted. She accepted the responsibility for her own gullibility and misplacement of trust. Johnnie was simply incapable of taking any personal responsibility for his dishonesty—ever. None of this situation could be allowed to touch him or his family. Beatrice could not possibly tolerate another humiliation. She must never know about the pregnancy. No, somehow he must get Ali to the abortionist and end this before it devastated his expertly scripted life. It simply would not do.

He added, "And I must say, it is unbecoming behavior in a cultured lady such as yourself. I am *disappointed* in you. We must take care of this and with all due haste."

There it was again—the golden dagger—the very same one James thrust into me time and again. Father was disappointed in me. And now so is Johnnie. A great sob escaped from deep within her soul. She turned to Johnnie and for the first time in their time together, she spoke unvarnished truth to him.

"You are *disappointed* in me? You have no right to be disappointed in me! Johnnie, I am with child, *your* child. It was not an immaculate conception. A child I already love because of my love for you. I am carrying a part of you within me, a part of you that no one can have but me. Beatrice cannot ever have this piece of our love that belongs to me, to us. Any yet you are not concerned about our child or my welfare or the fact you have shattered me today or how you are ruining my reputation, my life, and my ability to provide a respectable life for our child. You are concerned only with how you can extricate yourself from this—what did you call it again—predicament—unscathed so nothing will sully your name or Beatrice's reputation. You cannot bear the possibility that anyone might discover that your strong Christian marriage—a primary school infatuation, fairytale-come-true relationship—is a farcical lie. Or maybe you don't want your children to find that you are not the honorable hero they thought you were.

"Stop and think, Johnnie. In a very short time, it is going to become evident to all around us that I am expecting a child. We cannot hide our feelings. You know as well as I do that the people who know us well will see it on our faces and know this child is yours. How shall I respond? Where shall I live with our child? I certainly cannot bring further shame on Edy. I cannot. I will not. As soon as she discovers I am pregnant, she will be ruined along with me if I stay.

"I cannot go back to Wilmington and now, to placate your jealous wife, I do not have my position at the bank. It's not enough that you end your relationship with me; she wants to take my position and means of support as well. How threatened she must be! This situation is not primarily about you, Johnnie, nor is it primarily about me. It is about our child and what is best for him or her. How can you abandon me in this, and in doing so lie to me with words of love? How can you leave me to face my grandfathers alone, with child, and without a husband? No amount of money can cover my shame while again you remain untouched by scandal. None of this makes sense. How could I have been so wrong about us? You are a master of manipulation, Johnnie."

"Now, Ali, as I've said, I do intend to help you. I've said that over and over. I will not abandon you. I will see this through to the end, but that end cannot be the birth of this child. That will not do. It will bring us both down. Surely you see that! Your reputation will be tarnished and in tatters if you go through with bringing this unwanted child into the world. The far-reaching ramifications are untenable with the effect this will have on my wife and family as well as your cousin Edy. You will be responsible for the ruination of many lives unless this can be nipped in the bud. And now."

"You intend that I kill our child? Our baby? Jesus, Mary, and Joseph, help me," she pleaded as she crossed herself. "You have no decency, no conscience, no morals. You are devoid of honor altogether. And you are a stranger to me. You want to destroy everything that matters to me and take my soul too."

"My dove, I am afraid we have no other choice. I will not allow this one indiscretion to destroy my wife, my children, my position with the bank, nor my standing in this community. What has to happen will happen. There is no use in arguing or discussing it further. If you make the unfortunate choice of not going through with this, I will make sure no one in this town will receive you or believe I am the father of your child. I have a long-established reputation here, and you are a newcomer with an unknown history. Just a few words from me and the ones who matter here will never even speak to you. Do you understand me? You will be ruined. I don't want to see that happen to you, of course, but I will not allow you to hurt my family."

"Knowing that I would never, ever betray you or our love, you would do that to me? You would purposely ruin me? Oh, Johnnie. I have no more words."

"Then this conversation is over. I've told you that I will take the responsibility for arranging and paying for an abortion that will be best for us both and I will. I will contact you when the arrangements are made. I'm certain once you are more lucid and not so emotional, you will realize this is the only choice."

Johnnie reached to put his hand on Ali's shoulder, but she jerked away from his touch.

"*Never touch me again.* Never speak to me again. And never contact me. Forget me because if I commit this horrible, unspeakable sin, it will destroy my soul forever. You have stolen my innocence, my trust, my faith, my love, my dreams, and now my child. I will purge our child from my body, and I will purge you from my memory. You are as dead to me as our child will be."

Ali knew she would never again be able to remember the days they spent together here in the Tybee cottage or their long lunches at the hotel. She would no longer be able to look at his face or even hear his voice, that soft, Southern drawl that used to be so charming to her. His touch on her skin that used to feel like silk now burned like a branding iron. His lips that were so luscious and soft she now saw as the vile, hateful portal from which his poisonous words vomited on her.

She knew this act of murder would end the vision she had of her first born and possibly the only child she might ever have. *God only knows how I will survive this emotionally if I survive physically.* She had read and heard of many horrible deaths of young women who had sought out abortions. After it was done, Ali held the hope she would die rather than face life after this. She had already passed the "quickening" stage of pregnancy and felt that heaviness in her womb as well as that first faint flutter of life. Johnnie had committed the ultimate betrayal of her and the child she carried, his child.

"You repulse me," Ali said flatly.

Ignoring what she hissed, Johnnie flatly stated, "I will make the arrangements in the morning to resolve this. We must be completely discreet, and you cannot reveal names or addresses of these persons who will help us. I don't need to remind you that they must work in secrecy. Come into work tomorrow as you normally do, and I will have all arranged.

"Now we must hurry to catch the ferry back to town. Please betray this to no one, Ali. This is what is best for all including the, um, child. Better to end it now while we can."

Ali's brain shut down. She could take no more today. She was completely saturated with this trauma. Her mind was reeling and her body felt weak from eating nothing all day.

"Please take me home. Now."

Johnnie paused on the porch to lock the door to their "little piece of Heaven." Now it seemed as if she were on the very hinges of hell here.

She and Johnnie boarded the ferry in silence, not touching, not looking at each other, barely acknowledging they had ever come there together in the past. Jack noticed and gave Johnnie a raised eyebrow in question. Johnnie subtly shook his head to dissuade him from asking any questions.

Johnnie drove to her home on Lincoln Street, in silence that was deafening.

"I will see you in the morning, Ali. All will be well. I promise you."

Ali snickered and said sarcastically, "Well, we both know how dependable your promises are, do we not?" Ali had never felt so completely and desolately alone in her life.

Not waiting for Jonhnie, she got out, left the car door open, and slowly walked up the steps. No backward glance, no goodbye. Only resignation.

Chapter 18
Separate Directions

After a sleepless night, Ali walked to work that mild September morning in a fog. The weather seemed bound for another sweltering Indian Summer day. She plodded with leaden feet and a sense of dark foreboding in her stomach. She felt as if she were being forced down a path she vehemently did not want to traverse. *I want this baby. I want Johnnie's baby. How can I go through with this?*

She entered the bank's formidable door as the doorman opened it for her. She walked directly to her desk, expressionless. She knew she had to meet with Johnnie this morning to receive the information he had for her.

Arriving at her desk, Ali removed her hat and sat down trying in vain to pretend she was working. She spied the corner of a folded note under her ledger. She recognized Johnnie's stationery. *Ha, careless of him.* Ali was surprised he had not thought to write on plain paper so that nothing could be tied to him if it were found. She shook her head. Just like Johnnie to take the risk of using his own stationery. *I'm sure he would find a way to blame me for that too.* She unfolded the note, trying not to draw the attention of her coworkers.

> *Take the streetcar to Indian Street at 3 o'clock*
> *this afternoon, where you will disembark and walk*
> *a short distance to 183 West Boundary Street.*
>
> *There will be a red vase of flowers in the window*
> *if it is safe to enter. Knock on the door twice, pause,*
> *then knock three times. They are expecting you and*
> *have been paid in advance for their services.*
>
> *I will be out of town until tomorrow but will be*
> *in touch to check on your health upon my return. Be*
> *strong, little dove. All will be well.*
>
> *—J*

The coward hasn't the decency to be in town while his lover is murdering his child at his command. Ali noted that the address was in a part of the city that Edy had sternly warned her not to go near—ever. Edy said it was inhabited by criminals, former chain-gang convicts, and immoral women who sold their bodies. Why was Johnnie sending her to an address in the District? Surely the person she needed to see didn't live there. And he expected her to walk there alone, unchaperoned, risking her life? *Johnnie, what were you thinking?* But Ali knew Johnnie was not thinking of her well-being but his own. Right at that precise moment, her brain resigned itself to the fact that Johnnie had never loved her. He was incapable of loving anyone but himself.

Ali made the motions of working but in truth accomplished nothing. She was dazed, just doing everything by rote, and watching the clock move slowly towards the appointed hour. Each second ticked off and Ali imagined it as her baby's heartbeat slowly ticking down to death.

At two o'clock precisely, Ali stood, retrieved her hat and reticule, and walked out without a word. She left earlier than necessary so that she could stop at St. Mark's to pray. She wasn't sure if she even had a right to pray given her plans.

She climbed the steps to the cathedral with its massive carved walnut door, the saints of her childhood engraved there. She felt they were accusing her. She put her hand on the door and pushed it slightly open, just enough to slip quietly in, her fingers instinctively reaching for the holy water to make the sign of the cross. Tentatively, she stepped into the sanctuary, then knelt to pray in the last pew. Crossing herself again, she mouthed the words of the Rosary, "Hail Mary, full of grace. Blessed art thou among women, and blessed is the fruit of thy womb, Jesus."

Ali choked back tears at the mention of "womb." For the first time ever, the words of the Rosary had great meaning to her. She felt a sisterhood with Mary, with the fruit of the womb within her. Her conception was not immaculate but nonetheless a miracle to her. Hers was fraught with sin, darkness, betrayal, and, ultimately, abandonment. Joseph did not abandon Mary, even though it caused him embarrassment and shame. People in society looked down on him. Joseph was the perfect example of manly integrity. He loved and believed Mary and stood by her side and cared for her regardless of what his family or friends said.

"Holy Mary, Mother of God, pray for us sinners now and at the hour of our death," Ali continued, praying as much for herself as her unborn child. "Be with my child at the time of his death," she added in a whisper.

She wanted to go to confession but could not bring herself to ask for forgiveness for the sin she was about to commit. She desperately desired absolution but knew she didn't deserve it. She was sorry. Sorry for the wretched affair that had brought her to this gut-wrenching moment in her life. She was sorry because at the time she knew it was sin but shut down her conscience because she loved Johnnie and craved his touch like an addiction.

She was about to commit the worst sin—a mortal sin—the taking of another human life, and this, her own child. How could she possibly ask for forgiveness when consciously hurling herself directly into sin? There was not one saint, whose statues were standing at intervals around the cathedral, who would intercede on her behalf now. Ali crossed herself and walked out. Leaving behind her childhood faith. Unabsolved. Unforgiven. Drowning in despair.

Chapter 19
Back Alley Butchery

She resumed her walk to the address Johnnie left for her and arrived at the appointed hour of three o'clock. She had ventured into the seedy side of Savannah, not far from the wharfs. Unlike the waterfront area of Wilmington, bustling with shops and activity, this was a dark and frightening part of town. She realized she felt nothing now. All of her tears had been cried and the well was empty. Her mind was shutting down, anesthetizing itself in preparation for this nightmare. She was a shell of a woman with but a tiny speck of humanity left within her. Soon she knew even that speck would be extinguished.

She remembered Johnnie's words to her, "Darlin,' how can you miss something that you never had?" How little he knew of motherhood. She would miss her child because he was a part of her. She had felt the flutters of life. These were feelings Johnnie could not possibly fathom. How she wished she had chosen another man to father her child, but, of course, that thought didn't enter her mind when she made love to Johnnie. She truly believed he was the perfect man for her.

Ali wondered if the thought of her and what she was doing would even cross Johnnie's mind at three o'clock today. Would he think of how his child was at that moment being murdered, ripped from what should be the safest place in the world—his mama's womb? Would he feel pain, she wondered. Would he look like a baby yet? Would they give him a proper burial or just toss him in the garbage like a sack of cells and nothing more? She couldn't think about it.

Ali had given a great deal of thought to all Johnnie said yesterday. His coldness caused her to shiver, and it broke her heart. She questioned her own sanity, wondering if she had just dreamt of a love relationship with him. Had all their nights together at Tybee and the hotel just been in her imagination? *Well, obviously not, Ali, or you wouldn't be in this situation now.* She tortured herself with these questions for which she had no answer.

She followed Johnnie's instructions to the letter, walking, descending further into the hell that was the notorious "District." The sights were disturbing, and the smells of urine, vomit, and rot were overwhelming and nauseating. With each step she was eyed suspiciously, perhaps even greedily, by the inhabitants. Yet, she was surprisingly unafraid. Numbly unaware of any possible danger afoot. She shut her mind down. It was the only way she could get through what she was about to do.

As she neared the address, she began shaking, barely able to walk. Fear and panic now overwhelmed her. She looked at the note and then up at the door, 183 West Boundary Street. Her eyes searched for the red flowers in the window, hoping there were none. They were there. She raised her shaking hand to knock twice. She paused. She knocked three more times. She waited several agonizing seconds until the door suddenly opened, and an unattractive and unkempt woman grabbed Ali by the arm and dragged her in. Ali was startled.

"Follow me," she ordered, "Come quickly! Did anyone follow you?"

Ali shook her head and obeyed silently. They came to a dilapidated kitchen at the back of the tenement, a smoking kerosene lamp providing the only light. The woman cleared the table, brushing off crumbs to the already filthy floor. Ali saw a bloody bucket by the back door and nearly fainted.

"Take everything off from the waist down," she coarsely ordered.

Ali flinched at her sharp command, prickling with embarrassment. Surely she could have some modicum of privacy to remove her skirt and undergarments. She looked around the dismal room and saw nowhere to hide herself as she undressed.

"Come on, girly! I have to get home to feed my youngins. I can't wait on your ladylike sensibilities. Don't know why you're so uppity about it. You didn't mind droppin' yer drawers for the mighty Mr. Meadows, now did ya? All them other women he's sent to me think nothin' of it either. Now git 'em off and git up on that table."

Ali realized this was just another stop on the path to total humiliation and degradation. She removed her skirt and undergarments and climbed onto the filthy table on which the woman had thrown a dirty cloth. Ali was angry, and she wasn't sure if the anger was at the woman's orders, the information that Johnnie was a "regular" at this business, or her own behavior that lead to this. The rage fueled her into action now. No longer afraid, no longer heartbroken, she snapped at the woman, "I'm on the table. Let's get this over with so I can get out of this filthy hole." Her anger was giving her courage to move forward.

Startled by her quick change of demeanor, the woman roughly secured her with makeshift leather straps made of old horse harnesses nailed in place to hold her hands by her sides and her feet perched on the end of the table, legs spread wide. The tabletop was hard and rough, but Ali didn't complain or move. She stared at the kerosene lamp on the cupboard and pretended she was on the beach and the light was the sun. The woman handed her a shot of whiskey from a dirty Mason jar.

"Drink this; you'll thank me for it later," she snapped at Ali.

Ali drank the fiery liquid down in one gulp. It burned her throat, and she felt it all the way down.

A disheveled man in dirty clothes and glasses came into the room. "Want another," he asked. "I think I'll have another!" And he drank a large portion down.

Immediately Ali was embarrassed because her lower body was exposed to his view. "Yes," she managed to squeak out. "Who are you?" Ali asked.

"I'm the doc who's gonna solve all your problems, little lady."

Ali was horrified that this dirty, slovenly drunkard was going to perform the abortion on her, but again she realized she had no voice in what was happening. Johnnie arranged everything and obviously had much experience in this realm.

"All righty, let's git this done, shall we?" The man asked to no one in particular. He sat on a stool at the end of the table, looking directly into her private parts. Ali prayed to pass out, but instead she was acutely aware of his every move. She steeled herself against what was about to happen, determined to leave this filthy place as soon as possible. She looked down and could see his greasy black and white hair. There was a breeze from the open window blowing up her bottom. She had never been through any experience so humiliating. James' relentless attacks on her were child's play in comparison.

Her anger dissipating and her courage with it, tears began streaming down Ali's cheeks. "Hail Mary full of grace…" she began. She decided she would say the Rosary as long as the procedure took to keep her mind off what that man was doing. Over and over she recited her "Hail Mary's." She felt the cold prongs of metal being inserted into her vagina. Horrified, she felt the man's fingers probing her while he pushed down on her belly.

"Well now, you're pretty far along. I'd guess around eight to ten weeks." He turned to the woman and said, "Better give 'er another shot—or two. This ain't gonna be as easy as I thought."

Ali stiffened with fear.

"Now don't be a clampin' down on me, Miss. I ain't yer lover and you'll only make it harder on yerself."

The woman held her head as she poured the cheap whiskey down her throat, burning, and then another shot immediately. Ali could already feel the somewhat sedating effect of it. But not enough.

"More. Please," Ali said.

The woman obliged giving her one final full shot. "Thata girl; just ease up there and we'll get that babe out of ye," the man said, not caring how his mention of a "babe" stabbed her heart.

The rough edges of the makeshift speculum he had inserted in her vagina hurt her. She had never experienced any such nightmare in her life. Ali hoped that would be the worst of it. Then the man inserted another instrument and began poking it into her insides and moving it around and scraping her insides. It felt like a hot poker in her, and she moaned in pain, biting her lip to keep from screaming, but it didn't work and a scream escaped.

The man told the woman, "Shut 'er up or she'll have the whole damned police squad down here!"

The assistant roughly shoved a smelly leather strap into her mouth and told her to bite it when it hurt. Just then she felt the man inset his hand into her and tug. Ali mercifully fainted.

The assistant wafted smelling salts under her nose until Ali came to. She coughed and raised her head as far as the restraints would allow and felt a horrible pain in her belly. She looked down and saw that her legs and stomach were covered with blood. The assistant unbuckled the restraints and ordered Ali to sit up. She was wiping Ali's stomach and legs with a wet rag in a feeble attempt to clean the blood off her. She handed Ali the rag.

"Here, finish yerself and get dressed. You need to leave out the back door there as quick as you can."

Ali was pushed roughly into a sitting position, and she nearly fainted again from the pain. Unbearable cramping as she had never experienced even with her menses caused her to vomit into a bucket near the table. She opened her eyes and saw in the bucket a bloody mess and the tiniest form of a developing baby and began sobbing silently. She knew there would be no sympathy anywhere for her, and the gravity of what she had done hit her full force.

Despite her pain, she slid off the table, nearly collapsing under her own weight from the pain and her drunkenness. She saw blood flowing down her leg, and, assuming there were no clean rags in the house, she tore her undergarments and fashioned them into a sort of diaper. She pulled on her skirt and jacket and tried to look as normal as possible. She still had to find her way home to Edy's house.

The woman went to the door, opened it far enough to look both ways, then said to Ali, "No one about. You'll be on yer way now, missy," as she pushed Ali out the door and slammed it shut behind her. She was standing in a dark, putrid alley, rats scurrying for cover. Disoriented, she walked towards the light from the street. Though she had rags packed into her private area to stem the flow, it was heavy, and she felt the sticky wetness of it running down her leg again.

Ali realized she could not possibly walk to Edy's house in this condition, so looked for a hack to take her home. Once she approached the indeterminate border of the District, she hailed a hack sitting across from the park. Giving the driver the address on Lincoln Street, she climbed into the carriage and steadied herself on the hard seat as well as possible. It seemed the driver hit every hole on the cobblestone streets. The five-minute ride felt like an eternity.

The buggy pulled to a stop outside Edy's house, and Ali thanked God that Edy would be out all afternoon helping with the Ladies' Auxiliary, rolling bandages and taking baskets to the poor. By this time, the blood had soaked completely through the rags and her skirt. She was relieved she had chosen to wear a dark brown skirt, though she had no idea it would be for this reason. She quickly paid the driver and stood facing him until he drove off so he wouldn't see her condition.

Ali let herself into the house and went directly upstairs to her room. There was enough water in her pitcher to wash up, but the blood flow was relentless. The chamber pot was nearly full of her blood and she saw large clots. She pushed it under the bed, hoping to empty it before anyone else saw its contents. She positioned several towels on the bed and tripled the rags between her legs. The sooner she laid down the better, she knew and she was a little lightheaded. Normally her soft bed smelling of lavender would be a comfort, but tonight it might as well have been a bed of nails. Every inch of her body felt aflame with searing pain, and she feared she may have a fever. Now, though, she was much too tired to think of that. Tears streamed down her face, and she descended into a deep and troubled sleep within seconds. Ali never regained consciousness.

Chapter 20
Bereft

Edy arrived home about an hour after Ali but avoided the embarrassment of knocking on Ali's door on her way to her room. She knew or suspected from the local gossips that Ali had been at her secret love nest at Tybee Island, and it troubled her deeply. Johnnie Meadows, the "highly regarded banker in Savannah," was in fact a seducer and the ruination of several women. Ali was vulnerable, but she was, after all, a twenty-nine-year-old woman, and there was only so much Edy could do to dissuade her from this disastrous path. At the end of the day, Edy was not her mother. Edy laid on her bed and slept fitfully.

A blood curdling scream startled Edy awake at three o'clock, and she knew it was coming from Ali's room. Not waiting to find her dressing gown, Edy ran to Ali's room where she met Mable, also awakened by the scream, just outside the door.

"What on earth…Oh, dear Jesus, no!" Mabel began as they opened the door. They both stopped, shocked to find Ali shouting and thrashing about in a blood-soaked bed.

"Oh, Ali, Ali, my sweet, what on earth…?" Edy cried.

Edy pulled back the covers on her once white bed to see that Ali was covered in blood from her waist down. Edy was hoping against hope that she would not find what she feared, but when she lifted Ali's night dress to find the source of the blood, she saw that Ali had towels packing her female parts—all soaked through with bright red blood.

"Miss Edy, we need to fetch Doc Anderson right quick! It looks like Miss Ali done got her a 'bortion," Mabel said fearfully. She knew this was illegal, and this looked very bad.

"Yes, Mabel, we do need to fetch Doctor Anderson, but this is not to leave this house to anyone other than the doctor. Do you understand?" Mabel nodded, eyes wide. "I'll do what I can here, but please hurry, Mabel. Please hurry!"

"Yessum, I understand. I'll run as fast as I kin. Miss Edy, try some ice to stop that bleeding," Mabel called as she ran from the room.

Edy attempted to use extra towels and tore up sheets for dressings. She applied ice as Mabel had suggested, but nothing seemed to stop the flow. Ali became combatant, pushing Edy's hands away and yelling, "I'll kill you if you touch me!" Ali hissed at her, "You stay away from me! You cannot have my baby! No one will take my baby!" Ali screamed at her.

"Oh, Ali, Ali, what have you done?" Edy cried. Ali retreated back into her fevered nightmare as Edy placed a cool compress on her forehead.

Ali sobbed in her fever, "I'm so sorry, so sorry, Mama. Johnnie, come back…"

Edy was too frightened to be angry, still doing everything possible to stop the bleeding. She didn't know how much blood Ali had lost, but she was as white as a ghost and growing weaker. All the fight seemed to drain from her with it.

"Ali, darling, do not give up. You must live; you must! It is not your time yet. Please fight, Ali, fight!"

By the time Mabel returned with Doctor Anderson, Ali was quiet. Her fever still raged, but she lay deathly silent. The second nightdress Edy had put on her was now soaked to her breasts in blood. The sheets and towels were saturated. Edy could barely believe a body had that much blood in it. Edy had dared to look at Ali's private parts when changing the towels, and to her horror, it looked as if Ali had been slaughtered like an animal on a butcher's block. Who had done this to her? How could someone do this to a young woman and just leave her to die? Edy, of course, knew of no one who would do such a thing, but she promised herself and Ali she would find the villain and see that he was prosecuted. He murdered a child, and, God forbid, if Ali died before this night was over, he was a double murderer.

"Oh, Doctor Anderson, thank you for coming. I'm afraid she has lost a great deal of blood. I have tried everything, but I cannot stop it."

Edy heard a weak whisper coming from Ali. She pressed her ear close to Ali's mouth to hear. "I want Johnnie," she managed to say. "Please, I need Johnnie."

Edy patted her hand. "I'll find him, my dear; you just rest." Edy knew full well even if she went directly to Johnnie's house with an engraved invitation, Johnnie would not waste one second further on Ali. She was of no use to him anymore and actually quite a liability. If Ali's grandfathers learned of this, they would be inconsolable, and likely Ali had just lost her only child if her private parts were any indication.

Edy knew exactly who had forced Ali into this abortion and who had paid for it as well. *If Ali does not live, I will hunt down Johnnie Meadows and ruin him.* She would be certain Beatrice and the community knew everything. She would make certain whoever butchered her sweet Ali would stand trial and be behind bars for this, and, so far as it was in her power, so would Johnnie Meadows for arranging and paying for these murders. All irresponsible hypocrites—every one of them. It was Johnny Meadows' carelessly sown seed that had brought Ali to this, and she would see to it that Ali would not be the only one to suffer. She felt certain, and the gossips had whispered, this was not the first time he had employed these butchers, and, if nothing was said, it wouldn't be the last. No. She would end this. Yes, let Johnnie come and see what he has done to this precious girl.

Beatrice was not to escape blame for this either. She had long appeared cold and distant from her husband, belittling him in public whenever she saw an opening. Though never spoken of, it was widely thought that women who failed to take care of their husbands' needs had no right to expect them to be celibate and faithful in a loveless marriage. Her social standing be damned! Edy knew Ali would never ever have succumbed to his charms if she hadn't had a solid promise that a wedding was in the near future. She believed all Ali had told her now—that he said he was leaving Beatrice and starting a new life with Ali. And he *knew* about the baby! Oh, how he had used Ali.

Tears flowed down her cheeks as she watched Doctor Anderson examining Ali. She tried to avert her eyes but felt compelled to look so she could later testify if necessary. She would serve as an eyewitness to the butchery.

"Doctor Anderson, will she…w-will Ali…" Edy couldn't bring herself to ask the question on her lips.

"She'll need a long recovery, won't she, Doctor Anderson? I will take excellent care of her until she is on her feet again."

"Mrs. Leonard," he began hesitantly, "If, and I stress *if,* Miss Malone survives the night…"

"Shhh! She might hear you!" Edy snapped.

"Madame, I assure you, she cannot hear nor comprehend a word I am saying. She has a very high fever from sepsis, I suspect. Dirty conditions. Dirty instruments. Half-ass medical skills. I've seen cattle butchered with more skill. She has lapsed into unconsciousness, which is a mercy. Again, if she survives the night, and it is very, very unlikely she will, her recovery will depend a great deal on how she is able to deal with the consequences of her decision to end her child's life. In all likelihood, she will never bear another child. It appears the person who did this to her destroyed all her female organs beyond repair. All we can do now is pray and wait. I have nothing more I can do for her. She has lost two-thirds of her blood volume, and I cannot stem the flow. With the sepsis, Mrs. Leonard, prepare yourself for the worst. This is a damnable situation. Mrs. Leonard, do you have any idea who did this to her or who the father of her baby is?"

Edy wiped her tears on her nightdress and shook her head. "I do not know who did this to her, but I know who will know and who paid for it and who the father is. I will not rest until he is called to account for this terrible tragedy. Your culprit is John Meadows, our fine banker." She nearly spat his name from her mouth.

"Well, my dear, you will have my full support in that endeavor," Doctor Anderson assured her. "Why don't you get some rest now, and I will sit with her. I'll awaken you if there is any change."

"Thank you, Doctor Anderson, but I could not leave her. I want to be here with her. If she indeed is dying, I will not let her transition without me by her side. She is like a daughter to me, and I was charged with her care. I'm afraid I have failed in my duty," Edy admitted as she began to openly weep.

Doctor Anderson patted her shoulder in comfort, knowing no words would abate her grief. Edy sat down on the bed beside Ali and held her hand.

An hour passed and Edy noticed that Ali seemed to have broken her fever. She was much cooler. She was startled to hear an inhuman sound come from her throat and then nothing. She placed her hand on Ali's head. Ali did not move, and Edy detected no breath. She laid her head on Ali's chest trying to hear a heartbeat, but there was none. Edy began to cry now, a hard cry, a mournful wail as a mother grieves for her lifeless child. Ali was dead.

Edy held her rosary and prayed over Ali, then tucked the rosary in her hand just as Ali had done for her own dear Mama.

Doctor Anderson touched Ali's neck just under her chin, checking for a pulse. "Miss Malone has passed. I am deeply sorry for your loss, Mrs. Leonard. I will send a message for the health officer's wagon. There will be a full autopsy and I suspect an investigation by the police into this. Abortion is a crime. Let's hope these butchers will be apprehended."

Tears flowed down Edy's cheeks, but determination was set on her face. "Anything, anything at all that I can do to assist in their apprehension, Doctor Anderson, please let me know. I promised Ali I would find her butchers, and I intend to keep that promise."

Doctor Anderson patted Edy on the shoulder, replaced his instruments in his black leather call bag, and went downstairs to await the coroner. He felt a heaviness in his chest, his heart today. *Such a cruel and unnecessary death—and so young—her whole life in front of her.* Doctor Anderson was sickened in spirit and even more determined to find Ali's abortionists. He was repulsed seeing this happen to young girls in the community. He would do all in his power to put an end to it and see the perpetrators imprisoned.

Chapter 21
Indictments

D r. Anderson met the coroner at the door when he arrived and handed him the Certificate of Death.

Certificate of Death

Sept 25, 1906

Name: Allison E. T. Malone

Aged: 29 years 1 months 3 days

Sex: Female **Race:** White. **Nativity:** No Ca

Single: Yes. **Married:__Widowed:__**

Occupation: Accounting Clerk

Date of Death: September 24, 1906

Died at: 142 Lincoln St

Cause of Death: Heart Failure due to Septic Peritonitis and Puerpetal Septicaemia, the result of a criminal abortion.

Duration of Disease: Only seen date of Death

Place of Burial: Wilmington, NC

Name of Undertaker: Sullivan's Mortuary

Attending Physician: E. H. Anderson, MD

"And you are certain of this, Doctor Anderson? If so and for the sake of Mrs. Leonard, we can keep this out of the papers."

"Absolutely I am certain of the cause, and you are absolutely not to cover up the reason for her death. Mrs. Leonard is in complete agreement with me that the murderers who did this to Miss Malone need to be brought to justice with all the severity the legal system will allow in their judgment. You are free to release the cause of death to the *Morning News*.

Speaking of the murderers, Mr. Brunner, Mrs. Leonard believes she knows the father of the child and suspects he is the same man who suggested and paid for the abortion. If pressed and to avoid any undue attention that might tarnish his reputation, such as it is, I believe he will provide the names and addresses of the abortionists."

"Thank you, Doctor Anderson, and you, Mrs. Leonard. I am very sorry for your loss and will do my best to bring indictments against these criminals."

"Thank you, Mr. Brunner. I am available to you at any time if I may assist you in bringing about their arrests. I know Ali kept a journal, and perhaps it will have some answers or corroboration in what I have told Doctor Anderson regarding John Meadows," Edy spat out his name as she said it. She loathed John Meadows and the way he had so smoothly insinuated himself into Ali's life, made her fall in love with him, toyed with her at her most vulnerable time. He promised her the sun and the moon and the stars only to yank them right out from under her when he realized she was pregnant with his child. *You will pay for this, John Meadows.*

If it takes me to my dying breath, I will see you pay for what you have done to my Ali.

Mr. Brunner motioned to a man standing just outside the bedroom door. He coughed, still uncomfortable with the situation. "Perhaps, Mrs. Leonard, you would be kind enough to make a cup of tea for me?"

"Yes, of course, Mr. Brunner, right away," and Edy turned to leave the room, then turned back, "Mr. Brunner, please, be gentle with her. She is so precious to me."

"Do not worry, Mrs. Leonard. We will treat her with the utmost respect and gentleness."

Edy left the room to prepare tea for both Doctor Anderson and the health officer. Mr. Brunner's assistants entered after Edy had descended the stairs so as not to upset her. They were accustomed to handling these delicate affairs, and this was certainly a particularly delicate situation. Ali's body was wrapped with the sheets from her bed and moved to the stretcher after the men did the best they could to wipe the blood from her body. They covered her with a heavy dark blanket and began carrying her downstairs just as Edy was coming into the foyer to take the men their tea.

"Oh, oh. Oh no," Edy whispered and turned her head so she couldn't see Ali's body being removed from her home— their home. *Ali, Ali, my darling child. How I shall miss you!* And again the tears slid down her cheeks. She dabbed at them with a delicate lace handkerchief but to little avail. It was already soaked through. She looked down absent-mindedly. It had Ali's blood spattered on it in several places. Edy knew she would never wash it or try to remove that precious spilt blood. It would be a reminder to her of what John Meadows stole from her. She would not forget it, and she would not allow him to forget. He may not be sent to prison, but she would erect invisible bars around him so that he would not live a comfortable life while her dear Ali lay cold and dead. *It's all so unfair!*

Edy walked into the parlor where she and Ali had laughed and chatted while playing card games or talking about her life and work. She unconsciously smoothed out the chintz on the sofa, waiting for Doctor Anderson. Speaking to Able's portrait, she silently asked him to watch over Ali.

After several minutes, Doctor Anderson entered the parlor, worn and wearied. Edy warmed his cup of tea and sat silently for what seemed like an hour, though it was only minutes.

"Doctor Anderson, thank you for coming tonight, for all you did in an attempt to save Ali's life. I…I'm sorry the circumstances were so base. I know you had no desire to be involved in such a sordid affair." Doctor Anderson held his hand up to stop Edy, but she continued. "Ali was such a sweet, kind girl. I know this must be hard for you to believe. She was led astray and into John Meadows' debauched scheme.

I normally don't believe gossip when I haven't witnessed the behavior firsthand. What has happened to Ali has confirmed to me that all I have heard of John Meadows is absolutely true. I am not a vindictive woman, and God forgive me, but Meadows must pay for what he did to this precious girl. Do you know he actually told her he was going to leave his wife and marry her before the end of the year? When he learned of the baby well, you see the result. He paid for and sent her into the hands of those butchers! He murdered his own child. And he murdered mine.

Now it is time for him to face his dirty little secrets, and, if I have anything to do with it and if God is just, he will live out his life in misery—in or out of prison. Please keep me informed and let me know what I may do to assist in the prosecution of these murderers."

Doctor Anderson finished his tea and placed the china cup and saucer on the side table. He stood to take his leave. "Mrs. Leonard, again please accept my deepest sympathy. I am quite certain your Ali was a lovely young woman, and I am saddened this has happened to her. Such a horror. You may be assured I will do my utmost to follow this gruesome and bloody trail to its end. Now I must go to the health officer's office to begin the paperwork for the investigation. I have left a sedative on the bedside table upstairs for you in the event you need it. Please try to get some rest. This has been very traumatic for you."

Edy thanked him and walked him to the door. She shut it behind him and leaned for several minutes against its strong wooden frame, trying to grasp all that had happened. As she began to cry, she collapsed to the floor, sobbing as she hadn't since Hannah passed. This hurt no less. Mabel came down the stairs, stooped, and took Edy by the arms and helped her up, leading her upstairs to rest. Mabel thoughtfully had closed the door of Ali and Hannah's room, but not before she had tidied the place, cleaned up the bed, and put the bloodied towels in the washing basin to soak. She wasn't sure she could get out all the blood and had changed the water several times in the first couple of minutes. Edy didn't need to see it or relive it. She needed rest.

Edy allowed Mable to lead her and tuck her into bed as a child would. She had none of her own strength left to even hold her head up. She must have been asleep by the time her head touched her pillow.

Edy slept from that early morning until early afternoon. When she awoke, she found herself disoriented, not because of where she was but because something wasn't right. It was then that the events of the early morning came crashing back and with them the sorrow. There were no tears now. She was nearly afraid she had cried out all the tears of her life. Able. Hannah. Jo. Now Ali. All of her loved ones gone. How alone she felt. She had been accustomed to being alone until Ali came to live with her. Now she felt wholly bereft of family.

She sat on the side of her bed with a strong determination to assure that John Meadows knew the same sorrow. The loss of family. Surely Beatrice would not be so silly as to stay with him now. Edy hoped she would have the courage to leave and take his children with her. It would require more pride or greed than Edy could imagine to stay with him once all was exposed. And it would be exposed; she would see to that. Her first action would be to go to the cathedral and have a conversation with the bishop.

Edy's conversation with the bishop proved fruitless. It seemed that Johnnie made rather large donations to the church and, in particular, the Priests' Retirement Fund.

She realized the bishop was not likely to bite the hand that would eventually feed him. He assured Edy that he would have a serious conversation with Johnnie.

"Will he be excommunicated, Bishop?" Edy could not imagine that she would have to sit in the same mass with the murderer of her dear Ali.

The bishop was unwilling to commit to excommunication. "Mrs. Leonard, surely you understand that we cannot excommunicate Mr. Meadows simply on hearsay. Surely it would be extremely difficult to prove that he was the father of Miss Malone's baby and further that he was responsible for the abortion."

"Bishop, I have her diary which details her relationship with Mr. Meadows that I happily shall make available to you, and if the Savannah Police feel certain enough to arrest him for murder and throw him in jail, the evidence is compelling enough for the Church to excommunicate him!"

The bishop patted Edy's hand and asked her to pray the Rosary and ask for forgiveness for gossiping and making unfounded accusations, and to not seek retribution as that was in God's hands.

"I certainly will not ask for forgiveness, Bishop, because I am as certain as the police that he murdered my Ali and her child. Your reluctance to treat this seriously is appalling to me. I suggest *you* pray the Rosary and ask for forgiveness for your blindness."

The bishop was stunned to silence, and Edy took advantage of his lapse and quickly left rather than face the possibility of her own excommunication.

Chapter 22
The Wages of Sin

The day after her death the *Savannah Morning News* was awash with preliminary details of the crime. The headlines read, "Alleged Crime Was Unearthed," and discussed Ali's death and Doctor Anderson's subsequent report to the health officer, Mr. Brunner. The article stated that given the circumstances of Ali's death, Mr. Brunner initiated an investigation. He submitted his findings to Savannah Police Detective Murphy, which were compelling enough to warrant the subsequent arrest of three people for assault with intent to murder. The three included John Meadows, a Doctor Smyth, though his title as doctor was in question, and a midwife by the name of Lizzie Spinner.

Much to Edy's disgust, John Meadows was released on bail of $1,000, posted by his wife, Mrs. Beatrice Meadows. The "doctor" was also able to make bail, but Miss Spinner remained incarcerated. Edy was shocked that Beatrice would stoop to bail Johnnie out, but she suspected it was more a matter of preserving her lifestyle than love. Edy felt certain Johnnie might well have preferred staying in jail than coming home to the wrath that surely awaited him.

After visiting the bishop, Edy's next stop was the bank as she assumed Johnnie would not miss work and risk having people think he truly was a womanizer and murderer. As she approached the bank's doors, she took a second to gather her wits, take a deep breath, and picture Ali lying on that bed of white in a nightdress soaked with bright red blood to her neck. She realized this was not a matter of "if" she could do this. It was a matter of not being able to live with herself if she did not confront John Meadows.

Edy realized that ever getting any kind of satisfaction or apology from John Meadows or even an acknowledgement of his role in her death would be impossible. He could see no fault in himself. He placed himself above others, wiser and cleverer than most, worthier than those of lower status. Ali was merely a toy for him to pull down and play with when he felt the urge and when she became inconvenient, he cruelly tossed her aside.

She was certain he had not consciously intended for Ali to die, but this had become an extreme embarrassment and inconvenience for him. Rather than a murderous intent, John Meadows simply did not give a damn what happened to Ali nor to their child. Though he and the Bishop it would appear, placed himself at the top of society, he was nothing more than a fraud and the lowest of the low. He was not fit to breathe the same air as Ali.

The Pinkerton agent opened the door for her, and she walked into the main lobby. She knew enough from Ali's description of her office that she worked up the ornate staircase in the glass-walled area, where John Meadow's office sat separately to the side. With a determined air as if she had been here many times on bank business, she walked up the stairs, through the accounting office without looking at Ali's empty desk, and straight into John Meadow's office without first knocking on the closed door.

He was sitting behind his impressive desk at least pretending to work on a stack of papers, but Edy suspected he was bluffing. He looked up to see her and was caught off guard by her presence. "How—who gave you permission to come directly to my office, Mrs. Leonard? You must leave at once. I am not having this conversation with you today."

He rose to escort her to the stairs, but Edy blocked the door. He would listen to her.

"No need for conversation, Mr. Meadows. I have come with a message for you. You will sit down and listen to what I have to say because I am certain you would not like any more of a scene than your arrest has already caused. You would not like to hear me proclaim to all within earshot that you are nothing but a filthy, arrogant, philandering murderer of no conscience."

"It appears you have me at a disadvantage, Mrs. Leonard, so please say what you came here to say and then leave. And don't come back."

"My Ali was a fine, innocent, kind, and loving girl when she came here at a very vulnerable moment in her life. She had just lost her mother and was in need of love and care.

"You swooped in and swept her off her feet with your romantic gestures and offers of marriage. She was quite dazzled by you. I'm sure you are aware of this as much as I am sure you intentionally used this to your advantage.

"Ali was a virgin until she met you—a married man with children who had no intention of ever marrying her no matter the lies you told her. I tried to tell her this, but she was gullible and believed your fairytales. You took her virtue without thought of the impact it would have on her. Without a thought of consequences. Without a thought for her reputation and future. Ali desperately wanted to be loved and have a husband and children—many children.

"Even if Ali had lived through your despicable actions, the horrible murder of your child, she could have *never* borne children. The butchers you employed so completely destroyed her female organs they were unrecognizable. They looked like mincemeat. Raw. Torn. Gashed. Bloody. Defiled. Destroyed. You, John Meadows, *you* destroyed and defiled that innocent and precious young woman. You took her dignity, her love, her future, her reputation—her life.

"I make this vow to you now, John Meadows—I will not rest until I see your life ruined because of what you did to my Ali. I want you in prison and I will testify and use Ali's own words from her journal—oh, yes, she wrote all about you—your lovemaking, your promises, and your deceit. I will make certain to enlighten the public, as well as your wife and children if they are seemingly unaware at this point what kind of a man you are—a liar and a murderer, completely bereft of conscience, integrity, and honor. You will be fortunate if you are allowed to leave Savannah without being tarred and feathered. Even that would be too good for the likes of you.

"I intend to speak with Mr. Woodworth to inform him of Ali's murder and your hand in planning and paying for it after impregnating her with your child.

"I've already met with the bishop, but he seems to be enamored of your weekly contributions. I will go above his head, and I will not stop until you are excommunicated by the Pope himself if needs be.

"I will go to the newspaper and publish Ali's journal if I must so the Savannah society knows all about their esteemed John Meadows. I will attend every garden club and book circle until Beatrice would not dare show her face in society again. Hopefully she will see the kind of man she is married to and divorce you and take your children and her daddy's money with her.

"Because you murdered Ali just as if you stuck a knife in her yourself, and I will not rest until you live the rest of your life without so much as a dime to your name, a friend to console you, a family to love you, or your freedom. Any comfort or privilege you have enjoyed up to this day will be gone when I finish. Your charmed existence ended when you sent my Ali to that back-alley butcher and not only murdered your child but Ali herself.

"Mr. Meadows, I hope you live a very, very long life and that every time you look in a mirror, you see Ali's dead face. I hope with every morsel of food you eat you remember Ali never again will taste. I hope whenever you hear music, you remember that Ali never will dance again. When you experience any comfort, which I predict you won't from this day on, I hope you see a bloody and butchered Ali, stone cold and alone in death.

"More than anything else, I pray that God turns his back on you and denies you peace and forgiveness even if the bishop hasn't the backbone to do so. I hope you experience the same feeling of being lost that Ali experienced on that butcher's—*your* butcher's—table as she awaited having *your* child savagely cut from her body."

Before Johnnie could answer, and Edy could tell he was only half listening while he composed his rebuttal in his mind, she exited as quickly as she had arrived. He was left gobsmacked. She would speak with Mr. Woodworth once the entire investigation and trial were completed.

Edy also delayed going to the newspapers because the police were holding Ali's journal presently. It was evidence for the trial.

Doctor Anderson had upheld his promise to testify what he had found when he treated Ali. He would be called upon for the trial as well, but he had secured the indictments and she was thankful to him.

Edy's final tribute to Ali would involve seeking out the Suffragettes and working on Ali's behalf to have the law changed so that women never again had to resort to back alley abortions. She knew the church would have a difficult time reconciling her choice to promote legal and safe abortions and birth control without a husband's permission, but surely they could see the need if a mother's life was in jeopardy or a young girl fell victim to a devious man such as Johnnie, resulting in pregnancy. She would never sanction an abortion as birth control, and from what she had read in some British medical literature, most abortions were requested by married women! She could not condone this ever. She was near certain the church would not agree with her logic or even listen to it. Perhaps she would have to work "underground" as her faith was dear to her. If she were found out, she wouldn't be surprised if she were excommunicated before Johnnie Meadows. *Ha! Wasn't that an irony?*

Edy hoped Ali would be proud of her. She wasn't one for causes, but this was more than a cause. It was a crusade for the rights of women to have safe, clean, available medical care without judgment. She wanted to vote for Ali. She wanted to control her estate for Ali, which she wouldn't have been able to do as a single woman. Very simply, Edy would spend the rest of her life fighting for equal treatment for women under the law. It might be a long way off in the future, but she would lend her voice on behalf of Ali. How she wished she could be doing the work with Jo, Ali, and Hannah at her side, but she could at least do it in tribute to each of these precious women she had loved so dearly.

Chapter 23
Justice Denied

If Edy had expected swift and harsh punishment for Johnnie, she was to be sorely disappointed. According to the *Morning News*, there was "suspicion" that Ali had been the victim of a "criminal operation," based on the autopsy, and the coroner's inquest would be held the next afternoon at four o'clock. Subpoenas were issued for several witnesses and any evidence presented at the original indictment hearing. Readers were warned of the salacious and gruesome nature of the exhibits as well as the news articles based on the inquest.

Coroner Keller placed Mr. Brunner in charge of the inquest after his investigation along with the autopsy and suspicious death certificate indicated criminal activity. Mr. Brunner stated that the evidence he intended to present would be clearly evident to the layman's eye that this was a criminal operation. He did not anticipate further arrests at that time.

At the inquest, the defendants' attorneys had prohibited their clients from taking the witness stand. As a result, the jury was unable to hear the facts that the coroner may have relied upon to affix their guilt. After a short deliberation, the jury found that Ali died as a result of a "criminal operation performed by an unknown person."

One of the attorneys had argued a point of law that he claimed made the inquest without warrant of law. He read a portion of the law which revealed that an inquest could not be held without the presence of the body or without having the corpse within easy access to the jury. He argued that Ali's body was now out of the jurisdiction of the coroner as it had already been transported by train to Wilmington, North Carolina, the week before.

The State's solicitor disagreed with the attorney, but the attorney presented more law that pointed out that inquests were held to determine the cause for issuing warrants, and warrants had already been issued in this case. The statute was sustained and, when John Meadows was called to the stand, his attorney invoked this statute. The other defendants, the "doctor" and the "midwife," used the same defense so as not to be compelled to testify.

A crowded courtroom was disappointed at not being able to hear from the defendants, but it was assumed even without this defense the defendants would not incriminate themselves. The crowd was appeased somewhat due to the gruesome and horrific evidence that included parts of Ali's anatomy which the coroner had removed during the autopsy to preserve for the inquest. These body parts were used by the physicians to illustrate the damage sustained by Ali during the illegal abortion as well as the cause of death. It was reported that the cause of death would be evident to the most untrained eye.

Detective Murphy testified that his investigation indicated that Ali's appointment with death was made by John Meadows, who had prior experience with the house of ill repute where the abortions were carried out. He further testified to the unsanitary conditions and crude instruments used for illegal abortions.

He provided evidence from medical journals, which any physician would have access to, that because of the work of Doctors Pasteur and Lister, it was proven that most deaths in childbirth or abortions were the direct result of unsanitary conditions, lack of hand-washing, lack of clean surgical gowns, and lack of the use of sterilization and disinfectants. He opined that Ali "didn't stand a chance in that hovel under those circumstances."

It was pointed out that even being fully aware of the abysmal conditions of this establishment, Mr. Meadows secured the appointment, paid for it, compelled Ali to go there, and neglected to provide medical help to her or even a hack to take her home afterwards, and in fact, he absented himself from Savannah during the procedure.

During Mr. Brunner's testimony, he indicated he knew of only five doctors in all of Savannah who would do a thing of this kind. He said, "One of these five has done this to Miss Malone, and my investigation has led to that man sitting there," and he pointed to the defendant's table. The coroner had determined that the operation was more than likely performed by a doctor due to the manner in which the abortion was performed.

He further commented that "heart failure," which was originally on the death certificate presented to him by Dr. Anderson, seemed suspicious to him due to the general overall health of the victim. Upon questioning Dr. Anderson further, the death certificate was amended to "criminal operation."

The inquest reached no further findings, and the defendants were still out on bond. It was surmised that the case would now go before a grand jury and be remanded to the District Court of Savannah. There would surely be another large crowd for the trial due to the morbid curiosity in the case. The prurient interest in the community however, dissipated after Ali's organs were put into evidence in court. Everyone knew the rest would be procedural and uninteresting.

Ultimately, John Meadows was never brought to justice for the murder of Ali. There was some discussion that manslaughter charges might be brought against him, but nothing came of it. The appropriate strings were pulled, money pressed into eager palms, and under the table agreements made.

He received an insignificant hand slap, a small fine, and the case was swept under the rug. The scandal did cost him his position with the bank, and he ended up selling groceries. By this time, Beatrice had indeed taken their children and moved back to her parents' mansion, where she lived out her life in obscurity. The damage to her reputation due to Johnnie's arrest and subsequent news of his affairs and having used the abortionist on several prior occasions ruined all prospects Beatrice had of re-entering society.

The Catholic church eventually excommunicated Johnnie after the divorce, primarily because of Edy's letters to the cardinal and the Pope. Her work on behalf of women's rights and in particular the access to legal and safe abortions and contraceptives caused her excommunication as well. She was tireless in her personal crusade until her death and decided she would allow God to sort it out when she met Him in Heaven.

Before Ali left home on that fateful day that was to be her last, she must have had a deep foreboding about what was to come. Edy found a letter in an envelope addressed to Johnnie. While on one hand it disgusted her that her dying thoughts were of her eventual murderer, Edy knew Ali well enough that she would have written in love to him. Remembering her catechism, she intended to pass the letter on to Johnnie as part of the principle that loving your enemy by doing good for him was akin to heaping hot coals on his head. She would not violate Ali's privacy even in death by reading the letter. She knew this was why Ali entrusted her with its delivery.

Just after the inquest and without any hesitation, Edy chose to deliver the letter directly into Johnnie's hands—at his residence—and hopefully Beatrice would witness the exchange. She walked up the brick walkway to the large, ornate door to their impressive home and knocked with determination.

A servant opened the door to her. "I am Mrs. Edyth Leonard here to deliver a letter into Mr. Meadow's hands from Allison Malone. Please inform him," Edy pushed.

As she suspected this message not only quickly brought Johnnie to the door but Beatrice trailing not far behind.

"Mr. Meadows. Beatrice. I am here to fulfill Ali's dying request, which was for you to have this letter. Though I would want you to have no solace whatsoever after what you did to Ali, I have respected her privacy and respected her request to deliver this to you. I cannot do otherwise, but I cannot do so without the hope that it will bring you to your knees in anguish and humble repentance for what you did to my dear Ali. As surely as if you had picked up a knife and stabbed her, you murdered her. God forgive you, for I certainly never shall."

She placed the envelope in his hand and walked back to the waiting hack. She heard Beatrice's shrill voice call loudly after her, "If you dare come near our home or family again, we will have the sheriff prosecute you for threatening us! Stay away from us! Johnnie was not convicted!"

Johnnie simply stood in the open doorway, silent, looking down at the envelope in his hand. He saw Ali's beautiful script on it. "Johnnie" was all it said.

Having finished her tirade against Edy, Beatrice turned to Johnnie and demanded, "Well, let's just see what the little trollop had to say," and she reached to snatch the letter from Johnnie's grasp.

"No! Beatrice stop! As the envelope states, it is addressed to only me, and I too will honor Ali's final words by keeping the contents private. This is, was, between Ali and me. I have no intention now or ever of sharing it with you. You have already had more than your pound of flesh from me, and Ali deserves much better than she received. I will not harm her further. I am going to my study and I do not wish to be disturbed. Do you understand, Beatrice?"

"Well," huffed Beatrice in indignation, "I nev…"

Before she could say more, Johnnie held his hand up in front of her face and commanded Beatrice to remain silent. "If you know what is good for you, you will never speak to me of Ali again. Do not even let her name rest on your lips," he said in an unnatural calm.

Beatrice took a step back and turned to resume her packing, having seen this brewing rage in him before.

"It is over, Beatrice. This is the final word and it is not for your eyes. I suggest you be thankful for this life," he added as he swept his arm to indicate their lavish home and their children in the next room. "All you have ever wanted, could ever want, and certainly more than either of us deserve. Let this go or I will go. If I go, you will see a substantial decline in your social standing in this community."

He turned and climbed the stairs to his study. Beatrice uttered not a sound but stood mouth agape, still in mid-sentence, not daring to make another sound.

Johnnie closed the door to his study and leaned against it, fighting off the emotions that threatened to overtake him. To date, he had not shed one tear over Ali's death nor that of his unborn child. He had been far too busy trying to shore up his shaky position at the bank and defending himself in court. His defense? Denial. That was all. Just denial of everything—his relationship with Ali, his finding and paying for the abortion, then compelling her to go. None of it sat well within him. He did it out of self-preservation, but damn it, Ali had meant something to him.

Johnnie first received the news of Ali's death the next day when Edy showed up at the bank. He knew that she had not come into work those past two mornings but assumed it was because she was recovering from the abortion. That same afternoon, he received the further distressful visit from Mr. Brunner accompanied by two police officers. In handcuffs, he was led in disgrace from the bank.

Now, in the quiet of his study, he wept the tears he could not when he was told Ali had died because of his actions. *I did warn her of the possible disastrous consequences before I bedded her though.* No, these tears were not because Ali had died; they were for his forever-altered life as a result. She was an adult and made her own decision. He could have walked away with his pride intact even if she had refused him. *I wish she had walked away! Damn you, Ali! You have ruined my life—just because of your foolish fantasies! I told you I would never leave Beatrice.*

Dear God, how he wanted to leave Beatrice—many times! And now here he was, constantly listening to Beatrice tell him all the ways he had been a disappointment to her as well as their children. How he had disgraced himself by being let go from the bank. By being arrested, jailed, and tried in court. That he was a failure just as her daddy had warned he would be. It was relentless and he was weary of listening. She would soon be back with her daddy though which was a relief to him.

Johnnie walked to the overstuffed chair next to the fireplace where a fire was burning to warm the room. It was now into fall and there was a nip in the air. Even with the fire, he felt a chill and rising panic go through him. He sat in the chair and looked down at the envelope. As if trying to invoke the saints of his youth, he whispered a prayer, "Lord, I am not worthy that you should enter under my roof. Only say the word and my soul shall be healed." He crossed himself, then slipped his finger under the flap of the envelope, pulled out the folded letter.

Pressed dried wisteria petals spilt from the envelope into his lap. He knew instantly they were from the first day he had taken Ali to the Tybee cottage—that magical day he had captured her heart and her virginity. Was it guilt he was feeling or regret at being caught? He couldn't say. Whatever it was, he disliked it immensely. He was a man accustomed to walking away from discussions that made him uncomfortable. But how could he walk away from himself? He read her words, again haunted by just the recognition of her handwriting.

My Darling Johnnie,

As I write this, I am preparing to leave for work and later to go to the place you have chosen to kill our child. Every fiber of my being is revolting at this choice. I ask myself why I am doing this. Couldn't I raise our child alone? We both know this would never be possible. Not only would the wrath of the Catholic Church descend upon my head and our child's but society's as well. My acceptance into polite society would be ruined, and I would, therefore, never be marriageable to any gentleman of quality.

Our child would suffer; he would be labeled a bastard. He would never know who his father is and would spend the rest of his life wondering why he didn't have a daddy and he would feel abandoned. I have felt that all my life, and I will not bring that down upon my own child.

You have taken the choice from me, from our baby. So I will go to this terrible place today. I will do as you have forced me to do. I will become a murderess. And I will have to live the rest of my life knowing I have committed this horrible sin against God and my own child. That is my punishment. I will deserve every second of this sentence. God forgive me for what I am about to do.

I loved you, Johnnie, to the depths of my soul, and I would have loved this child I am still carrying. Now, I wish I had never met you. I wish I had not allowed myself to fall under your spell. I know now that you never loved me; you couldn't and compel me to do this. I was a fool and my foolishness has caused the death of an innocent child.

I will not be coming back to work after this. I will never see you, speak to you, or allow myself to think of you again. Because of you, I have ruined two lives.

Go back to Beatrice and your children. Live a long life. Never forget what you have done this day. God forgive you. I cannot.

With deepest regrets,

Ali

Epilogue
A Better Place

Suddenly a warm peace settled on Ali. Dr. Anderson and Edy noticed a dramatic change in her as she drew her final breath. There was a smile on her face, and they heard her last whisper, "Oh, Mama…lovely."

"I've never seen her so beautiful and peaceful—happy, Doctor. Anderson. Do you suppose she is…in Heaven? Yes, she must be with her mother, dear papa, and her child," Edy nearly whispered. This vision was indelibly painted in her mind from that moment on and she clung to this comforting hope.

The night after Ali's death Edy dreamt vividly, and she saw Ali in Heaven. Ali wondered if she were dreaming. All around her was pristine white. Could this be real? At that moment, someone placed his hands under her arms and seemed to pull her up and up through circles of clouds, like smoke rings. When she arrived at the white place, she was held in the arms of someone in the whitest robe she had ever seen.

"Oh no! Don't hold me close to your beautiful robe," Ali cried. "I am so dirty—and the blood—I will cause a stain on you." Ali felt ashamed of something, but she couldn't remember what.

In a soft voice, he replied, "My child, you are not unclean! Look at yourself! You are just as I am, pure."

She hesitantly looked down to find she was indeed wearing the purest white robe—so bright it almost shone in the sunlight. But how could that be?

"Who, who are you?" Ali asked timidly.

"I am the Archangel Michael. You prayed for my protection as a child. You are with us now, my child, in God's Heaven."

Ali looked around and in the distance, shrouded by clouds, Ali felt certain she had just seen her mother holding something in her arms and smiling beautifully as she did when she was well. Ali was too far from her to make out what it was she was holding, but whatever it was, it was making Mama happy, and she laughed! *Oh, what a beautiful sound,* Ali thought, *to hear Mama's musical laughter again!*

Ali was so thrilled to see her and called out to her. "Wait for me, Mama! I'm coming!" As Ali and her mother grew closer to one another, Ali could see she was holding a tiny baby. Whose baby could it be?

"Oh, Mama, Mama! How I have longed to see you again! I have missed you every second we have been apart."

Jo smiled, overjoyed to see her precious daughter once again. "I've waited for you, my sweet Ali, and so has this little one. He has only recently arrived, but I could see he had your eyes and smile," she said looking down at the baby in her arms.

Not understanding, Ali said, "But whose baby is this, Mama?" She caressed his tiny pink hand, and he gripped her finger as he smiled brightly up at her. Ali immediately felt a strong connection with the child and looked up at her mother, a questioning expression on her face. Her heart seemed to skip a beat as she gazed at the babe, and a longing pulled at her. Ali wanted to take him into her own arms.

"Mama, may I?"

With this, Jo gently placed the baby in Ali's arms.

Jo explained, "This is your child, Ali. He has been waiting with your papa and me for you to come to us."

Ali didn't fully understand, but something in her soul stirred and their hearts were joined. "Oh, Mama, he *is* mine, isn't he? He is so perfectly lovely, so precious. And, Mama, you are *happy*!"

From out of the clouds, a handsome young man approached and stood behind Jo. "I am happy, Ali. Now I have my precious Robert with me. This is your dear papa, Ali. We are together finally, and we are so thrilled that you and your child are here with us at last. Our family is all together now.

There is no more pain here, no sorrow, no tears, only joy. You will come to understand more in time, and we have all the time in the Universe now, for there is no time here, only forever."

With that, Ali felt a peace spread through her that truly passed all understanding, and she realized she was home at last. She did not question this realm again. She was here with her dear mama, her true and loving papa, holding her precious baby boy, and she was *happy.*

Edy awoke early at sunrise. A sunrise she wouldn't share with Ali. Instead, she was gathering the few things she needed to accompany Ali home on the train. She remembered the day she met Ali in the station on her first day in Savannah. What joy she felt having a new "daughter" to love. She hadn't been able to protect her, but she would do whatever she could to help other young women who found themselves in Ali's condition.

Her Grandfathers Thayer and Malone had mutually decided to disinter Robert Malone from the family mausoleum as well as Josephine from the Davies mausoleum and inter them together with Ali at the Thayer planation outside of Wilmington in the family cemetery. Both felt this was only right. They had not been allowed to live together as a family in life; they would have this privilege in death. Edy was comforted with this arrangement.

She had seen to the process of having Ali's body prepared to return home to Wilmington. She ordered Ali's southern pine coffin from Able's store, and she would accompany Ali to Wilmington for the funeral mass led by Father Maloney. This was one journey she would not allow Ali to take alone.

A notice had been placed in the *Wilmington News* without mention of the circumstances of Ali's death other than illness. The article did include a few statements to make attentive readers question the death. The most shocking part of the article, however, was the statement the grandfathers had mutually agreed upon and submitted.

Allison Thayer Malone (Davies), formerly of Wilmington, North Carolina, has gone to her home in Heaven, September 24, 1906, after a brief illness in her new home of Savannah. The remains will be returned to Wilmington where she will be interred alongside her mother, Mrs. Josephine Thayer (Davies), and her father, Robert Malone, Jr., who passed prior to her birth. Interment will be at the family cemetery on the Thayer plantation near Castle Hayne. The mass will be officiated by Father Maloney of the Basilica Shrine of Saint Mary. She is survived by her grandfathers, Colonel Robert Malone Sr. and General Forrest Thayer, and her second cousin Mrs. Edyth Thayer Leonard of Savannah. It is reported Miss Malone had adopted the name of her natural father as her own while living in Georgia. No further information is available at this time regarding the cause of death. The funeral will be a private affair, and the family requests privacy during this difficult time.

As four porters brought Ali's coffin onto the train platform to make the final journey to Wilmington, Edy placed her gloved hand atop it and whispered her last farewell. She silently prayed that her nightly dream since Ali's death was now coming true, that she was at this moment swathed in the warmth of her loving family in her eternal home. *Godspeed darling girl, Godspeed.*

Acknowledgment

This book would not have been possible without the love, support, generosity, and kindness of several very special people in my life and include the following.

My precious sons, Trevor, Nathan, Matthew, and Devon Tuttle. Never has a mother been so blessed to have four sons. You are my heart, boys. Thank you for your patience and for making me feel as if I could do anything. You aren't just part of me, you are the very best of me.

My beautiful granddaughter, Mackinnley Tuttle. My prayer is that you will never face the decisions of Ali Malone, and you will pick up the torch and fight the fight for equality for women.

Lucille Daniels, my precious mom, who loved me completely and among many gifts, gave me the joy of reading.

Edwin Daniels, my dad. A good and strong man who instilled in me that "nothing is impossible, the impossible just takes a little longer."

Dan and Jack Daniels, my big brothers who have had my back when times were tough and share my memories of home.

Jack's wife and my sister-in-law Janie Kempner Daniels, my eighth grade English teacher, who gave me a rock-solid foundation in grammar.

Ron Thompson, my dear friend, for his abiding presence in my life, pulling me back from the ledge when at times I'm sure he'd rather let go.

Ron Fields, a once-in-a-lifetime constant source of love, friendship, encouragement, support, and mentorship for many years.

Nita Phillips who shared with me her great aunt's life story that inspired me to write this book.

My dear friend and mentor L. Diana Henderson, writer, editor, and graphic designer at Realization Press, Convey Media Group and Creativetype (*http://creativetype.biz*; *https://grandfatherpoplar.com*).

Diana's husband and my dear friend and mentor Drew Becker, author, publisher, seminar leader, and wizard of media & marketing at Realization Press (*http://realizationpress.com*).

There would be no book without either of these very special and talented people. My deepest gratitude for your encouragement, support, knowledge, and mentorship. Through her kind comments and expert guidance, Diana has encouraged me to write my stories and share them. Someday, Diana will break my comma obsession forever.

My respect, gratitude, and love to my son Devon Tuttle for his skillful and creative cover design that perfectly captures the haunting temper of this story, and for traveling to Savannah for authenticity in his beautiful photographs. (Devon Tuttle @Tuttle_Recall; Tuttle.Recall@gmail.com)

About the Author

The author grew up with her four brothers on an idyllic small farm in the verdant rolling hills of Ohio. Ms. Daniels knew from an early age that her destiny was to become a writer. She was introduced to journalism in high school and was spurred on by Woodward and Bernstein's investigative reporting of Watergate for the Washington Post, to study journalism at Brookhaven College in Dallas, TX and at the University of South Carolina, Columbia, SC, where she earned a BA in Journalism.

As the single mom for four young sons, Ms. Daniels continued her education and earned a Master of International Studies degree at North Carolina State University. Russian history and culture is an area of particular interest for the author, and her Masters specialization focused on the country, culture, language, and people of Russia and the former Soviet State of Belarus in the aftermath of the Chernobyl disaster. Ms. Daniels was honored with an invitation to serve for a semester as a guest lecturer of American History & Culture at the Mogilev State University, Mogilev, Belarus.

Meeting interesting people around the world, studying other cultures, and being a keen observer of human interaction provides Ms. Daniels with a perpetual palette of personalities from which to draw in developing her believable and complex characters. She explains, "Everyone has a story to tell, but many extraordinary people from the past and alive today consider themselves ordinary and unimportant, yet their voices are saturated with wisdom and echo with relevance today. My purpose is to bring light and life to these untold stories, so their wisdom and lessons aren't lost. I was gifted with the basis for this story, In the Shadows of Savannah, during a conversation with an acquaintance who discovered while doing her family genealogy, the story of her great aunt who travelled from Wilmington, NC to Savannah, GA in 1906. There she had an illegal abortion, lost her life in the process, and that resulted in an inquest into the participants in the abortion. In the Shadows of Savannah is a fictionalized story of what her circumstances could have been, based on the times and a compilation of what other women have experienced. While tragic and a century ago, I saw the relevance and connection to today, and believe it was an important story to tell."

One reader commented, "With a missionary's fervor, Dianne has thrown herself into the writing of this book that will take us on a fictional journey through a time long ago, as she weaves the behaviors of the characters and the outcomes of their actions into a mesmerizing tale, leaving the reader in a place of virtual exhaustion and with a recognition of the past resonating even today."